D0935584

by Richard Llewellyn

Warden of the Smoke and Bells

RICHARD LLEWELLYN

Warden of the Smoke and Bells

Doubleday & Company, Inc.,
Garden City, N. Y., 1956

With the exception of actual historical personages identified as such, the characters are entirely the product of the author's imagination and have no relation to any person or event in real life.

Library of Congress Catalog Card Number 56–11503

Copyright © 1956 by Richard Llewellyn
All Rights Reserved
Printed in the United States of America
First Edition

Warden of the Smoke and Bells

Chapter 1

Franc watched the tiny head and shoulders of a man jogging toward the towngate along the path in the wheat, and at the same time he tried not to take his eye off the dust cloud, south, where the road went down toward Rome. A long furl of gold had been rising for two quarters of St. Rufino's bell-tower chime. Slow dust, he knew, came from marching men, but not so high. Cattle raised their own height in dust, he also knew, but they rarely moved in such a tidy column, and he could see nothing of drovers or dogs. Caravans could be told by the scouts riding ahead, but there were no little puffs to tell of horsemen in front of that long crawl, going steadily northwest toward hated Perugia's roofs and turrets on the far hill, and its length made him close one eye and guess.

The running man grew larger and kept his jog, although the hill was steep, and the sun had been hot enough that noon to make housewives throw water on their straw roofs. Nobody walked the town streets down below, for even the hardest feet blistered on the stones, so there was nobody to call to, and Keeper Mozo, at the gatehouse on the wall, would laze his hours until it was time to ring the night bell and raise the drawbridge till morning. There was nothing to do until the runner reached the outer grille and rang the bell.

Franc looked at the piles of brittle twigs stacked in the middle of the tower roof and made sure that the water bags were full and the wick of the lamp burned clear. A touch of flame to the heap, and a sprinkle of water, and signal smoke would give alarm to all the countryside. He reached up to touch the bound ends of the bell ropes and stretched his muscles to think how it would be to ring them all in peal of alarm. But only his father had done that, many, many a time under Perugian attack, though for him, since taking his father's place, there had been no chance. All was set at peace. Even the Perugians had stopped warring, perhaps because Il Cardinale had come to live near the new churches. Bandits never tried to raid outlying farms since it became known that the dreaded Count Althasar d'Orosa had returned from the Crusade to barrack his men-at-arms up at the Rock Castle. Condottieri troops feared to attack a town as newly walled, for the height, to say nothing of molten metal cast from the battlements, and red-hot arrowheads and half-ton boulders had wondrous effect upon the most desperate spirit. Often he had seen the robber bands ride past along the Roman road, going north or south to join an army or effect a pillage.

But in spite of his whispered plea, they rode on, and he was left in the watchtower high above the town, to look at the birds with every feather stretched and floating in nothing, or to roll his eyes all across the plain in front, and to detested Perugia on the far hill, and to the D'Orosa castle on the top of the mountain behind, and to the red tile and straw roofs of Assisi down below, and outside the walls to the new church of St. Francis and other buildings spread along the high rock, all trussed about with poles and rope like oxen before the roast. The carpenters and masons were in their wooden shelters snoring their siestas, he had no doubt. The laborers lay among the stones, hidden until they were called. All the headmen and master craftsmen were sleeping in their lodgings over the town, and every house was shuttered against the sun and flies and any noise.

Franc took greatest pride that he, the highest man in Assisi, kept watch and ward over all.

The jogging man went down in the dip and came up on the wider part of the track leading to the main gate. Franc insulted himself under his breath. He should have known that only Ob, the giant from the furnace and the best blacksmith on the plain, would have the strength to run in that heat. The furnace took a corner at the end of the track where it met the Roman highway, but hidden from the tower by a crest of the hill.

"Ob!" Franc called. "Ee-hai, Ob! What's afoot?"

Ob looked up and flipped sweat, glanced behind, and ran on, shouting. But the height was too much for his voice and there was no breeze to help. The dust cloud crawled on in a long, straight line, with the end still coming over the rise and the dust rolling off behind. Franc guessed at a column of wagons, horse-drawn, because wagons raise little dust, and horses, with their clean stepping, far less than oxen. That was too much to imagine. So long a line would mean hundreds of wagons. Hundreds of wagons meant at least double those hundreds of horses. The only time he had seen more than a hundred horses all together was when he was little, on the day the Perugian knights charged up the hill and captured the town and burned all the houses. But that was like a dream.

The outer-grille bell clanged and clashed as perhaps it never had before. Ob had an arm larger than most men's legs and his strength was in the pull. The door of the gatekeeper's house on the town wall opened, and Mozo's goodwife fluttered out in her wide skirts to look over the gate arch and scream. Mozo ran out in his shirt and hopped his bare feet about on the hot stones,

11

holding one and then the other. Distance made his curses tiny, and in he went again, coming out shod and pulling his gatekeeper's tunic over his head. His wife ran back to tell him what Ob had told her, and she pulled at the wheel to open the small postern. Mozo wasted no time, but ran to the stairway and down.

"Good Mother Mozo!" Franc shouted. "Ee-hai, Signora Clara, good Mother Mozo!"

She waved up at him, still turning the wheel.

"Near to having his throat slit!" she shrieked. "A troop of giants, all bigger than he is! They're coming up here. He said they robbed him of all in the place——"

Instead of finishing her story, she put a chock in the wheel to keep the postern open and ran inside the house. The bell had roused some of the townspeople. A few men looked out of doors, women peeped from windows, and dogs barked. But nobody went into the street where he could have shouted at them to get the news. He dare not leave the watchtower. There were more than tenscore steps, and to go down and up was the journey of half a quarter's chime. Apart from that, he had to keep watch, and if what Ob said was true, there was need of it.

If strangers had attacked the furnace, then they must have ridden under the crest of the hill. They could not have come from Perugia, or he would have seen them over the plain. They could not have come from the south or southwest or the west, which was all along his front, or from the northeast, behind his back. They must have come along the road the column was traveling, riding in shadow under the crest as sensible men would, to the furnace. In that way he could not have seen them, and had not. But if they had beaten Ob from his property, then they were less than harmless men, and if they belonged to the column, then the column was suspect.

It might be the transport train of an army, and therefore manned and led by robbers, pirates, and cutthroats of every people, and ready to take all their claws could gather, with bloodshed, burning, and destruction to follow.

But he had to be sure. Many in town had at first thought him too young for the post of Tower Warden. Many another was jealous of his place. Only Il Cardinale, that illustrious prince, had got him the berth by telling the town councilors that Giuseppe's son knew the duties better than anyone else from serving almost a lifetime of eighteen years in climbing the steps with his father's meals, in helping to stock the watch platform with bundles of twigs and water, and staying there to keep his father company through many an anxious night. No other townsman had served that apprenticeship. Franc, therefore, should be made Warden of the Smoke and Bells in his father's place, and the town might settle to its work in peace and dear content. Kindly thoughts of Il Cardinale were chased out of his head by Keeper Mozo, down in the street, bawling up at him and pulling Ob by the sleeve of his smock.

"Ho, Franc! What, do you sleep?"

"With both eyes watching the dust!" Franc shouted down, pointing out to the column.

"Send up the smoke. We're beset o' Satan!"

Franc leaned farther over the parapet and grinned.

"Not so, Keeper Mozo," he called. "How many stripes and kicks would I earn for bringing in the men on call to arms? And nothing to show but dust?"

"They are every man jack seven or more feet high!" Ob bellowed. "Bells! Smoke! Rouse up! To arms!"

"I'll rouse when there's need, good Ob!" Franc laughed. "So far, we'd arm for dust!"

Doors opened, and people ran out, calling to each other and crossing themselves against danger, and men came from their houses with swords buckled on, and their wives helped to strap them into their breastplates as they ran. Fat Gil had his on back to front, and his goodwife beat him over the helmet to make him stand still while she righted it.

Franc looked over the plain at the dust cloud, longer now and still hiding the procession. He looked toward the river's silver streak and on, to the hills and Perugia's roofs. Nothing moved. To the right and all the way around behind, nothing, except among the new buildings, where the laborers were coming out of sleep, ready to work into evening. Behind his back the mountain was bare, except for the olive trees. In the bulk of Count Althasar d'Orosa's castle the sun shone on the helmets of two men-at-arms resting on their spears up in the keep. To the left, the mountains, and olive trees on the slopes, and vineyards lower down, and then the plain once more, and patches of wheat, and the cleft of the road to Rome, and still the procession came over the rise and into the dust.

Behind ridges and in dells, wherever anything might grow, and on terraces cut into the hills, the townsmen worked in vineyards and orchards and in gardens and cereal fields. At the first shock of the warning bell, those nearest would run, and those too far away to hear would see the warning smoke and go for the town's walls and safety. But to bring them in for nothing carried penalties, not least the loss of his position and two pieces of silver a month, a free roof, bread and wine from the Cardinal's house for himself and his mother, a leathern working tunic and one of cloth, braided, for feast days every year, and the use of a pair of mules, Scabbard and Spada, to fetch wood and water for the tower, which he could lend to others for a fee. The loss of all those would be serious enough. But there was also loss of honor, for the tower watch had been held by his family since the time of his great-great-grandfather. Besides all, he knew he could be kicked about the town for a dolt by man, woman, and child and he might be lucky to escape with his life. Time in the fields meant food and money. To waste it was the worst crime of all.

"Never touch flame or rope till you see the enemy coming over the rise in front of the gate," his father had always said. "Latecomers can always get in by the postern in the field of the Little Brothers. The alarm gives plenty of time for everybody except the sluggard. And who thinks for him who thinks not for himself?"

He looked over the town roofs to the flower garden beyond the walls where the Little Brothers of St. Francis lived, each in his own little hut. Some were built of stone, some of wood, and some of sticks plaited with vines and plastered with mud. All the little houses, just big enough to admit a stooping man, and only long enough to let him lie on a straw pallet to sleep, ranged around three walls of a large square, and the fourth side was the town wall itself, with a postern gate that was never shut. The Little Brothers got up and said prayers at the second hour of the night, worked all day, and went to bed at sunset. The town Council had no wish to pay a guardian to look after a gate in such strange hours, and so they allowed the Little Brothers to name their own gateman. Besides, they knew that most people looked upon the garden as holy ground and never used the gate unless there was good reason, especially because of the bowl beside the door for those with a coin to spare. All knew they could enter the towngate for nothing, and no pull at the conscience.

The sun was third-hour high. The procession was almost halfway across the plain, and still there was no sign to tell what traveled in the dust. Only breeze moved in the wheat fields growing on the slopes before the town and the path was bare.

In the lane behind the forum, Ob and Keeper Mozo stood before the inn of the Leather Flagon, ringed about by dozens of men all listening hand to ear while Ob told his story between swigs at a wine flask. Franc saw Mother Mozo leave the wall postern, raising her skirts to go on her toes down the lane to the back of the crowd. She pushed through the outer rings of men

15

and, just when poor Mozo took his turn to drink, up came her fist and he got a buffet on the back that stretched him near to senseless, and the flask went up, over the wall of Signora Vala's yard, and sprayed her clean wash with red wine. Signora Vala screamed and reached for a broom and went through the house and out of the front door among the scattering men, swinging and poking at all in her way. Ob had Keeper Mozo over his knee, pounding his back to stop him coughing. Down came the broom in a crack that might have split any other man's skull, but Ob turned about and took it from her in one pull that sent it all the way over the inn roof, and Signora Vala went skirts-over-head into the horse trough. Mother Mozo took her husband by his ears and ran him through the forum to the gatehouse, and the innkeeper chased them, shouting for his money. Signora Vala's screams could be heard high above the laughter, but as fast as she put a leg out to stand in the street, somebody threw it in again, and somebody pushed somebody else in, and a couple more were thrown in, and soon the trough was full of arms and legs. In the turmoil of screams and splashes, Sesto, son of the coppersmith, climbed up and tipped the beam of the cistern. A wide green flood gushed out and hid everybody in or about the trough and swamped the lane to the knees, and the water curved down the forum's stairway in a great wave that laid flat all coming up.

Franc bawled down at the stall-holders opening for the evening's business at the foot of the steps. But none heard his warning, and the water fell on them and their customers and toppled their baskets and bales of fruit and vegetables and the pens of pigs, poultry, and rabbits, all in a slop and swim.

Franc hopped around to the other side of the tower to see if the water might reach his mother's house. But a movement in the wheat fields brought him about and he ran to the parapet.

Over the rise, along the path coming toward the towngate, a cohort of ponies trotted in armor, ridden by armored giants trailing their feet in the earth. Ranks of drummers in front were led by a man on a white horse, carrying a scarlet shaft floating a long white and gold pennon. Behind him, a child on a side-saddle rode a white pony. Behind her, two boys in black rode black ponies. Behind them, ranks of soldiers marched in high red caps and steel coats, carrying curved swords three times as long as themselves. Then came palanquins, roofed with gold, borne on the shoulders of giants naked to the waist, and behind, more men in blue and yellow.

And not a sound from any.

Franc leaned over the parapet, shouting down at the crowd. None looked up because none heard. He ran to the tower-house side. But Keeper Mozo and his goodwife were within, and he could hear the small sound of their discussion.

He reached for the bell ropes and paused, measuring the size of the procession. No more were behind, unless they were hidden. So few could well be repulsed by the men-at-arms in the town. The main gate was shut. An alarm was surely not necessary.

A strange sound beat in the hot shimmer rising from the miles of swaying wheat. Drums hummed and thudded, voices sang, and cymbals clashed. All the men riding the ponies got off, and with the drummers and the soldiers they first knelt, and raised their arms and put their foreheads down on the ground. The rider with the long gold and white pennon rode on toward the gate, and behind came the girl in white on a white pony, and behind her, the two boys in black on black ponies.

One palanquin, roofed and curtained in gold and scarlet, left the cohort, and the half-naked bearers trotted in time to a drum-beat and stopped at a command. The curtains were drawn aside by servitors, and a man in black got out and stamped his red-pomponned shoes in the dust to ease the cramp in his legs. He went to the girl on the pony and bowed low, and two women followers knelt, one behind the other, and two others helped her to dismount, using the two kneelers as footsteps. She came up to the man's waist, a child. The two boys slid off their ponies and stood behind the little girl. The rider with the pennon backed his horse away, and the man in black went toward the towngate with the little girl beside him, and followed by the little boys.

Franc waved his cap, hoping to take the eye of somebody in the street below to warn Gatekeeper Mozo. He saw one of the kneeling soldiers string his bow and shoot. He ducked behind the parapet, and the arrow struck deep in the wooden pillar, nicking his cap by a thread. That was warning enough, but a flight of half a score hit in the same place. Before he could move, the drumming stopped and the sound of the townspeople squabbling over water in the streets came plain.

He put his head over the rail and saw the rider with the pennon raise a long silver horn to his mouth. But instead of the trumpet note he expected, there came a voice, so loud that it leaped the walls and brought all in the town to silence, except the pigs swimming about coops full of angry hens.

"Hear ye!" the voice bellowed. "O hear, citadel of the mighty and most gentle Francis. One comes to pay homage. Set wide these Assisi portals and admit a governor of Cathay, one Messer Polo, christened Marco, sometime of Venice, now of the Court of the Great Kublai Khan, Lord and Emperor of Cathay. Open, I say. Hear ye. Open!"

Chapter 2

He heard Emantha climbing the steps with his supper long after her usual time, but although he was hungry he could have missed it and never given a penny-piece, so busy were the streets down below with so much to marvel at.

The forum and all the steps up from the towngate were thick with Cathayan soldiery and the gathering of townspeople trying to talk and find some sense in what each other said. The streets going left and right were massed with crowds standing about fires under the visitors' cook pots, and every inn was noisy with bibbers. Torches flared golden hair among all the palanquins lying side by side like so many golden ships, and light fell upon the Cathayan banners and flags, and all the pennons streamed, making shadows on the silken tents and pavilions strung outside the walls in tidy lanes as far as the churches. Sunglow reddened the straw roofs and the sides of St. Rufino's clock tower, and the night's blue came with breeze from the cooling plain.

"Dark drops too soon," Franc grumbled. "Here am I, and nothing to see!"

"You see enough," Emantha whispered, getting her breath after the climb. "Who sees more? And you're better here than in the streets. Strange women abound, in height barely to my shoulder, and brazen!"

"How, brazen?" Franc asked, ears a-cock.

"They wear a shift tight to the throat," Emantha said, breathing easier. "It reaches to the ankles. But from there up to the hip, it is split wide, and wider when they move. Our lads were all gone stupid in a stare!"

"And I up here!" Franc groaned, wringing his hands. "Take my place only for the space of a quarter's chime——"

Emantha laughed and shook her head, and turned her back to take the lid off a clay pot of soup and put a twist of wheat bread and a ball of sheep's-milk cheese and a bunch of grapes beside it.

"I am promised to wash and wipe tonight for the kitchen of the Three Silver Men," she said. "They are full to the doors in the tavern and not a bed or stalk of straw to be had in the lodging. They say that every beaker in the town is being tipped one to every dozen throats. Your mother told me to say she gives thanks you are up here and not mischiefing below. She works in the hospital of the Poor Clares all tonight. They are full of Cathayan women with sore stomachs from bumping in the wagons and swollen eyes from the dust. More of them reach us by tomorrow's noon. Il Cardinale is going out himself to give welcome to a princess of the blood of Kublai Khan, they say——"

"Soup, bread, and water!" Franc spat. "Where am I served different in a dungeon?"

"A comfortable one, too, with profit and reward," Emantha said softly, and kissed his cheek. "That, from your mother, with a message to put the woolsack under you against the cold. Under, not over. The nights grow damp after a day's heat——"

"A rotting melon for the damp," Franc sulked. "See the sport

I miss. How the lads'll jeer at me, roosted up in air, while they're out and frolicking below. Slit to the hips, you said?"

"From the ankles." Emantha nodded, turning for the stairway. "But they have soldiers to guard them every step. They carry great swords that slice a hair with the sound of a ringing bell. I heard it, and I know. As do others. Slit skirts or not, nobody turns eyes or head, lest he turn neither back. Up here, your head is safe enough. Eat, before the soup grows cold. Good dreams, and holy safeguard through the night!"

"Kiss my mother, and sleep well, both," Franc said, breaking bread. "Be early up with my festal tunic. And here, take my cap for a stitch or two. Il Cardinale will want to see all in place, remember. And kiss Leda for me——"

"Kiss her yourself!" Emantha spat, pushing the cap in her belt. "Think not to make me jealous. Fat and fumbling ditherwell, she is!"

He laughed aloud, hearing her creak down the wooden ladder and across the window platform to the stone steps. All that was needed these days to bring the gentle Emantha into teeth and cat's claws was to say aloud the name of Leda, daughter of the proprietor of the Three Silver Men, perhaps because she had been told of late that Leda's lace cap was set for one, and none other, and his name was Franc. Not that he cared a broken twig, although he knew well enough that many were after her because one day she would own her father's hostelry. She was the best catch of all, if youth and beauty counted, besides her dowry, to say nothing of property, with more than a thousand pieces of pewterware at the Three Silver Men, and sets of silver platters, and a wine vault judged to be the fullest north of Rome.

But if Leda was a-fortune with riches, Emantha had none, except her nature. In beauty, she was Leda's mistress. Master painter Messer Giotto had said that only she was fit to stand as model for the angels he was painting on the church's walls. He went in person to the house where she lived with her married sisters, a few doors down from the Three Silver Men, and pulled her by the hand to his studio, whether she wanted to go or not, and made her stand for many an hour while he used a brush on cloth and made her likeness live.

Leda was a month or two the older, and she wore the tallest lace cap in town or out and a precious turquoise necklace, brought by her father from Florence, that the jealous ones said was haggled of a thief and therefore had a curse upon it that brought all men to look at her, though she looked only at Franc, and he only rarely at her.

Emantha wore a cap of linen spun by herself that held her hair, the color of wheat tips in noon sun. Her eyes were her only jewels, bluer than Leda's necklace, and Messer Giotto said of them that if he could capture their light in paint, the church would need neither candle nor dip, nor any single window.

Leda, too, he had drawn and painted upon the walls, but as a woman of the Court, in mauve and white finery, and her dark red hair hung below her waist entwined with a wild rose, and her eyes looked black, peering up there as she always did behind her father's counter to see if there was something secret she ought to know that might be told on the sly to others. Not that she was a bad girl, or chance-tempered. Franc thought that it was only because, having no mother since a babe, she had ever twisted her father by his forelock and made herself the airs of a grown woman long before her time. Leda worked, yes. But only to serve a flask and show her smile to the best patrons or to take money from any other, best or not. She washed no crock or beaker or swept any floor, and if she went near the kitchen it was only to screech at the wenches or fill her trencher with another helping.

But Emantha swept, washed, mended, and cooked for three families and still found time to help at the inns when hands were scarce and patrons were many. She worked for any coin that would fill the wooden shoe against the sum needed to take her sister's son, Ubaldo, to the school at Bologna. Her elder sisters all worked for the same reason, in households in the town. Hortensia and Rosina cooked at the mansion of Rovi di Rovigo, chief mason and master builder of the works at the churches. Maldina cooked and cleaned for Il Cardinale in his small house beyond the walls. As the months went by, so the wooden shoe became heavier with silver pieces. The heavier, the happier the voices of the sisters to think that one, at least, of the family would have a life outside the town, beyond the toil of the fieldman, and bringing them honor by the might of his scholarship and the fount of his learning. The three married sisters had lost their husbands in battles with the Perugians. Emantha's father had been lost just after she was born, though none knew how, except that he had been taken prisoner by the Count d'Orosa's father and dragged into the castle gates on the end of a chain. Some said he had perished under torture, but none knew, except that he had gone. Few women in the town had the husband they first had married. Fewer children had a living father. Thus it was that the works about the new church had come as a great blessing, for many of the workmen had taken themselves a wife, some with growing families of children, and laughter had come, little by little, bright to the town again.

Franc spooned down the soup and sopped bread and gnawed bones, thinking of them all, family by family and street by street, for he had watched most of them from his high perch and knew far more than any crone a-gossip. But he said nothing, for his mother had taught him that everybody's business was his own, with no weight to him and less to say of it. He plucked at the grapes and left the peels on the parapet for the birds that sang him awake in the morning, long before the town bell struck the rising hour. He swung his legs over, leaning

23

against the pillar, watching lights flicker near Perugia on the hill. The land was dark. All the way around, only the watchman's fire lit the poles red about the works on the churches, and the sentries' braziers shone in the keep of Count Althasar d'Orosa's castle.

But the town below was alight with torches at every door and all around the forum, and fires burned down the middle of the stairway to the towngate. Oil wicks blew like carpets of leaves on all the tables in front of the taverns, and lanterns threw light on the cobbles in front of all the doors. The market place shone from the evening's wetting, alive with the shadows of stall-keepers still shouting their wares. Housewives picked here and pulled there to see how they would spend, and then argued about the price and raised their faces and hands to the night, calling all heaven and every star to witness how they were robbed.

He had seen it all before, though the town had never been up as late, and the streets and lanes had never been so crowded. Again, he gloomed to sitting up there while others of his age were down below keeping a watch, he was certain, on foreign women with split skirts, which might earn them a chop in the neck with a blade that could split a hair with the sound of a ringing bell. That danger was reason enough to watch. He remembered the stories of his father's old friends, about foreign women with fishtails instead of legs. Ordinary women's legs were nothing to see and less to be sliced in the neck for. But a fishtail, now. It seemed to him that even a fishtail was little enough, unless, of course, it was walked upon. Even so, walking on a fishtail could only be painful to watch, much less to do, and Emantha had said nothing of it. But it would be little, in any case, to compare with watching the way Emantha walked, as in the times she carried the water pot balanced on her head, hands on hips, and barefoot over the stones.

He sat up in sudden wonder, trying to see why he should feel

24

that others were lucky to see a foreign woman with a skirt slit to show a fish's tail. He could find no reason why she should be looked at except with pity. If she had legs and feet, then she was nothing to look at, for all women had them, not one more than another, although in some they were more catching to the eye, and with others they were logs and hoofs. Perhaps, with the women of Cathay, there was some extra reason to put the town lads in a stare. He wished he had kept Emantha talking a little longer to find out. He also wished he could run down the steps for a minute or two, just long enough to have a word with any passer-by.

But there was nothing to do except sit and dangle his feet above all of them, wishing he was down among the light and laughter.

The door of the capstan tower next to Keeper Mozo's house squeaked open and cracked against the wall. Goodwife Clara came out holding a lantern to see where she was setting her feet and turned to give light behind. Shadows passed, one after another, to the middle of the wide wall. Keeper Mozo came out with a pine torch in fine hiss of flame. His voice carried tiny on the breeze, but what he said was lost. A long line of men came out carrying heavy burdens and lengths of timber. A fire started in the middle of the wall, and dry leaves were thrown on, and sawdust, to make a clear blaze for a working light.

Franc got down and went to the side nearest, the better to see what went on. Most of the men were Cathayan soldiers in red tunics. They laid the timber flat on the floor. Bales were unrolled, and cloth was pulled out. Men paced here and there, measuring distance. On a long whistle of many shrill notes, four white pavilions were raised, ropes were tightened, pegs were hammered in, and on the sides a dozen small white tents went up at the same time.

At one moment, nothing but darkness, fire-flame, and a lantern. The next, a small city of white streets, with light shining through the walls and a fire before every doorway. Keeper Mozo took the men off, and Signora Clara stood alone at the big fire in the middle.

Franc sat straighter.

Through the door came one, six, a dozen, twenty, thirty and more, of the women of Cathay, all of them not even up to Signora Clara's chins. They went into the tents with their bundles and came out to go down again, and came up with furnishings and carpets and pots and pans and every sort of pack and coffer.

When all was up and every tent showed the shadows of its furniture against the white walls, some of the Cathayans went to Signora Clara, and bowed low, and turned her about, and shut the door on her. Some gathered in groups and clapped their hands and sang, though little of the music reached him. Others tended the cooking pots, and good smells played touch on the breeze, bringing him, full as he was, to hunger again. All went to a table and took round platters that flashed gold, to be helped to food, and all went into a tent to eat, so that for a while there was nothing to see except shadows dipping and putting hands to mouths and jaws champing, and dipping again and champing. First one finished, and another, and water splashed silver in washing the platters, and many sat about the fires to sing and pick at long-handled lutes but without the lute's soft tone. More wood was thrown on the fires, and flame blew higher. Shadows were blacker on the white tent walls, and all the women went in and tied the doorways for the night.

But he was unhappy that all he saw were clearly ordinary women, and not a fishtail among them. There was no doubt about it. Every detail was a shadow on the walls, undressing, talking, walking, lying down.

He yawned and stretched. The town was still alight down there, and the streets were full enough. Nothing moved, and no glim was in the plain. The little white city was darker, pink, in the dying fires. Only faintly he could see the shadows of Cathayan women lying on their sleeping mats, and fainter still he thought he heard the sound of sleeping breath.

The fancy made him sleepy. He pulled the woolsack, dry from its bed among the twigs, and laid it over pine branches. The soft leather blanket covered him to the eyes, and he yawned again and slept.

His ear seemed to have known of the steps long before he woke. He opened his eyes, seeing by the stars that morning was yet far off. But the steps were plain, of three people treading soft and slow, and not yet at the window platform. He pulled on clothes and shoes and hung his sword in the belt hooks. With a stone floor and an iron trap, he could keep an army from getting in. He lit tinder in a basket and clamped a chain to the handle. When the flame came high he went to the trap and swiftly lowered the bucket into the darkness.

"Who comes?" he called. "Names, and business!"

The basket swung a little way from the top, showing two Cathayans in red uniforms, each with a bundle, and a man in black, cloaked, with a black hat, feathered.

"Peace!" the man in black said softly. "We come unarmed."

"In what matter?"

"In the serious matter of showing proper welcome for her exalted highness the Princess Na-Nou, beloved daughter of the Great Khan, on whom may the sun ever bend his most lustrous benevolence!"

"Your words push at my mind and have no substance, for this is a public building," Franc said. "I am Warden of the Smoke and Bells. To enter here, you must ask permission of the Mayor and Council——"

"Asked and got," the man said. "The Mayor and Council are now at the Three Silver Men, where they have been my guests since sundown. They are at this moment most worthily stretched, each one, under the table!"

27

"Nevertheless," said Franc, "an order is an order. None may enter the tower without the signed permission of the Mayor and at least two councilors——"

"Could you read if such were got?"

"Present the order and let us see!"

"This will take time, and I wish to fly banners the length of the tower in greeting to the sun and moon's most perfect daughter——"

"By permission of the Mayor and Council!"

"My name will free you of all blame. I am Marco Polo——"

"Which has no meaning here," Franc said, and pulled up the fire basket. "Three better names, the Mayor Gandolfi's own and two of his councilors, or she'll lack any welcome from this tower, that's certain——"

"I am Marco Polo!" the man shouted in anger. "Do you dare contradict me?"

"I dare shut the trap——"

"In risk of your head!"

"A look at a slit skirt might have lost it for me this very night," Franc said. "And, from what I have seen, for nothing. Am I now to lose it for something? A much better bargain——"

He let the iron trap fall in a clanging thud to let them know that many more would be needed to open it without his help from above. That done, he brushed his hands, pulled down his tunic, and strutted, well satisfied, back to the woolsack.

Sleep might have crept upon him before he knew, but his name, cried from the street, awoke him. A stick rattled on the railings of the garden, and he knew Emantha was down there. Each time she passed, the stick rattled to let him know it was she, on her way to market, or erranding, thinking of him, but without time to come up.

He leaped to the parapet and looked over.

Emantha stood among a group holding lanterns. Messer Polo's feathered hat caught light, and also the feathers in the hats of his servitors. But the camel-hair gown and the wide-brimmed red hat with the tassels could be worn only by one, and he, great and good and gentle man, should long have been in his bed. But he stood beside Emantha.

Il Cardinale looked up, waving his hand, but his voice was lost in the high breeze.

"Open the trap, Franc!" Emantha called. "It is proper and in order. Messer Polo brings men with him to fly banners in greeting to the Princess. See, his excellency gives you blessing!"

"To which I return thanks," Franc shouted, kneeling on the parapet. "But only the Mayor and Council have authority here. No other word has weight. This is no cark of mine. The orders are here, in front of me, cut in bronze."

"The Mayor and Council are drunk!" a man shouted.

"Sober them up!" Franc said, content.

"Open the trap!"

"The trap is shut," Franc replied. "Take a lesson!"

The little group's heads got closer together, but what they said took flight with the owls. In a moment all had turned to walk toward the Three Silver Men, though he saw Emantha hesitate, as if she would have a last word.

He thought, knowing the Mayor and the Council, that if they were full enough of wine to slide under a table, then not even the trump of doom would waken them before their goodwives dragged them home in the morning and put them to bed and purged them with stoups of herb-soak and set them a-foot with cloths made icy with well water plumped on their paunches. Mayor Gandolfi, for one, from all known before, would take a good three days before a sober word would escape his head. The Mayor was a barrel that, once full, could be rolled to any corner and left.

He took a turn all about the parapet. Most of the town was dark. Here and there the rags of a torch burned and sparked. Nobody moved in any street. Owls made gray patterns in the air and flapped away. The little city of tents on the wall glowed white, without sound.

"Franc! Franc, good fellow! Hear me!"

He ran to the parapet on the north side and looked over, barely able to agree with his ears. But they were right. The Mayor, in his red cloak, and a couple of councilors were down there with a group of others.

"We are agreed in Council that Messer Polo should enter into the tower," Mayor Gandolfi shouted up. "He comes with sundry others to prepare greetings against the visit of her illustrious magnificence, the Princess No-Na——"

"Ah, no!" somebody objected. "Na-Nou!"

"Ah—— No——"

"No! Na-Nou!"

"No—no——"

"Her exalted highness, the Princess Na-Nou!" a voice shouted, cold, sharp, distinct.

"As I said, to the syllable," continued the Mayor. "Therefore, we, Mayor and Council here foregathered, do pronounce and pass the order that the tower shall be opened, and all facilities shall be afforded, short of cost to us in any kind, now or in the future. D'ye hear me, Franc?"

"I hear, Messer Mayor. The order is obeyed!"

"Then open up, and let the rest of us find lights and a fire and a pleasing flagon. I'm froze to every bone and starched o' thirst!"

Chapter 3

It was not, thought Franc while he glowered down at the forum, that he minded where Emantha went, or which one she spoke to, or why she laughed at jokes he never shared, because she could never remember them, or if she did, and told him, she always forgot the part at the end that held the laugh. He tried to tell himself that it was little to do with him what she did. He was not sworn to her, nor did he much think of when he might be, and neither was there thought in his head of marriage, although his mother had been hinting that one in his twenties would be better off in a house of his own with a girl like Emantha to look after him. That was well said, and he had nothing against it, nor against any notion of marrying anybody at all. He was not given to thinking of marriage, and he never thought of girls, much less Emantha. She had been part of his years of growth from infancy. They shared all joys and any sorrow. They knew each what the other knew, and how it came to be known. There could be no hope of sharing with any other. His mother said they were already one creature, each a half without the other. He said no word, willing it should be thought so.

But to catch her laughing, arm in arm, with a couple of Messer Polo's upstarts in velvets and lace, and to call down to her and see her look about and wave and go on, skipping and cackling as if he meant so little, that was too much. They had played together since they were beyond crawling, and were ever a-tumble in one another's houses, or chasing out in the fields or about the lanes and over the walls. As they grew, he took her to look for birds' nests in the spring, and to scrape the blight off the vines or stone the crows off the wheat in summer, and pick the grapes and gather hay in autumn, and throw snowballs in the winter. When she grew tall enough to help in the house, their time together was shorter, but she always found the moments to come with him up to the tower to take his father's noon meal, and sometimes she came up at night to sing with him about the fire to keep his father company. When his father died and he went up alone, then she made herself his turnkey, for his mother had no breath to climb the stair, and he had no sister or any to serve instead. It had never been in his mind that some other might take Emantha's hand and set an arm about her waist and toe a measure down the street. Not, certainly, one in velvets and lace, for those were marks of wealth far outside his dreams and long beyond his grasp.

But two of them, one each side, and she between held close, hip to hip, all three neighing laughter, was no dream, but fact and nightmare both.

The long silk banners nailed to the tower roof flapped and cracked in the morning breeze. Yellow, blue, red, and black, with strange writings all the way down in gold, each twice the span of a man's arms in width, and in length almost the height of the tower, all sailed out and up and around, as if they would fly their greetings before the Princess got near. More silk blew from the roofs of the pavilions and tents of the little white city on the town wall. The Cathayans had washed and scrubbed, and flowers had been planted in boxes, with small trees in pots, and the space on the wall that had been empty looked as if people had always lived there in comfort and with an eye to a garden full of colors and living green. All the furniture and the bundles brought up by the soldiers had come off the line of wagons in a camp down at the furnace under the crest of the hill. Ob had been foolish to run. He was a big man and a brave workman, none better. But in brain he had a sparrow's worth, and when the Cathayan scouts had ridden up to take his service, he thought himself attacked and ran for help. Only that morning he had ridden out with the rising bell among a troop of those he had once thought were his enemies. He had the more to sing and laugh about because of all the Cathayan horses and ponies to be fitted with shoes, each set a florin of silver, and so many to be done that none could count or even make a guess.

As with Ob, so with the town. The streets seemed to run with fortune. The inns and hostelries were crammed so that the walls had to be propped. Every house that wanted had lodgers. Saddlers and tailors and cordwainers and cobblers were all heaped high about their walls with work. Nobody in any street but had profit. Even the sweepers and watermen earned extra by serving the visitors' needs in grooming their horses or cleaning their camp stables.

All in Assisi, from master to scullion, gained fortune except himself, separated from any coin and all excitement by the height of the tower and the course of his duty.

But if that were not enough, here was Emantha making a fool of herself with a couple of saplings, neither of them of any size in the leg or shoulder, and the two together not a match for a man, expecially one given to some hours of daily exercise with quarterstaff and buckler, longbow and shortsword, tilt-lance and javelin. The hours in the tower soon passed in that rough company and left behind toned muscle and a clear eye. He looked at himself in the smooth surface of the water bucket and pushed his cap over the black curls and grinned at the frown over black eyes. It was easy to lose temper, his mother taught, but better to lose it entirely, and alone, and in peace.

Across the plain in the cleft that held the road to Rome, a dust cloud started to rise and grew longer with the minutes. Little puffs of galloping horsemen went to meet it, and other puffs came out of it, and the head turned straightway, led by the puffs, toward the path to the furnace and up to the town. The little puffs, he knew, were Cathayan horsemen. The long cloud was the caravan of the Princess Na-Nou, daughter of the Grand Khan, and mothered, it was whispered, by the moon itself. Emantha had told him she heard it at the market, but she had time only to put his clothes and morning broth over the edge of the trap, and down she went again. He understood her hurry when he saw her not long after, dallying with the lace and velvet. He was angry to think of more of it coming with the Princess's suite. He could see Emantha's waist being squeezed by droves of vaunting gallants, and himself held by duty to stay in the sky, helpless. He looked at the dust cloud and wished it gone, for all it meant was more crowds from Cathay, more animals to be tended, more lodgers for the houses, more profit for the townsmen, more velvet and lace springalds to set arms about waists, and, among it all, nothing for himself except a view from above.

Getullio, the baker, called up, wanting to borrow Scabbard and Spada to fetch a load of flour, and put the fee of four copper pence one by one in the hole between the stones.

"They are with Brother Egidio on the mountain, close to the mill," Franc shouted. "Take them when he is finished——"

He watched the dust cloud winding a long loop toward the track to the town. A cavalcade rode before, and sunshine glinted on lances and helmets, and the colors of flags and pennons blew clear with the trumpet notes. The plain toward Perugia was free of traffic, except for a couple of farm wains. Further to the right, workmen the size of a little-finger nail climbed all over the poles and ropes binding the walls of the new church, and teams of men on the roofs laid down the sheets of lead, and fire pots passed between them, sealing all inside from the weather.

One more bell chime, and the plain being clear toward Perugia, he might go down for the space of an hour to kiss his mother and see a few friends. He prayed that no cavalry might appear, or anything else that might require a watch kept on it. He prized his free hours, which came only sometimes at night, or when the plain and the hills were quiet by day. One hour was the space of his freedom, for it took an hour for those coming from the north and south to reach the edge of the plain, and the further hour or more they had to ride to reach the town gave ample space for him to leap the steps and set flame and ring bells to bring the fieldmen in.

The chime came, and nothing moved on the plain or beyond except the long wagon train of the Princess. He put on the braided cloth tunic and picked up his cap and jumped out of the trap door, sliding the ladder to the window platform, taking the stone steps in leaps of four, going down a flight in five leaps, each flight set against each of four walls, with ten flights until he reached the foot, and through the arched doorway, out.

It was always warmer in the street than up in the tower. The festal tunic and the weight of the town's gold badge on the chest sat heavily after the first few minutes, but he put up with it for he knew that in all the world there was not another like it, which set him apart, and besides, people liked to touch it for good fortune, and his father had told him that they should not be deprived of comfort for the sake of a little healthy sweat.

He called and waved to this one and that, and blew kisses to housewives and had them blown in return, all on the run to his mother's house, near the garden of the Little Brothers and only a hop away from the new church. His mother's house was strongly built of stone, with a fire-clay-tiled roof, all the work of his father. Three rooms, and a small yard on the street level, and one small room built above, made it one of the largest houses in the town. The roof room was his, built by himself with help of Emantha and whoever passed by. The rest of the roof space was caged to hold the birds he brought from the tower, for in bad weather they flew in, tired of flight, or hit into the brickwork and broke pinions or twisted a wing. A kestrel, an eagle half grown, two falcons, and a pair of owls had cages to themselves. Doves and pigeons were in others, and smaller birds, splendid in summer plumage, had a big cage with a stone bowl for bathing and branches of pine to sit upon and sing.

In the roof room, which he could read in for an hour here and there on odd days, he kept his books, given by some of the Brothers and by Il Cardinale. They were not many, and their parchment leaves were ragged with much handling, and the ink barely showed. But they were books, and from them he had learned his letters and words. Hours of practice had made him a fair one with a quill, and a good reader, not only in Latin, but in the new language of the scholar, Messer Dante, that was spoken by Il Cardinale and by learned professors coming to visit the new church, and heard from them when they sat at meat in the Three Silver Men. Leda and her father and Emantha were helpful at those times, for they let him in by the back way so that he could stand behind their chairs, pretending to serve at table, and so listen to their speech.

But in that way, too, he was nearer the looks and nudges of Leda, though he gave none back of one or other, content to keep an ear on what passed in talk. And there were many subjects among the wise men that puzzled his brain, but he could get no answer even from Il Cardinale. He remembered a discourse about the blood, how it was made, what kept it warm and gave it color, why every man, woman, and child should have so much and no more. The arguments pro and con were those he might have made himself, but he heard nothing of a reply that satisfied, and Il Cardinale told him that it took time for the light of knowledge to come, and to be patient, for, lacking light and patience, eyes were useless and ears would ever deceive.

The house echoed to his call. His mother was out. A fire of twigs was on the stones, and a pot boiled. The bench was set against the wall. The table glistened from beeswax, and the two stools were under it. Sun shone on the tiles, fresh from a washing, and he feared to enter lest his feet leave marks. He went around the yard and looked in the window of his mother's room. The bed place was filled with pine branches stacked ready for the woolsack, and the leather cover was folded on top. In the next room, the loom stood in mid-roll of white sheep's-wool. A hank of wool soaked in a dish of red dye, and another in blue. He climbed the ladder to his room. All the birds greeted him, and he dropped seeds into the smaller birds' cage and, in the others, beetles he had caught in the tower.

His room had been cleaned not long before, and lilac hung in the leathern bucket on the table. His books were set against the wall, held upright by two polished pebbles the size of his head, and carved as birds by Simone, an apprentice stonecutter in Messer Giotto's studio. One wall was painted with a scene at the hunt by Tivi, Messer Giotto's senior apprentice, and the other with a map of creation, drawn in with charcoal, but not yet painted. On the wall above the table a set of plates in colors showed the arms of soldiery, all made by Laz, another apprentice of Messer Giotto's, and on the fourth wall hung his great-grandfather's longbow, arrows, broadsword, and throwing spear, which had all been dented and battered with use on the walls of Acre and Jerusalem in a war of the Crusade.

But he smiled to see the carpet, made by Emantha from pieces of old cloth and a wool shawl she had loomed, broad and soft upon the floor, pleasant to the resting foot.

Instantly he made up his mind that his hour would go, not

as it mostly passed, in reading, but as he had decided, in finding her and setting the froward gallants in their places.

He went about, and down the ladder, and ran through the street to the Three Silver Men. Cathayan soldiery sat at the tables, a-many. But not one drank wine. They sipped at little beakers that might hold a mouthful, if the mouth was small. Leda's father, Soffolo, stood before the door and gave him welcome.

"You are come at proper time," he said. "See these cattle. They slop hot water fluxed with leaves. What, am I come to own a public trough? Some rock salt and a brush, and they might also wash their feet!"

"If that's their custom, let them be welcome," Franc laughed. "Is not hot water cheaper got than wine? And, by the griffon's ruff, the same price here, I'll wager!"

"More, for their swollen dewlaps and bursting pockets," Soffolo said, though not loud. "This dribble they call tea. Slice a piece of burning rope in water, and boil it, and there's your tea. And these are called the Khan's Infallibles!"

"I seek Emantha," Franc said.

"Gone to the house of his excellency." Soffolo nodded at the new church. "Il Cardinale sets dinner for the Princess and her Court, and a feasting for the town in her honor. Every woman of sound health is up there for an hour to dress places, or clean a fowl, or in some way put her art to use. Your mother makes her pastry. Leda took my silver. There's added value!"

"And you are left to make profit of hot water?"

"More, because the leaves they bring with them, and the cost to me is nothing. Drink a beaker of my best?"

"I'll taste these Infallibles' hot water, and I may?"

"Into the kitchen. The pot's there. The water must be fresh to the boil, and boiled in the space of a count of twenty. Then put in the leaves, a pinch to every person, and one for the heated vessel. Pour on the water. Let sit for the space of an attempt at murder. Serve out and drink, praising none and cursing the rest. Then the murder's done!"

But the drink, when made, was fragrant on the air and delicate to the palate and brought a feeling of peace in body and mind. Franc went out and looked at the Khan's soldiers, at their height and breadth, and at their faces, which showed nothing.

"There they sit, hour after hour," Soffolo said. "A-swole on rope and hot water!"

"I thought it good," Franc said. "I'll take some leaves and brew myself a pot tonight——"

"Better, take a flask of honest wine——"

"Have you forgotten? Not a mouthful in the tower, for any reason. Therefore, I'll take the leaves for a potful——"

"Take a capful, and drown!"

"I'll make a knee to his excellency first, good Soff'. Tell your Leda I was here."

"Come back and tell her yourself. Your Emantha plays duck to a couple of these young drakes from Messer Polo's corps of valets and fellows of the household. Leda holds herself from such. As perhaps you knew?"

"Ten silver pieces she's with Messer Polo himself!"

"Not taken. You are free with your money."

"When it's safe as in my pouch. Adio!"

Franc ran on up the hill past the postern of the Little Brothers' garden, waved to Brother Matteo on duty, and went through the lane behind the courthouse, past the Mayor's residence, and beyond the walls to the house of Il Cardinale.

Women sat plucking poultry in a float of feathers. Butts and casks of wine were being rolled to places at the side. Meats were being cut, and sheep and oxen were spitted ready for the coals. A roof of canvas was up, and women set places at tables under it and piled bowls and platters on others. Cauldrons of broth sent steam from a line of fire trenches, and more women peeled vegetables, or washed fruit, or carried stoups and crocks, or folded squares of linen, or made pastry, or kneaded dough. Wherever there was space to look, there the women worked.

Il Cardinale's house was smaller than most houses in the town, of two rooms, and one of those a kitchen. In the front he set his table and high chair and a couch of elm with a straw pallet and a wool shawl. On the walls all around, floor to ceiling, books in every size. On the floor a mat woven by Emantha and her sisters. In the kitchen a square hearth of stones, three crocks, and a cauldron. On the walls a rack, with a pot for soup, a platter for meats, and a beaker for water.

Il Cardinale lived within the rules of his Order, and they, he said, enjoined that each should have enough, and no more, lest others go without. Hortensia, Emantha's eldest sister, put her head from the door and laughed greeting.

"Nobody home," she called. "His excellency is at church. I am here. Maldina is here. But Emantha is with your mother, cutting flowers in the Mayor's garden. Will you eat? Drink?"

"Neither, with my thanks. When do they return?"

"Within the chime, or I'll be after them."

"I'll take myself to Messer Giotto's studio for a halloo at the lads. I'll return in time to kiss my mother. My respects to his excellency, if he should notice them, or me."

"When he does not, then I'll have none to cook or make a bed for, and long forfend the day!"

Franc ran on up the hill to the courtyard leading to the churches. A new building was barred at the gateway by a painter's color board with a clutch of worn brushes all tipped a different color thrust through the thumb hole, and the painted sign of an open hand, palm out, warning all to stop and turn back. Franc went on, into the room where outer clothes and caps were left, and through the small store racked with kegs of colored powders and pots of oils and spirits. A storeman grinned welcome and pulled a string, lifting a latch that opened the door to the paint room, bright with light from long windows and white walls, drawn on and streaked with brush strokes of every tint and tone.

Boys squatted in long ranks with square stone vessels between their legs, pestling colored ores into powder. The rolling, beating, and crunching pestles made a rhythm, and every rank had its own, which agreed with all and yet was different, but the song they all sang quietly together was the same. At the head of each rank a junior apprentice sat at a bench, mixing the ground powders with oils into a paste. As a boy finished his pestling, he raised his hand and was beckoned out of his place. But if the powder was not fine enough, he got a clout in the ears and went back with a couple of hours' extra work for penalty. Franc had watched for many an hour and could have stood for many more, looking at the long ranks, one of different shades of blue, and another of reds, from deepest carmine to palest pink, and another all yellows to blazing orange, and greens, mauves, browns, and grays among the black and white, and in a separate corner the gold beaters and silversmiths. Brushmakers had a bench beside the door, and on the other side a couple of old men graded charcoal sticks and racked them in furrowed boards that the artist could hang about his neck, making his choice at will.

The junior apprentices all gave him greeting, though silently, for none was permitted to speak during hours of work. He passed them, and a charcoaler opened the door for him to enter the studio of Messer Giotto. The master painter only rarely went there, preferring to work on the scaffolds in the churches. In the long, light room, among easels and rows of wooden models and racks of men's and women's dresses, the chief apprentices and picked juniors prepared paints a day in advance of the Master's need.

The walls of the room billowed with linen cartoons of the paintings that had been done, and those in progress in both the churches. Each sketch, in the Master's black brushwork, was key to the color scheme to be used in the panels, and all the figures were numbered and dabbed with the chosen colors, with the sky and buildings in the background. A board showed what paints were required each day, and how much of each color was to be set ready as the Master required, and which apprentice was responsible for each tint and quantity. Tivi, Mok, and Laz had all learned since boyhood with Messer Giotto in Padua, Florence, and Orvieto and were about worked out of apprenticeship and ready for their time as journeymen. Not one of them wanted to leave the Master. Rather, they stayed on, learning much by earning little, and the happier. All three were pale from staying out of the sun, for when they were not in the studio they were in the upper or lower church, and their day began before the town's rising hour and ended when the morrow's last dish of paint was ready for the Master's brush. Tivi, the tall Venetian, gray-eyed and nervous, ruled the corps of apprentices as a father. At a word he could banish any boy from the paint room or bring another in. Even so, he made no weapon of his power, for the only rule was that of work. The idle, or the time wasters, had no place. Many a father was willing to pay gold pieces to say his son held place with Messer Giotto. But gold had little way with the Master, and even less with Tivi. To both, gold was a paint to be put on a wall, and the only coins they knew were those which paid the workmen, bought food for the paint room, straw for beds, and the powders, ores, and oils for the day's work.

Mok, the second apprentice, had come squat and bowlegged from the pastures in the hills, and wise in the art of staining sheep the better to be told from another's, with a special gift for mixing tints from all kinds of earth that none had ever taught him. The third apprentice, Laz, had been found by the Master drawing figures on the paving of a street in Florence. None other had more knowledge of mixing blues, either from gentian blossoms or from rocks, and his whites were whiter than all others, and the Master sometimes said they were white as light itself.

All three were lean with muscle from building and taking down scaffolding, and strong-armed from years with the pestle and mortar, and they were dressed together in Messer Giotto's livery of red hosen, orange doublets, and lemon shirts, and their smocks over all, Tivi's in dab of any color, Mok's mostly of reds and browns with some smudges of green, and Laz always a sky-flourish of all the blues.

"Ha, bellman, what then?" Mok greeted him. "Are we now free to be roistered of droll Perugians, and no watch kept?"

"I am free an hour," Franc said. "No nonsense, then. The Princess's suite approaches, that, yes. All else is quiet, except Mok's mouth."

"Fill it with your mother's pastry, and I'll promise merry silence," Mok grinned. "Who should see you a-skip in gold and azure this day?"

"The Mayor and Council, who bought it," Franc said. "Who has seen Emantha?"

"I," said Laz. "With two stern fellows of this Messer Polo's court."

"Stern?"

"Stern to be about the business of tip and tattle. Lace and washed fingers, both. But Emantha grew in their ogling. Before my eyes, she burst a-color. The Master said——"

"He saw her?"

"Could any not? That blush of hers would hue a ton of steeped lime——"

"Which blush is this?"

"That one which came of what they whispered——"

"What was that?"

"Should I know? Which whispers bring a blush?"

"There's much here to learn," Tivi said with interest. "Tell, good Laz. What whispers?"

"Those spoken by a tattler with a maid in mind," Mok grinned. "What's alack, Franc? Are you strait of a whisper? Spend a quarter's chime with us now, and we'll set out an armory. First, there's the whisper of her beauty. Tivi, take the lute——"

"A plague of spitting toads upon your lute!" Franc shouted. "Where are these spindreams to be found?"

"Did I not see them moments ago as I crossed by the Mayor's garden?" Laz whispered, closing his eyes to dream. "Did I not see Emantha cutting blooms? And both of them beneath the ladder, whispering up? And she scarce to be seen for the rosy halo all about?"

"Beneath the ladder, say you?"

"Beneath," Laz said, as though injured in a nicety. "Beneath the ladder she had climbed to cut the blooms. Where else do tattlers stand, except beneath?"

"And this rosy halo, now," Mok inquired. "Was this some artifice of hers——"

"Not so," Laz said. "What could it be but blush upon blush setting a certain rosiness upon the air? They, beneath the ladder, whispering up, and she up, blushing down——"

"Enough!" Franc shouted. "The Mayor's garden, ha? I'll cut a bloom or two before the hour's out, by the blade o' Jason!"

He ran through the room to the door at the end leading out to the courtyard and the lane going past the Mayor's garden. The wall was high enough to keep the winds from the nectarines, but Franc leaped and caught the top and drew himself up and over.

The ladder showed in the flower garden, and he heard voices and, plainly, Emantha's laughter. He jumped down and quietly made way along the path to the wall arch. The garden trembled color in hot sunshine, and so thick grew the flowers that, two arm spans away, all in front was hidden. He picked his steps down to the curve and around to a trellis blocking the way.

"Fa-la, you say these so, but how should I take your words?" Emantha's voice hovered in laughter above his head. "You make me gifts which I refuse, and silks and stuffs I cannot wear——"

"And why not?" The man's voice came from nearby, perhaps in the shade of a tree laden with scarlet flowers. "The service I require is small——"

"But not in my gift," Emantha said. "First ask my sisters. They are senior and have the yes and no."

"You are old enough, and also beautiful," the man said. "Therefore, make an end of play. Were this elsewhere but a village pimpled on a rock, you'd reign as queen——"

"Though I do not," Emantha said. "Let be. I must take these flowers before they droop for want of water——"

"Though I may droop for want of loveliness," the man said. "Say now, what will you take? Name any gifts, in jewels or coin, or properties soever——"

"I am not the one to ask——"

"Each is responsible for his own acts——"

Franc tore at the trellis and ripped it down, jumping through the broken sticks and flying leaves to an open space.

"Be responsible for yours, clappermouth!" he shouted. "Draw steel, an' your able——"

He leaped on the man beneath the tree and felled him, and rolled him face-to-light and took him by the collar and shook him once, twice.

And loosened his fist.

A man, no youth, in black velvets and gold chains, stared up at him. Leaves clustered in his hair, and straws had stuck in the mustache that curled in Cathayan style, long and narrow from top lip all the way down to the jowl.

Messer Marco Polo stared with eyes of hard white crystal, sparkling wide in some amaze, and then smiling, though blinking never.

45

Chapter 4

"Well-a-day, Franc, and what is this?"

Messer Mayor Gandolfi looked down, but his face was almost out of sight behind his great girth, belted with gold and buckled with a silver tortoise, and all that could be seen of him jellied up and down with laughter.

Franc stood, finding a knot in his tongue, and tried to help Messer Polo, but the two servants were there first. The knot stayed tied, allowing no word, and the laughter round about made it tighter. He dared not put an eye on all the people, from their sound, a crowd. He looked up instead and stared, for Emantha laughed down at him from the door of a bird cage built of slender branches and painted gold. Leda and a dozen others of the town girls looked out from the bars, and some of the giant Cathayans were at work, adding more branches and more gold paint, and town carpenters were building a wide stairway beneath.

"Is this the way you use an honored guest, good Messer Warden?" Mayor Gandolfi asked soberly. "To leap, a very Perugian, upon the unsuspecting?"

47

"I make no complaint," Messer Polo said in good part. "He thought I spoke beyond my proper bounds. What's this young dart to you? And how is he called?"

He spoke in laughter, as if his dignity had never rolled in a flower bed, settling the lace of his collar and looking up at Emantha.

"He is Franc, though called Francesco on the holy day," Emantha said. "He is my play-brother, born an hour before me——"

"But what is he to you? Is there tie of marriage?"

"None."

"Or of troth?"

"Not."

"Sworn?"

"No."

Messer Polo shrugged and sighed, and both together in relief.

"Then still I ask, since you are not sworn, or trothed, or tied, will you be white nightingale and wear the feathered robe and act those things which I have told to you, all in welcome to her most resplendent highness? Or do you act the mule?"

Emantha shook her head.

"Again, I say, you must ask my sisters first, and they will ask his excellency," she said. "But I may not dress a part, or play-act, or disport myself without permission, or take any gift——"

Messer Polo turned in chagrin to Messer Gandolfi.

"You have a town of but-mongers here, Messer Mayor," he said. "They lack all, wanting an order!"

"And wanting that, have all else," the Mayor smiled. "Let the girl ask her sisters. They will ask Il Cardinale. If he says yes, then she may play this white nightingale. If not, there are others."

"Without her beauty," Messer Polo said. "And none so innocent. The perfect white nightingale——"

48

"Who, or what, is this rare one of feathers?" Mayor Gandolfi asked.

"A songstress of the White River, in the great province of Li-Chen," Messer Polo said. "She is the guardian angel of the Great Khan's house. Where she greets, she blesses. Where she is present, she protects. Where her song is heard, there also is happiness, and no regret."

"Then how could you travel without so sweet a bird, in person?" Mayor Gandolfi asked, almost in blame. "Would it not be better to cage her and spread her notes for all of us?"

"There, you see, good Messer Mayor, is error," Messer Polo smiled. "For in the province of Li-Chen, nothing grows except the sleep-trees and the slumber-grasses, and the White River flows only to the arms of Mu-Hsiang, mother of all. The white nightingale is herald of her love and appears in her children's dreams, though most to the innocent and certainly to the beautiful——"

"What, now?" Mayor Gandolfi frowned. "I have three daughters, all ugly, I swear it, to other men. Fat, freckled, and straight-haired. Does this white one not look to them?"

"Ever." Messer Polo nodded. "For in everyone is part of Mu-Hsiang, and what is ugly in a woman except a certain blindness on the side of the beholder? If his eyes saw truly, he would see her beauty——"

"But my eyes see truly," Mayor Gandolfi asserted. "I tell you, as their father, they are three prizes, and the man who marries one for her looks is a fool, or he's ready to suffer for my money——"

"Not so," Messer Polo said gently. "Each of those girls is of splendid heart——"

"None better!"

"And excellent health——"

"Draft oxen, each!"

"In tooth, bone, muscle, and skin, optimum——"

49

"Pictures!"

"Of enormous appetite——"

"To my cost!"

"Attentive to the wishes of their parents——"

"Ever——"

"Wanting nothing, in short, except this ephemeral quality called beauty——"

"With that, I could marry them to fortunes. As it is, I shall lose a fortune with each!"

"So you judge beauty by what is to be gained?"

"By what it's worth to others, and why not?"

"Because then, friend Gandolfi, good Messer Mayor, it is no longer beauty, a quality to be seen and enjoyed, but a commodity with a price to be weighed——"

"And where's the difference? A beauty is a beauty——"

"And what is ugly is that part lacked by the beholder——"

"You say I, father, lack a part in looking at my daughters?"

"Exactly that sum in each that is lost to you. By that sum, they are ugly——"

"Then, if you find them beautiful, good Messer Polo, why do you choose another?"

"And cause a quarrel among three sisters?"

"Ah. True. But Emantha has sisters——"

"Married, did you not say?"

"True again——"

"Emantha is single. She is of poor family, owning nothing except beauty. She I choose above all others. Who denies me, except Emantha?"

"I," said Franc, with the knot out of his tongue. "I deny you on three counts."

Messer Gandolfi turned his mayoral girth to look surprise, but Messer Polo turned no more than a shoulder and stroked the mustache with fingernails long and curved and, like little sabers, sheathed in gold with many jewels.

"Name them," he said.

"First, she is Emantha, and no nightingale, or you have never heard her sing. Second, where is her pleasure to stand in a cage? And third, who would believe her?"

"Trapped, by the jug of Ganymede!" Mayor Gandolfi laughed. "What answers Messer Polo?"

"This. That where the heart is good, all else follows. What do we wish to do? To make warmest welcome to one who comes, a stranger, many a weary step from her own hearth fire and the comfort of her father's love. How do we intend it? That one from another land shall appear in robes of happiest omen to speak certain words the Princess has known since she left her cradle. How is she made happier?"

"You think at all times for this Princess," Franc argued. "If none else has Emantha's fortune in mind, why should I not think for her?"

"Her fortune is to give others pleasure," Messer Polo told the walnut tree. "Who gives more?"

"Enough," Mayor Gandolfi said. "Emantha, down, girl, and run to see your sisters. Franc, how long for the tower?"

"That moment to find and cherish my mother, Messer Mayor."

"Then away. And next time Emantha speaks beyond your reach, ha' patience. You might be lying here, cool clay. What then?"

"Why, then, good Messer Mayor, one blush from Emantha's store would bring me hot, and I would live again——"

"Which store is this?"

"That one filched often by these trip-shanks," Franc said, nodding at the two servants whom he recognized as her companions of the morning, both in livery of purple and gray, with slashed sleeves and breeches and purple pot-caps feathered in barred black and white. "These made her blush, and these I came to see. But in no coup of fortune, I trapped their master and I make serious apology——"

"Taken, and so let be, and I will deal with these codlings for unseemly speech," Messer Polo said. "You breed a plain speaker hereabout in this city of St. Francis, Messer Mayor!"

"With such a patron, and the city in such care, could he be less?" Mayor Gandolfi smiled. "And if less, should we place trust? Emantha, take his hand——"

"After he could speak so? Those of Messer Polo's Court said no word that stirred a blush of mine——"

"Well it were so," Mayor Gandolfi said. "Let none think he may assault the innocence of our maidens. I notice the Cathayans are jealous of their women——"

"This, by law," Messer Polo said, looking at the two servants. "As these will swift discover——"

"The poor youths made no wrong!" Emantha stamped in anger. "They are accused for no crime——"

"A warning will not fly amiss." Mayor Gandolfi nodded. "Come, be about your several business. I shall look for you in the tower before the next chime, Franc. Be there!"

Franc bowed and went to Emantha, but she turned and ran. He would follow, but in a pace he saw his mother behind baskets of cut blossom and went to her.

"How long since you began to act the lout?" she asked, clearing stalks of leaves. "I could have dropped with shame to think you could so use a guest——"

"Could I know it would be Messer Polo?"

"Did you look?"

"I'd thought him someone else——"

"Thought is the fool's hope. Beg Emantha's pardon——"

"For what?"

His mother whipped a grass bind about the stalks and put the bunch on top of all the others.

52

"Who are you to speak of blushes?" she demanded. "Have you said something to make her blush?"

"Never!"

"Have you seen her blush?"

"How should I?"

"Then speak of what you know. Who are you to choose what shall make her company? Or any word to be spoken? What right have you to play sneak——"

"I, sneak?"

"Sneak! You accused those youths before their master. Did you ask them to go aside for speech? Are they to be punished? Do you care? You are yet ungrown and unmannered."

"If I seek to protect Emantha——"

"Not in such fashion. You bring disgrace upon us——"

"I will go now and call those two into the street!"

"And what? Will it save them their master's punishment?"

"I will speak to him——"

"If he will speak to you. Who are you, except a warden in your father's place? Remember, you have room above to fill. Think not to be tower-tall. You are still little milk-fiddle with me. Go to your work and think of him who was there before you."

"May I go now?"

"Go. And remember. Make pardon with Emantha!"

He went off down the path, looking at none, glad to be gone, feeling in height no more than a cricket. He ran through the crowd of workmen and idlers, but in a flick of silk Leda was beside him, hurrying step for step.

"What I would give to hear you speak so for me!" she sighed, out of breath. "That Emantha! Ungrateful!"

"She had reason, thinking herself demeaned——"

"By Messer Polo's choice? Demeaned?"

"By me. I spoke without knowing——"

"You spoke truth. We in the cage with her know how they

spoke and how she answered. She makes pretense of her blush. Have you watched? She blushes more for thought of beauty in herself than from any words of others. Wait now, and see. I'll wager anything she's taken high enough with her own airs to float above the walls if her sisters say yes, and Il Cardinale says yes, and she becomes this nightingale. Remember this word and the wager——"

"There is no wager without price, both sides."

"For my part, say what price you will——"

"A kerchief of silk for my mother, of the same that you wear on the holy day."

"It is agreed. And if I win?"

"Name the price."

"A kiss, at a time of my choosing——"

"Remembering I have but little free time, and by day——"

"That. Are we agreed?"

"Agreed. But this is not a price."

"What should I ask? Silver pieces? Florins? I'd make the more in a wager with Ob or any merchant. What, then? Gold? As soon the moon——"

"I am Franc, and poor, yes, though I'd work to pay a debt——"

"What need, when the work's a kiss? And dearer than a price because of Franc. Poor, yes, but not in kisses!"

"Cheap to come by."

"How, would you kiss anybody?"

"Not I."

"Then who? Name them."

"None I know——"

"You see? Not cheap, Franc. And I know. Have I not also watched? Think on me, remembering our wager. Adio!"

He watched her run down toward the Three Silver Men in billow of apricot and pale blue silks. It made him pensive that she would speak so, warm and quiet, hands together, almost pleading. Emantha never did. She was more his mother, joking, or kindly or plainly sharp, and treating him as if he wanted in everything except how to climb a stair and light a smoke fire and ring six bells. He found Leda's way of speaking more to his pleasure, new, and a little strange. He never had thought of her before except as helper in her father's hostelry, and one, the gossips said, setting her cap for him. Which, he nodded to himself, was little enough thinking.

Crowds in the streets and filling the forum before the towngate brought him to the moment. He chose the lanes behind, the sooner to reach the tower, and ran up the hill behind the Temple of Minerva, and out to the front. All the old women selling herbs and simples on the temple steps gave him greeting, and the scripmen waved from their desk boxes, and countrymen and their wives going in to offer garlands to the goddess called his name and prayed him to give thought to them and keep sharp watch.

"That will I," he laughed. "Do you ask Minerva for some small share of her wisdom upon me——"

"It is done!" Ferraci, a farmer, shouted. "But she will have less distance to reach when you gain the tower. And you, too, believe on our goddess?"

"And on all that give benefit, even to the flies and beetles that feed the birds," Franc said. "Why do you lay your garland on her altar this day of any?"

"Our son will be examined in Florence tomorrow," Ferraci said. "If he succeed, he is fit to enter the profession of law. Think, that a lawyer should come from us!"

His wife covered her head and wept, and he put an arm about her and made salute, and the two went up the steps, carrying the heavy laurel garland stuck with grain stalks and lilies, between the pillars and into the temple.

"They have no trust in any but the old gods," Tassio, one of the scripmen, said. "He'll suffer loss of his market if Il Cardinale hears of it——"

"Not so," Franc said. "Il Cardinale harms no man for what he thinks."

"He sent the son to school on promise they looked away from all other gods——"

"Not this, either. For Il Cardinale said he would place the son beyond the reach of barbarians, did he not?"

"It is the same——"

"Never! The son is saved——"

"And if he succeed to become a lawyer? Which prayer was strongest?"

"None. His own effort carried him——"

"Effort isn't all, or it would carry many another. Even some of us——"

"And brains, good Tassio. Or else you sit upon the steps of the temple of wisdom day by day and write scrip for those who cannot write for themselves, or read their scrip for those unlettered. And I stand watch in the tower. Prayer makes light of trouble, though it digs no road or plows any furrow. Or who would lift his finger or have any need beyond a prayer?"

"You speak large for one so young——"

"I've heard many a discourse in this, to my profit. But if I stay gabbling here, I'll cross Messer Mayor with no profit and many pains. Adio!"

He ran in the arch of the tower and up, three steps at a time, without pause, hearing the noise of the crowd fainter with every flight. But at the top there was loud rumor of small shouts, and he ran to the parapet.

The dusty procession had traveled all the way across the plain and in toward the furnace and the path to the town, but the tail was still in dust at the cleft in the hills.

The town walls and the archway of the gate had all been looped with green branches and flags, and the little white city of tents was palled in flowers and banners, so thick that not much of a tent could he see, and though it was crowded with Cathayan women, they were hidden except for a glimpse, and then they appeared dressed in a finery of red and white and wearing tall headdresses that dripped gold and tinkled as they moved.

Drums echoed on the mountain behind. A fugelman, carrying the D'Orosa banner, led the company of men-at-arms in glitter of steel. Count d'Orosa, in golden armor, rode a bay horse wearing the same gold feathers in its bridle as he wore in his helmet. A hymn started from the garden of the Little Brothers, and the monks walked two by two in the gray cowled habit of the Order. After them there came the choristers of the churches in purple and white, with the priests and their attendants, and the nuns of the Sisters of Poor Clare, and behind, Mayor Gandolfi and his Council and the insignia of the town. Last, under a red canopy upheld by four of the Brothers, Il Cardinale walked in the old camel-hair gown that blessed his ankles, and with both hands settled the wide-brimmed threadbare red hat to shade his eyes from sun.

Outside the walls, boys ran up the path, shouting and pointing behind. Keeper Mozo waved to silence them, leaning over the battlements and pulling the wrinkles out of white hosen, straightening the skirt of his plum-colored tunic, ready to put his weight into swinging the gate open with one heave on the wheel.

The town guard swept the crowd in the forum back to the doorsteps to make a place for the procession, and those lining the stair were pressed to the walls. Brass horns blared and drums beat. The people threw up hats and kerchiefs for Il Cardinale, and he held out his arms to both sides and called to this one and that, and waved to those in the windows, and often left the canopy to talk to somebody in the crowd, and then ran his old knees back to his place and laughed at the cheers on his way.

Over the rise and up the path outside the walls, ranks of Cathayan drummers and pipers marched toward the gate with banners and pennons behind, and after them Cathayan soldiers on foot, with the giants first, and others in body armor of bars of gold and tall helmets with ear flaps, and spears flying streamers of silk. Cathayan women trotted after, in ones and twos and then in a crowd, all playing little cymbals and singing in high voices but not in tune. The palanquin of the Khan's daughter, larger than any yet seen, was borne by a score of giants, and in front the little girl danced and the two boys played music for her, but they were too thick in the dust to be plainly seen.

From a place before the towngate, Messer Polo in Cathayan robes of black and gold walked out to meet the captain of the Princess's legion. The drummers and soldiers went to the side, and Messer Polo walked on until he was met by the crowd of women, and, in a crush, they waited to meet the palanquin. Messer Polo held up his hands, and the palanquin was halted, and all the women knelt, bowing their heads to the ground. But Messer Polo knelt on one knee, upright.

A hand came, flinging a jewel's brilliance from the palanquin's curtains, and Messer Polo touched it with his finger tips, and stood and signed, and the music started again, and the soldiers took their places and marched on. Messer Polo walked beside the palanquin with his hands in the wide sleeves of his robe, head bent. At that time the town procession passed down the steps and into the archway, but Il Cardinale and his suite waited at the edge of the forum.

Messer Gandolfi held up the seal on the chain about his neck as sign of authority to open the town, and Keeper Mozo took off his cap in salute and straightway swung the wheel to part the middle gate.

58

The mayoral procession passed out, beyond the town walls, and Messer Polo met Messer Gandolfi and his councilors and accompanied them to bow and address the curtains of the palanquin. Nothing moved within, and no hand reached out. The long scroll of welcome was unwound, and the town scribe read, though not a word could be heard in the din of cymbals. Down in the forum, Il Cardinale left the canopy for a talk with people in the crowd, strolling from one to another.

Paolo, son of Councilor Corti, one of the richest merchants in town, had dressed for others' envy in a crimson doublet and white breeches, and puffed himself in front of the Mayor's suite, pushing the smaller choristers in their places and trying his best to act as a great one over the little. He cuffed a small chorister, but he made bad choice in a colt from the family of Tillio, the champion drover. The little one slapped back and put spirit into it, so that Paolo lost his hat, on which he kicked and the little one sprawled.

But Il Cardinale had seen the kick, perhaps from the corner of his eye. It was said of him that he missed little, and that, worthless. He paused in walking back to the canopy and stroked his chin, looking down at his sandals. In no hurry, he made way through the ranks of the choir and stood a little off, looking neither at the chorister sitting on the cobbles nor at Paolo brushing his hat. He spoke instead to Ciro, his purser, tall as the tallest Cathayan and nearly as strong as Ob. Ciro put two fingers down Paolo's neck, never minding his size, and swung him across the bent back of the town Wand Bearer. Thereon, Ciro took one of the willows from the bundle in the Wand Bearer's leather case, long and slender and flat, and easy as a whip. The red hat nodded, and the wand smacked dust from the tight seat of Paolo's hosen. Il Cardinale stood with his hands clasped behind, looking up at St. Rufino's bell tower as if the drub of willow on wool held no interest. But every time he nodded, the wand whistled and thwacked and the crowd said

59

"Ooh!" and Paolo shrieked like a girl at play. When the Wand Bearer stood straight, Paolo fell off, rolling on the cobbles and clutching his hams and howling, and the more of each, the more the crowd laughed.

Il Cardinale spoke to the chorister and took his ear to put him back in the choir and bent over him, shaking his finger. He gave Paolo no look. But he spoke to the Wand Bearer, and he made a gap in the crowd and shoved Paolo through it and pointed to be off home.

The sound of the drums and horns told where Count d'Orosa's troop marched under the walls. The Count rode out in the open and saluted Messer Gandolfi and Messer Polo and lifted his lance to the palanquin. But hats off, or knees bent, or heads bowed, or lances up, there was no sign from inside, and no jeweled hand to give greeting.

Everybody stood for a little in rolling dust and stamped his heels to raise some more. In a sudden, the little girl in white with the two little boys in black started to dance toward the gateway, and all the Cathayan women followed. As if instruction had been given, everybody moved on.

But there was little order in the entrance on the town side.

A rank or two of Cathayans and a few of the band and some of the women spurted from the archway, out, and up the steps to the forum, and then more, with a few of Count d'Orosa's men-at-arms and a couple of councilors and more of the band, everybody trying to hold a hat on or lift weapons out of the press, and using knees and elbows not to be flattened, all tight together and squeezed against the waiting crowd. The palanquin came out, tipped up and sideways, because the bearers had to turn this way and any way to ease its width. But it was out at last, in gold and brocade, and the crowd's patience burst through the town guard and all the people pushed forward, among all the Cathayans and the women and the choristers, and nothing was left of any procession, and less of any order. A ring of Count d'Orosa's men protected Il Cardinale, and the Count rode among the crowd to clear a way for the palanquin. Not because there was room or way, but because of the press of townspeople trying to see who was inside, the mass began to move up the steps and into the forum and along the street toward the Mayor's residence, and the faster they moved, the faster they might because of more people shoving up the steps behind. In little time most of the crowd was gone, except for soldiers and some townspeople picking about to find hats or kerchiefs or bits of uniform pulled off piecemeal in the crush, or some limping from a trodden corn or a twisted muscle.

Franc watched them, every one, until they had all found what they looked for, or in want of it cursed a thief and went anyway. He sighed, thinking of all the sights to see, and the free feast, and the adventure he was missing.

"So-so!" A little voice said behind him. "You make one-piece big breath, lo. I say not is very good! This is what talk?"

He turned his head slowly, thinking that he dreamed, and hardly thinking at all.

The little girl in white stood in front of the two little boys in black, all of them smiling and nodding their heads and bowing, hands in sleeves, all the way down to the floor.

Chapter 5

Franc wanted to say a great deal, but all he thought of seemed sillier than the next. He was going to ask how they got up there, but he knew they could only have climbed the stair. He could have asked by what right they had climbed, but they were strangers, knowing nothing of rights, and the door was open, without guard. He might have asked what they were doing there. But he could see for himself they were standing, smiling and bowing, and nothing else.

For a moment he stood with his mouth open. And all the time they bowed and smiled. But he saw with great surprise that the little girl was a grown woman, despite her smallness, and the little boys were also grown men with whiskers a-lip as long as Messer Polo's, though softer, as if the barber's knife had never touched them.

"What do you want?" he said at last, all gentle manners and any form of honest greeting forgotten.

"This piece-house yours, chu, what do?" the woman asked, with a beautiful smile that folded her peachblossom cheeks, and her eyes almost closed, yet shining even out of the sun.

"It is the watchtower," Franc said, wondering how he should explain. "I am Warden——"

"You at here do what?" she asked in her little voice.

"I look," Franc said, waving at the plain. "If I see enemies, I warn the town."

"You wait him do what, when look?"

"I make the smoke and ring the bells."

"So-so!"

She turned to the little men and spoke to them, and they nodded and laughed all together. The two men carried, one a drum underarm that he tapped with his finger tips, and the other a set of bone pipes and a pair of cymbals no larger than a florin that he beat together with first finger and thumb.

"You do, lo, make happy with bells," the little woman smiled. "You make many-piece fire, smoke-smoke. You sell this piece house, how much?"

"I cannot sell. The tower is the Mayor's——"

"How much you sell?"

"You can't buy it——"

"I buy one-piece house, smoke-smoke. How much?"

"This tower belongs to all the people," Franc said slowly, that she should understand. "Nobody can buy it——"

But the little woman shook her head, smiling, holding out her hands.

"Visitor much happy, sing many-piece joy, chu, how much?"

Franc tried to make her understand. All three laughed at his frown, and the little man with the pipes played a tune and ended on the cymbals.

"One-piece fire, smoke-smoke," the woman tried again. "When I do? Make happy with bells, I how what, lo?"

"Ah," Franc said, looking for the right excuse. "When the White Bird flies from the White River. Then you shall also ring bells——"

64

He stopped because their smiles were gone. Their eyes stared. Their mouths were straight.

"How, what say, White Bird?" the woman asked in her little voice, a baby grown up.

"We give welcome to the Princess Na-Nou," Franc said, patience itself. "The White Bird will sing for her. When she sings, I make smoke and ring bells."

"So-so!" the woman said, and all the smiles came back. "We make many-piece joy. What name you, lo?"

"I am called Franc."

"I Hsi-Soong." She pointed. "This Chi-tsi, One-piece. Two-piece, Chi-tse."

"Chi-tsi!" One-piece, the drummer, laughed, nodding and tapping the drum.

"Chi-tse!" Two-piece, the pipe and cymbal player, nodded and laughed, playing too.

"Hon'ble Flamp, I go," Hsi-Soong said. "This two-piece man, he go. We find gold piece, make buy——"

"Nothing buys this tower——"

"We chop-chop go find Plinseps Na-Nou, highness very good, buy this one-piece house, six-piece bell, smoke-smoke. So-so, lo!"

They bowed and smiled, and Hsi-Soong went down first. Franc saw what Emantha had meant by the slit skirt. Hsi-Soong wore a dress that from the high, close-fitting collar to her waist looked like a second fleshing of white silk, and from the waist down to the tips of her small feet was just wide enough to stand in. But when she moved the skirt swung open from hem to thigh bone on both sides. The drummer went next, and the piper last, for a moment showing a smile above the trap. They began to sing going down the steps, and drum and pipe music came up all the way, loud even from the floor and out in the street.

He watched the three dance, Hsi-Soong in front, over the

forum to the towergate postern leading up to the little white city of tents on the walls. Hsi-Soong pulled the bell rope, and the door was opened from above. They went in and some moments later came out of the capstan-house door, and there were hidden, except for the noise of laughter among all the Cathayan women.

The town was quiet. Not even a dog walked the forum. The tables in front of the Leather Flagon lay on their sides with the benches piled on top. No pigeons flew and not a town guard leaned in any doorway. All that moved were the weathercocks, creaking a point or two in hot noon gusts, and the lines of washing in yards or pegged over the streets.

A coach and a small troop turned in to the chapel of St. Francis out on the plain. Nothing else moved all the way to the river and up to Perugia. No workmen climbed the poles about the church. The paths among the Cathayan tents and pavilions were clear. Only the olive trees shook gray-green heads in the hills, and cloud shadows were all that stirred over the stretch of rocks up to the castle behind, and there was stillness all the way around to the cleft in the hills where the road went down toward Rome.

He began to feel hungry, and small wonder, for with the chime he found himself more than an hour beyond his mealtime. It was excusable because his mother would be among the first in Il Cardinale's service, and Emantha could do no less than help her sisters. And if all the hundreds of guests were to be served there was plenty to do, and little time to think of one going hungry, and less to slip off with a dish all the way up to the tower and back.

Brother Egidio waved to him, hurrying along the lane behind the temple, and entered the archway below. Franc slid down the ladder to meet him at the window platform, wondering if there might be a message from his mother or Emantha.

66

But the platter wrapped in a white napkin stayed his question.

"I was passing the Three Silver Men and Leda asked me if I would bring this to you," Brother Egidio said, handing it up. "Your mother works hard, good woman. So many people and all eating twice, as you'd expect——"

"And Emantha?"

"Emantha is dressed in white feathers and she sings in a cage with some of our girls," Brother Egidio said, frowning. "In the Mayor's garden, and surrounded by Cathayans. Leda was with her, but she returned to the inn——"

"She remembered me when Emantha did not——"

"Emantha is guest of Il Cardinale and sits at his table with the small Cathayan dancer. It goes through the town that this Messer Polo has offered to buy her——"

"Emantha?"

"Mayor Gandolfi made good answer. He said he would sell Emantha if Messer Polo would sell the Princess, but for ten times the price——"

"This is language they understand!"

Brother Egidio nodded his thin-cheeked head, almost as brown as the habit, and smiled kindly eyes.

"They place great faith in coins," he said. "I have a favor to ask. Brother Dario will finish building his hut tomorrow. If we might again borrow Scabbard and Spada for an hour to pull a load of stone from the fields——"

"For as long as you will——"

"In payment——"

"It is made. Share the good things in this——"

"I ate at dawn. But my thanks. Pax!"

Franc went up the ladder faster than he had come down. The napkin held a silver platter with a stuffed chicken and salads, sausage and breads, many kinds of cheese, a tartino of strawberries, and fresh fruit, and a flask of the Three Silver Men

67

wine. Leda knew as well as anyone that he was not permitted to drink wine on watch, or even to have it in the tower. But he grinned at her willfulness. It was like her. He sat on the parapet and picked the chicken clean, and went through all to the empty platter, and leaned against the pillar to rest with loosened belt and no shoes, thinking of Leda.

He saw that the coach and troop of horsemen were leaving the chapel of St. Francis, and an outrider waited to turn them on to the path leading to the town. Only the saint's bed, table, and stool were inside the little stone hut, all he had owned and lived with in his lifetime, except for a few books that Il Cardinale had taken out of the damp to his house to keep in good repair. But, even for so little to see, the pilgrims of many lands went there by the drove day by day, and the rough stone walls were made smooth by the fervor of their kisses.

He thought of Keeper Mozo and his goodwife making free of the food and wine at the feasting. The little troop and the coach would have to wait outside until one or other Mozo came back. Nobody else was there to open the gate.

Unless he left the tower, sprinted across, swung the wheel, and sprinted back, with nobody to see or ask questions. That would be a good turn for Keeper Mozo and a boon for the visitors.

He waited until the outrider came over the crest of the path leading up to the gate. A look across the plain showed only a straggle of pilgrims. He slid the ladder and leaped the stairs and ran across the forum to the gatekeeper's postern and up to the top of the wall. Keeper Mozo's doorway was locked, but he pulled the grille off the window and went through the room to the capstan house next door and loosened the bolt holding the wheel. He ran back to the window and out, and swung his weight on the top spoke, and felt the gates below opening under the ease of the turn.

A look over the arch, and with the last horseman in, he swung the wheel back and went into the house to replace the bolt. The small horn window in the capstan house let in enough light to darken when shadows crossed it. For no reason except that he wanted to see the little white city of tents nearer to, he pulled aside the bolt, and the frame opened on cracked leathern hinges that squeaked from age. Cathayan music covered the noise, but even so he was content to stare through a narrow gap. The tents were richly hung and carpeted, and furnished with trees in pots and flowers growing in boxes, and Cathayan women in many-colored robes laced in gold sat in a circle, with wondrous dressings of jewels in their hair. A tall-backed golden chair made Hsi-Soong look like a baby swathed in white and sitting on a scarlet cushion waiting for her mother. The small men in black, One-piece and Two-piece, played music and a girl danced, if such was a dance, with a foot turned up, and a hand bent to the forehead, and a foot placed, and fingers held to the chin, and staring at nothing. At Hsi-Soong's feet an old woman, withered and lined, held a fan of black feathers and waved at flies. But the sadness in her face lifted only when Hsi-Soong reached down to pat her hand and chatter.

He closed the window carefully, thankful for the drumming and music that covered the squeak of the hinges, and went in to the Mozos' room and out on the wall, making certain that the wheel was firm, and ran down, across the forum, and up to the tower, all without seeing a soul.

A new sound of music and drumming came loud from the direction of Il Cardinale's house. He stamped the stones, thinking of what he was missing and wondering how Emantha might appear in the feathered robe, and if the two pip-fingers were dancing attendance, and what they might say to bring her to blush.

A movement in the lane behind the Temple of Minerva brought him to look down. A dozen Cathayan soldiers ran in the shadow, each carrying a bundle. They came into the lane leading to the forum and halted, unwrapping the bundles. Packages were taken out and tinder was sparked to light a torch. Some of the Cathayans came to the front of the tower and caught the ends of the long banners one after another, tying a package at each corner. When the lower corners of all the banners had been weighted, the Cathayan with the torch ran around the four sides lighting the strings falling from the packages into tips of fire and tails of gray smoke.

Franc had no fear that the stones of the tower might burn. The banners belonged to Messer Polo, and if he wanted to destroy his property, it was his to do so. But the burning banners could throw up smoke which might be mistaken for an alarm. He shouted down to stop them, but nobody took notice, and the strings went on burning and the banners flaunted, and the Cathayans ran down the lane and crouched, looking around the corner as if they feared something evil to come.

A clap of thunder shook below his feet, making the bells echo. He looked up in fright at the sky's blue, without a cloud, and all about the plain. But another clap broke, and another, and blue smoke puffed over the parapet and made him cough, and the sound of the thunder was greater than any storm he had ever heard, and the tower rocked as if kicked by a thousand stallions. The banners flew out in long rags, but the edges were burning, and at every yard or so the silk flamed and made a small thunderclap, and all the banners streamed and burned, and as they burned the small flames burst in their own small thunder, and the world seemed full of terror that hit the ears with force of a buffet, and smoke tore the throat, and a shaking made the tower lean from side to side until he thought it might break in two.

The banners burned black to the top, and the cinders blew away. The shaking stilled, and the noise. His ears rang worse than they might in standing too near the bells in full peal. He lay on the floor, feeling as if he had fallen off a horse at full gallop, wondering if his bones were whole and if he could stand and what he should say to the Mayor and Council about the Cathayans. Something would have to be said, and the men would have to be taught that they must not use fire, in joke or out, and certainly they must behave within the precincts of the forum and the watchtower.

While he dusted himself and twig-brushed the platform free of cinders, he tried to think how he should explain the Cathayans' thunderclaps and what words he could use to describe them and their effect. It was as plain at the end as when he began that, try as he might, he had not the words. Each of the sounds had been like the slam of a devil's door, far louder than the closing of the town's great gates. Nobody would believe that such a noise had come, not once, but a hundred times, from packages tied on the end of the streamers, or that a sound almost as loud had come from places in the edges, never mind that he was witness. Cloth, he could hear them saying, is cloth, even silk. It makes no sound except in folding or tearing or when brushed. Thunderclaps, no. He wondered what he should say not to look a fool, or if he should keep a discreet tongue, saying nothing, and let all go on as before.

But the Cathayans must be warned, guests or not. Laws were laws, and townsmen daring to make nuisance in a public place would have been tied up and flogged raw. To go further and threaten the safety of the watchtower and to make smoke and fire which could have been mistaken for an alarm were crimes that might have brought a public demand for the transgressors' deaths. It had happened in his father's time.

He looked up from the pile of sweepings, frowning at whip-cracks and thunderclaps, the one between the other, seeming to come from the little white city of tents. Cries and music and singing went on without pause, and the postern gate opened and a procession came out, with Hsi-Soong first, and after her One-piece and Two-piece, and then a veiled woman, and the Cathayan women in a crowd all around, dancing and singing down the hill toward the new church.

But the thunderclaps came louder, and with a great wailing of shrieks and shouts from the place outside the house of Il Cardinale. Smoke puffed in clouds above the roofs, and the ground beneath the tower shook and the platform rocked. But the Cathayans went on and out of sight.

Stiro, corporal of the town guard, hurried up the hill and paused, holding the wall with one hand and his stomach with the other, and lifting a face at that distance redder than his tunic.

"Ho, Franc!"

"Ho, Stiro!"

"Think no harm to the noises and rumors. The Cathayans make a game with sticks and fire. Messer Polo entertains his excellency. And we are all in a pin's-breadth of being lift from the seats of our breeches——"

"I was near to being tossed from the nest. Is more to follow?"

"Saints forbid! Messer Gandolfi sent me to assure you that within the walls all is well."

"My thanks in return. Is Emantha yet in the garden?"

"She is sitting in style in a gathering of his excellency and many nobles, with the Count d'Orosa, Messer Polo, and this Cathayan Princess. Emantha is a white bird, and Messer Giotto sits in front of her, making his marks with charcoal——"

"If you see my mother, wish her well. Tell her I had savor of my midday meal!"

"Ah! Good things were gulleted this day, I swear it, the like never before. Some new boiling of long strips brought from Cathay by Messer Polo that slid down by the platter. Everyone has eaten and drunk for three——"

"And I up here!"

"Ha, good Warden——"

"Ha, bee stings and pepper corns!"

"Pax!"

"Adio!"

He watched Stiro go back the way he had come, still in a hurry, as if he feared to miss pleasure. A stamp about the stones on all four sides cooled anger. It was enough that the town and every bird on the roofs could eat at rest, safe in knowing that Franc stood guard. But he wished he could go down to see what went forward. Eyes could give more joy than mouths could ever tell, and he wanted to see Emantha in her feathers sitting up among the great.

It surprised him, although he tried not to think of it, that his mother could have forgotten to send his midday meal. She would be there among the grandames, helping all others to chew and swill, and surely a thought of her son hungry at his post must have come to her mind. She had never failed in all the years of his father's duty, and never during the time he had been up there. He thought that perhaps she was angry he had begged no pardon of Emantha. She might be punishing him, as she had when he was small, by letting him go short of a meal.

A thought of Leda came, in softest voice, and a plea, and memory of a silver platter full of a roasted chicken, with a tartino, and a flask she knew was forbidden. He looked over the plain. Horsemen, perhaps a hunting party, were riding toward Perugia. Other horsemen rode toward the furnace. Four wains traveled toward the river. Too much was afoot to go down even for the space of a chime.

Scabbard and Spada clopped over the stones, and Getullio rode them into the stable and came out and looked up.

"Where was this storm without rain?" he shouted.

"It was entertainment of Messer Polo's," Franc shouted back. "No harm, no damage!"

"To others, perhaps. I lost an hour's work. My bumpkins dropped the last sacks and ran back to the mountains in a roaring fright. Half a day's work lost while others lick their fingers.

73

Is all scraped and gone at the feasting, or do they still pass a platter?"

"So said Stiro, the town guard, not long past. Go, set yourself before the largest——"

"Or two of the smaller. My appetite is truly earned this day——"

Getullio looked about, as if to see how many were listening. But, though he saw none, he signed to the door and went inside.

"Did you see D'Orosa ride out from the castle?" he whispered urgently up the stairway.

"This morning," Franc whispered through the trap. "To greet the Princess——"

"He rode not an hour gone under the back wall——"

"He sits in gold at Il Cardinale's table——"

"We saw him not an hour ago in steel, heading a troop from the castle's back postern, with his banner before——"

"Why should they go such a way? Except to hide themselves?"

"We think alike. They took the path that fords the river near the Perugian highway."

"What, then? Does he invite battle?"

"With a bare score of men? And the town not risen or the yeomen in arms?"

"Did you speak of this to another?"

"And lose my tongue? Not so. For myself, I am a baker, having no other affair except an appetite. Should any ask, forget my name!"

"Be it so. Good tastes and proud filling!"

Franc sat out on the parapet, watching the river toward Perugia. If the Count d'Orosa had left the feasting, he must have gone around the walls on the far side, for certainly he had not passed through the towngate. But the Count liked to ride behind the horns and drums and to exercise his privilege of passing through the great doors without showing sign. All others, even the Mayor, had to show seal of authority, except Il Cardinale. It was enough that he appeared, and Keeper Mozo flew.

But the Count had that morning ridden down in gold armor. Even so, to ride up to the castle and change from gold to steel and ride out all took time, and yet no horn had sounded, and that again was unlike the Count d'Orosa. Further, if he wished to reach Perugia or anywhere near, the easiest way was through the town and down the path to the furnace. Going over the mountain behind the town walls took longer and harder work for men and horseflesh. Getullio must have seen some other, and he could go burst for a fat fool, the fatter after his repast, and the more fool to burst.

But there was discomfort in the thought that if Getullio were right and the D'Orosa banner had flown at head of a troop, then only the Count could have been behind. None other, whether he were captain general and grand admiral in sum, could ride behind another's banner unless in company of its master. If the Count d'Orosa were not of the troop, then the banner would not have flown.

Therefore, if Getullio and his helpers were not dreaming, some other had usurped the Count d'Orosa's place. Or worse, it told that the Count had chosen a time when all in the town were steeped in a feast and not likely to notice movement on the mountain or to be vigilant in any matter except eating and drinking. That alone carried warning. But first it were prudent to find out if the Count made one at Il Cardinale's feast.

The plain was free of any traffic except pilgrims afoot. It would be an hour or more before the troop from the castle could pass over the mountain and appear along the river. There was time enough to run down to Il Cardinale's house and stand at distance to see if the Count sat at table or not.

Between thought and action was no time, and he was down the flights and in the street, listening to singing from the townspeople and a roaring chorus from the men-at-arms and strange sounds from the Cathayans all mixed together. The hill and the houses kept the noise from rising to the tower, though in passing through the gateway to the churches, he thought he had never heard so great a caterwaul.

The space before Il Cardinale's house of grass and wild flowers held the town and its guests, standing if they were able and lying down if not. Crowds ringed the casks at the walls and drank from any beaker. Dancers tripped it to pipe and fiddle, and singers shut their eyes and bellowed at the sun. Children played in shrilling hordes, and mothers sat in rings with food in their laps and fed their infants, and, far out on the verges, lovers held hands and watched, saying little.

Under the long canvas roof upheld by pillars wound around with colored cloths and garlands Il Cardinale sat at the head table, with an eagle-beaked man in a blue cap at his left, and, on his right hand, a veiled woman in Cathayan dress richer than any he had seen in the little white city of tents. That, he thought, must be the Princess Na-Nou.

At her right hand sat the Count d'Orosa in golden armor, and over his face the white hood he wore to cover the scars of his wounds, which kept him, so it was said, from marriage, since he feared his ugliness might cause any gentle-born to perish of fright.

There he sat, and Getullio was twice wrong, for the banner was hung behind his chair and his squire served all those sitting near except the Princess, and she had servants enough.

In shadow of the wall, he saw Getullio steep his fingers in a dish of yellow tapes, each a finger wide and an arm's length long and covered with a steaming sauce of tomatoes, holding it up over his head and letting the ends fall into his mouth until it was crammed, and munching, as if he tasted manna, with the sauce dribbling about his chops.

"Ha, good doughmaster!" he hailed. "Where now is this one we spoke of and his banner and the troop———"

"Soft!" Getullio spoke at the dish. "I am a grown man wanting little in what I should know for my trade, and in no hurry to learn of any other's. What I told you came as duty from one living in the town. I, too, saw the one in gold sitting there. I saw his banner. I see his troop of men-at-arms there at the further cask. But I also saw one of that banner carried over the mountain, as I told you, at head of a troop. Enough. I know nothing!"

"We have equal knowledge. What is this lengthy mess you eat?"

"A dish brought from Cathay by good Messer Polo and cooked by your own mother, of the thrice-blessed heart. It is of a flour and water, and yet is not bread. A poor man's treat and like to be his staple——"

"How is there taste in such?"

"Here. Dip and see——"

"My thanks. But I have little time. Adio!"

He ran down the lane to the back door of Il Cardinale's house, and found both yard, space at the back, and kitchen crowded with women, all wet-faced from the heat and working at tubs, or dishes, or peeling vegetables, or cutting fruit. His mother sat watching a group of women rolling yellow dough on marble slabs.

"No girl could I find to climb the steps," she laughed. "I was held here and Leda said she would find somebody. Brother Egidio told us you were fed in silver and napery——"

"I would rather have eaten some of this Cathayan wonder," Franc said.

"If we finish making it. These few girls have stuffed the town double and again, and still they crawl. It seems to bring the more appetite the more it is eaten."

"Remember me tonight. I shall hunger the more, seeing this——"

"Did you see Emantha?"

"Not yet, nor any sign——"

"Look well at Il Cardinale's table, at one in a covering of white feathers between Messer Polo and Messer Dante, to the left of his excellency."

"Messer Dante, you say?"

"He arrived not long ago——"

"By coach?"

"The same. A scholar, it is said, and he tells her pretty words, and in a place opposite Messer Giotto paints an angel. But the Count d'Orosa has an eye upon her. That misery!"

"Small harm if Il Cardinale speaks a word——"

"And she behind the castle walls? Who would hear that word, or any?"

"The Count has dared much. But not so much——"

"How many would dare him?"

"Il Cardinale——"

"Too late to help her——"

"Where is the certainty?"

"In the eyes behind the mask——"

"You fear this?"

"I have worked in the heat of these fires since noon. But the river in winter runs no colder than I feel, top to toe. I saw him look and I was lost to warmth or words."

Franc kissed her cheek and left the busy place. But in running back he saw that the feast was ended for those at the long table, although the townspeople looked as if they had just begun.

Il Cardinale walked between the Princess Na-Nou and Messer Dante, leading the procession of guests to the Mayor's garden. Messer Polo walked beside Emantha, and two Cathayan pages in scarlet robes upheld a long train of small, close-stitched white feathers hanging from her shoulders, and her eyes were in shadow from a cap of feathers and a long

78

golden beak. Next to her walked Messer Giotto, drawing shapes in the air with his hands.

Behind walked Count d'Orosa.

Franc saw the eyes behind the hood, a falcon's, scarcely blinking, staring at the feathered robe in front, and the rest of the face hidden by white linen and framed about by the golden visor.

But Emantha had no look for any beyond Messer Polo, or when he leaned to hear what Messer Giotto said she turned her head with his and listened too, and laughed if they laughed or nodded if they nodded, and all the time in a smile of lips and teeth that came, he knew, only at times when she was given a sup from the jam spoon or if Il Cardinale patted her cheek, or for some strong favor not to be got by anybody else.

He pushed his way through the crowd, hurrying to get in front to take the short cut through the back of the garden to the Three Silver Men. Il Cardinale paused to wait for Messer Polo, and the Princess and her suite went on toward Messer Gandolfi's house.

Franc went through the trees and over the wall. Cathayan music and drumming began nearby, but the growth hid the players. He went silently, keeping off the pathways, not to be seen.

But in his hurry he almost ran into a broad, cleared space where screens hung and mats were laid, and in the middle, not a yard from him, the gold palanquin of the Princess Na-Nou shone a glory in the sun. The curtain was not quite closed on his side, and he saw the Princess being helped in, and servants patting and smoothing and bowing in all they did.

He stood still, in shadow, breath drawn, fearing to move.

The Princess sat cross-legged on a cushion and took off her veil, and a click of the fan sent the servants away. But the withered face in the color of a peeled walnut was that of the old servant sitting at the feet of Hsi-Soong in the little white city of tents. He saw her sigh and bow her head and rock back and fore.

He inched away into darker shadow and chose his path and ran.

Chapter 6

With the first strokes of the evening chimes a stick rattled on the railing below, and he ran to the parapet in time to see Emantha enter the archway. He slid the ladder to meet her on the window platform and took the bundled platters, but when he offered help up the ladder she snatched her hand away and turned to go down.

"How, am I blamed for this morning?" he demanded. "Are you leagued with my mother to make me bend a knee? And which reason? That I had no liking for these nice-necks of Messer Polo's?"

"For the reason you had them put away from duty!" she raged suddenly in a voice that half the town could have heard, doors shut and bedcovers over head. "Is this a man? You had to accuse them before their master, no word to them——"

"Nor ever will be!" he shouted back. "Tell them, if they wish, to point a place and a time. Say I will meet them with the weapon of their choosing, longbow to quarterstaff. Or any of their imagining. What, then, are we in Assisi to knuckle for lace and finery?"

"If you are better, show them so!"

"With all pleasure——"

"They show manners——"

"They'd show bruises——"

"Any fly can sting——"

"You think of me as a fly?"

"What else? A nuisance. To me. To your mother——"

"Speak for yourself!"

"As your mother spoke, not long gone——"

"She has no word in this!"

"She is ashamed that two visitors, guests of Assisi, should be treated so. As I. Two boys, punished for no crime except that they laughed and made pleasant talk——"

"With blushes!"

"Your own, for thinking so!"

"If you are set in this, why do you come here?"

"To bring your food. Who else is there? The basest dog should not be left to starve——"

Franc took the bundle, balancing it in the palm of his hand and leaned over the ladder to throw it through the window.

"Here's one base dog ready to starve, yea or nay!" he said softly. "Tell my mother so. I'll eat no more of her hand or yours. Out!"

By evening light he saw the tears shine and the mouth shake. But she turned too soon.

"Be it so," she whispered. "Nothing suits a fool except his foolishness——"

"Back to your Polos and silk-simples. This dog howls alone!"

She ran down the stairway and turned, a dark shadow in darkness.

"This was cooked only for you!" she called through tears. "When some were tired of the day and dropping, yet they remembered you——"

"But you did not. The basest dog turns from a kick——"

"I did not kick!"

"With words. That apply harder to the mind than any boot to the rear——"

"If I gather it up, will you eat?"

"From the street? As a dog?"

"You threw it there. How will you eat this night?"

"Not by your kindness. Go!"

She went further down and stopped again.

"This is done for Leda's sake!" she whispered. "She fed you at noon——"

"Better than any before——"

"Then let her feed you this night, and tomorrow, and ever——"

"I pray she will. I'll grow the fatter!"

"Swim in your grease!"

"Better than rattling bones——"

"Then these are the thanks? We are now so taken of the Three Silver Men that nothing less will do——"

"And kindness, a gentle word——"

"Poor many-suffering thing!"

"Not to you. Tell my mother so——"

"I'll tell Leda so. I work there this night——"

"Then listen well, and take lessons!"

She ran all the way to the foot, and the moon sent her shadow long across the arch.

"Nothing is broken!" she called. "If I bring it up, will you eat?"

"No!"

"Then starve for a dog!"

"Howl for me!"

He went up the ladder, and looked over the parapet following her, running down the back lane toward the Three Silver Men. Town guards came with torch carriers to light the streets. Cathayans marched to the tower postern and rang and entered in.

All the townspeople awake from their siestas walked the forum at will, wives on arms and children behind. The Leather Flagon became noisy with song and the rattle of pots, and Cathayans filled the tables but only to drink small beakers of tea.

He peeled a twig and shredded the bitter pith. But the taste made his appetite the sharper. Hunger chewed the empty space somewhere inside. Thought of the bundle lying down there brought desire to fetch it up and eat. But to suffer sat better with pride. Certainly his mother would regret, if nothing else. He hoped Emantha would go straight home to tell her, for on the morrow any sacrifice so many hours old would earn a sniff or less, and perhaps an extra ladleful of soup or a larger twist of bread, no more.

He thought of the tea, brought from the Three Silver Men and as yet untried. A filled pot on a flare of twigs soon started to sing, and he remembered to heat the crock before putting in a pinch of leaf for himself and one for good fortune. The bits grew soft and opened in the heat, and the boiling water brought it to the top in black rags that sank.

Somebody shouted below and he went to the trap.

"Answer, good three-eyes!" Mok called. "Are we welcome up?"

"As far as the window platform, and no noise," Franc said in a tower whisper. "Who is with you?"

"Simone, the stone carver, and Laz. We have favors to demand and much to tell you. First, let me defeat this plague of steps. I breathe as a beldame cracked o' lung. Did you discover the source of Emantha's blushes?"

"She did not, and you, you dogs, stretched a leg for me!"

They started to laugh and howl as dogs, but he stopped them with a warning to use quiet.

"Many listen. Therefore speak low. Will you drink tea?"

All three stopped, looking up.

"How is this?" Laz whispered. "The town is become a morass of this windy tipple. Has it, then, reached to this height?"

"I got it from the Three Silver Men——"

"Aha! And that's not all, from what we hear——"

"Tea, or no tea?"

"Tea, and pray for me!"

"Wine, if you prefer——"

"I'd thought this place a stronghold of virtue——"

"And is. The flask's unopened——"

"Then let it stay so, and we'll swallow this juice of Cathay."

"Here, as far as the windows. No further."

"Take these in hiding," Simone whispered. "Keep them safe until we have need of them. Care!"

Each piled his arms with a weight of heavy packages that made the climb to the platform a matter of step and balance. He took the pot and a couple of beakers down and sat at the foot of the ladder, and they squatted on the window sills.

"You heard the loud knocks of today, no doubt," Mok began. "These were set off by the Cathayans. It is a powder of sulphur and some-such that with fire will blow many times its own weight into the air. Messer Polo calls it gunpowder. He says the Cathayans are as used to it as we to bowstrings, even their children——"

"So we made away with some to try what we may do," Simone said. "I have certain stone to split——"

"Stone!" Laz laughed. "He means he has certain walls to tear down——"

"I tell you again," Franc warned, "your words may be heard below."

"Behind my paw then," Mok whispered. "Our lodgings are not safe. They might be searched, or some fool of a bedmaker might catch a toe upon them——"

"They are safe here," Franc said. "What else?"

"Messer Dante talks tonight at the Three Silver Men——"

"What I'd give to hear him!"

"Hold, and listen. We are apprentices, and the law forbids us the delights of tavern, hostelry, or any public place, except we have as guardian one reliable, of proper trade, and vouched for by a justice. We ask you, as one having all these, to take us in——"

"Why not some other?"

"No other so gaily fits our company——"

"I have not the money——"

"You need none——"

"I spend no other's——"

"Do not. Drink tea, and Emantha will bring hot water——"

"This is honest bait. And good talk by great men?"

"Messer Polo has invited Messer Giotto and Messer Dante to sup with him. There is word that Il Cardinale will join them afterward. They will speak of wonders. Now do you know why we seek one to vouch for us?"

Franc thought of Emantha and his mother, and their tone of speech to him as if he were half grown, and all but laughed aloud.

"I cannot leave the tower before the last chime. Look for me at the fountain a moment after it has struck——"

"Good!" Mok said. "Simone, tell your tale!"

Simone drank the tea and held the beaker between both hands. A cool wind flew about his whispers and carried off the tea's steam. He said that his stonecutter at the river quarry had told of a troop of men-at-arms coming from Perugia and meeting another troop from the direction of the D'Orosa castle. Both troops had gone off to a place among the trees to lie in the grass and snore. But the two officers had sat at the river's edge talking for the space of three chimes. Then both called their troops, and forded the river toward Perugia.

"How did he know this troop came from the castle?" Franc asked.

"Brother Egidio was out gathering stones with Brother Dario. They saw the troop. They agreed the banner was D'Orosa's."

"And make no argument that the Count d'Orosa sat at meat with Il Cardinale," Mok interrupted. "We saw him there. But the stonecutter saw his banner elsewhere. How is this?"

"However it may be," Franc said carefully, "what is it to us that we should speak of it?"

"We know this butcher's handy man," Laz whispered. "Has he not laid waste in every quarter except this? Bearing the marks of his trade on his frontpiece? Are not the tenants of his lands beyond the mountain in terror of his whims? How many men and women are his victims, even in these past months?"

"He has the power," Mok said. "When will he use it toward us?"

"What would he do with Perugians?" Simone asked the tea.

"What, indeed, while he sat at Il Cardinale's table?" Franc said.

"If," Laz said, in doubt. "He is in as much danger as any of us in dealing with them."

"They would stretch and slice him as well or better than any of us," Simone agreed, and handed the beaker to Franc for a filling. "Why should he treat with them or they with him?"

"What is our concern in this?" Franc asked.

Laz stood up and stretched out his arms toward the churches, white in moonlight through the window slots.

"Twice have I see dear towns in smoke from unholy pillage," he whispered. "Always the master speaks to us of his fear that our work may be for nothing. Shall we sit by, knowing of matters that might lead to sack and destruction?"

"What made you silent to your master?" Franc asked. "His word carries weight enough——"

"Supposing we told him, and supposing we were wrong?"

Mok said. "We would be racked and flayed within the hour. How would this serve us? No. We came to you——"

"I, a warden——"

"With the ear of Messer Gandolfi, fat, but no fool, and many times a match for any D'Orosa. Further, we are ordered to go to the Rock Castle by Messer Giotto to look at the great hall and see if panels may be drawn thereon to please the eye of the noble Count——"

"He has in sudden come to art for solace!" Laz sneezed. "We go up tomorrow to take measures."

"Do you come too," Mok said, and drank the tea and gargled. "You have free time of an hour. Make it two, with permission."

"And what will I do at the castle?" Franc demanded. "With or without permission?"

"With us, use eyes and ears," Mok said. "Men-at-arms talk as chapwomen, having nothing else in their blocks——"

"And if there is something to be found?" Franc inquired.

"Then all speed to Mayor Gandolfi," Laz whispered. "And we'll look to D'Orosa's health with sticks of this gunpowder. Above us are enough to raze the castle from the mountain."

"And now the secret's out," Mok said, resigned. "So, Franc, good friend, a word from you and our flesh hangs in the forum before the morrow's noon——"

"Instead we'll tread it to the castle," Franc said. "And what of tonight? Only to hear Messer Dante?"

"A-many blessings rest upon his noble head," Simone said, standing. "No. To be near the Count, even from the room's far side. I have seen him on his visit to the studio. He has a scar on the knuckles of his right hand. If the Count sits there, some other rode out and spoke for him to the Perugians."

"And for which reason, except to sack Assisi and so destroy our work?" Laz whispered.

"Forgetting Messer Polo and his Cathayan Princess and the

sums of their ransoms," Franc said. "There are riches here in horses alone. But what of the Khan's Infallibles?"

"A few more than fourteen score I have counted," Mok said. "The rest, copers and ostlers and valets. Bring in triple those numbers from Perugia and add the Count's troop for surprise, and where are these of the Khan, except on the stones?"

Franc picked up the empty pot and beakers.

"It is well," he said. "Within a minute of the last chime, at the corner by the fountain."

He listened until they had gone through the arch, and went up to the platform. The town took gilding in torchlight, and the plain blew gray with heat mist, and no light showed anywhere in front, at the side, or up at the castle.

Simone's story bore out Getullio's. Somebody treated with the Perugians under the D'Orosa banner. No Perugian breathed unless with enmity for Assisi and all its people. Any whisper that D'Orosa's banner had ridden with a Perugian troop could have meant panic among the townspeople. For that reason Getullio had been wise, wanting nothing to provoke disorder, and yet intent to do his duty.

Franc looked about to assure that all was to hand and, satisfied, took cap and slid the ladder, and leaped the stairway, pausing only at the arch. The lane was silent, and he ran, choosing back ways and climbing walls to be seen of none. He reached the side of the Mayor's house and went in shadow to the kitchen door. A cook stirred at the fire and maids rattled pots in the pantry. He went through to the dark inner room and touched the long table to find a way to the door and out to the chimney place.

The Mayor's three daughters sat at lap-looms, and the Mistress Gandolfi made stitches in a pattern. Messer Mayor sat asleep on the longbench inside the fireless chimney place.

Franc made his bow and begged the goodwife for a quiet word with Messer Mayor. The three girls might scream, but the goodwife slapped one to silence, whereon the other two pretended no interest. The whispers awoke Messer Gandolfi, and the longbench groaned with his stretching. He cast a red-bead eye at Franc and instantly sat, pointing outside, and the women ran with no word.

Franc assured himself of closed doors, and his whispers made certain of deaf ears.

Messer Gandolfi nodded throughout and, at the end, went on nodding.

"The fruit is yet in the bud," he rumbled. "It wants but fair weather and proper moistening. Go up with Messer Giotto's fellows in the morning. Poke and find the number of troops up there and anything else of interest. Come to me here afterward. These of Messer Giotto's studio are closemouthed?"

"As their own devices upon the walls. They seek to protect their art first, above all things——"

"Rightly. And I, the city and all within. I have no trust in this D'Orosa. His father was ever an animal. I expect nothing more of the son. Stiro shall take your place in the tower. Did any tell you that Messer Polo would buy the tower and bells? I said we would sell the smoke!"

Franc left by the door in the garden. All the leaves were yellowed by lights in the pavilion built about the palanquin of the Princess Na-Nou, and the air was filled with odors from Cathayan cook pots. He ran along the path toward the tower, and halted among a group of women with music and torches going the same way. They made a lane for him, and at their head Hsi-Soong smiled, with One-piece and Two-piece bowing and smiling behind her.

"Hon'ble Flamp!" she called in the baby voice. "You go, how, what do?"

"I meet friends."

"I come, make many-piece joy, chu, one-piece house you got, tomorrow?"

"Not tomorrow——"

"I come tomorrow, I buy, take away, chu, one-piece house you got?"

"You must also take me——"

Hsi-Soong clapped her hands and jumped up and down, talking to One-piece and Two-piece, and all the women bowing about her.

"I speak you," she said. "I come one-piece house, bells, smoke. I speak, lo, hon'ble Polo, buy you!"

He laughed at her laughter and ran on. Simone met him at the fountain and said that Mok had gone in to find a place, hidden, and yet near enough to hear the great ones at their talking. They went between the tables outside the Three Silver Men, crowded with Cathayans and their town friends, and through the tavern and serving rooms to the garden covered with a trellis of vine. Lanterns glowed over long tables full of the town's notables and their guests brought in for the night.

The middle table was set apart, and chairs were drawn up instead of the usual benches. Messer Dante sat opposite Messer Giotto, and Messer Polo next, and a Cathayan officer, and master builder Messer di Rovigo, and another Cathayan, and a couple of town councilors. The Count d'Orosa sat at one end of the table, helmet off, and his head in a white silk cowl with embroidered slits for eyeholes, and beside him there sat the Count Schiavon, his commander of cavalry, tall, pock-faced, and sullenly haughty, glancing at the rest from a blue eye, and always with one corner of his mouth raised.

D'Orosa lifted the goblet of wine, and the scarred knuckles of the right hand gleamed white.

"No doubt lies here," Franc whispered to Mok at a table in a corner where little light came, and yet within sound of the nobles' voices. "This is D'Orosa!"

"Certain." Mok nodded. "This one has been in Assisi every

hour since this morning. Therefore, who met the Perugians? How shall this be uncovered?"

Tivi made a sign toward the middle table. Messer Polo first looked about the room to assure himself of silence, and then waited for the coughers to stifle their mouths in their caps.

"It would suit all merchants the more if the lands were set in peace," he said across the table. "Who takes profit by blood? If the Khan's armies marched, they could cover all Italy with their feet without room to stretch an arm. Where is the profit in this?"

"In the land," the Count d'Orosa said in a high voice unfitted to the scars and armor. "In the fruits of victory, in slaves, in riches of every kind——"

"All of Italy can be put into one of the Khan's present demesnes and lost, never to be found again," Messer Polo said. "The province it was my honor to govern stretched a full month on horseback, north to south, east to west. Yet this was a minor part of the Khan's birthright——"

"We hear great figures," Count Schiavon said. "Lacking proof, they make nothing——"

"Does the excellent nobleman doubt my word?" Messer Polo inquired.

"Nothing is doubted," Count Schiavon replied with a wink for D'Orosa. "But such figures leap in my head. I can believe what I see——"

"Let me make you an invitation to visit the Court of the Khan. Thereafter you shall come to my governorship and under my protection discover its size for yourself. To avail yourself of the Khan's gracious hospitality you must prepare yourself for a journey of at least two winters by horse, and three if the rivers or fortune run against us——"

"We spent three winters before Jerusalem," Count Schiavon began.

"This is children's babble, and not to be discussed," Messer

Polo smiled. "I was at Jerusalem not three months past. Everything is to be got there, and food and lodging fit for princes. On our journey we shall encounter wastes of sand and ice and animals never seen before. The lion, and tiger, and mountain camelopard——"

"We are anxious to hear of cities," Messer Giotto said, glancing at Count Schiavon with little liking. "The buildings and the crafts——"

"None beyond Hamadan, worthy of speech, until Samarkand," Messer Polo replied. "I am told there are cities to be seen along the northern route. That way I shall try on my return. But little exists between the frontier of the Khan's empire and Samarkand except a wilderness peopled with savages. For that reason the Princess was granted a Cathayan bodyguard."

"Which make slop with this tea," Count d'Orosa said into his goblet.

"As do I," said Messer Polo, touching the small beaker before him. "Perhaps you know of a drink more flattering to the health and all the senses?"

"Wine," the Count said, and cracked the goblet on the table. "I'll set any wine-bibbing man-at-arms of mine against any of your tea-drips, and see them run off the field——"

"Name the extent of your wager," Messer Polo smiled. "You decide the events and place. My men are ready and so is my gold!"

"Now, Messer Millions!" Messer Giotto warned. "You are promised to me in certain sums for works agreed——"

"Have no fear. I shall have the more when this match is finished!"

"Let us say a thousand gold pieces, equal, on each event," the Count said. "If there are twenty events, prepare to pay me twenty thousand such!"

"They shall be placed in a coffer tomorrow. It wants only a

word from you when I am to send for the twenty I have already won——"

A shout outside and a shuffling to stand and a cheer from all inside brought Il Cardinale to the table with Messer Gandolfi. It took the company time to settle down, and the serving wenches ran to fill flasks and beakers. Tivi tried to find somebody ready to bet against the Cathayans, but every man's pouch was tight shut.

"I have watched the Cathayans drill, by foot and with arms," Mok said. "They are stricter governed and more dexterous than any I have ever seen. What say you, Franc?"

"D'Orosa's troop is veteran, brisk, and tempered," Franc said. "I shall pray to be out of the tower to see the sport——"

"You are out, and here," a voice whispered beside his arm. "Sit and enjoy a flask with me. And tell now, how did you find your noon meal?"

He looked about at Leda's smile.

"No man has eaten more or better," he began. "Where is Emantha?"

"Taken to serve for the Princess Na-Nou," she said with a frown. "You missed her?"

"Perhaps."

"And did you enjoy your supper the less because of it?"

"No," Franc said truthfully.

"Then? Your mother made you the pick of the feast?"

"But I did not eat——"

"No appetite?"

"No supper!"

Her eyes grew almost as round as her mouth. She closed both in an instant, and whirled about and ran. In a moment she was heard, above all the talk and clatter, screeching in the kitchen.

"Fortunate he who marries a pot, a crock, and a beaker," Simone said. "He lacks for nothing, lifelong."

"He'll lack less with a Leda," Tivi said, glum. "Think, to be master of this house. Late to bed every night in the counting of so much coin. Up late in the morning from a nest of eider down. A fire to toast the toes. A beaker ever at elbow. A king's bounty at every meal. What more could any man want?"

"A brain and work to do," Mok said, short. "A week of this, and which would be a whole man?"

"I, for one," Tivi laughed. "I would open my paint room next door. What would I lack then?"

"A master," Mok said. "Here would be your mistress, shrewing daylong——"

He fell silent at Leda's approach. She had beakers, a flask larger than any on the longest table, and kitchen wenches brought trenchers of bread, and meats, and a potage of vegetables.

"Eat and be full," she told them in a whisper, for the room had grown quiet. "There is plenty more!"

Tivi looked at Mok and shook long hair over his eyes.

"Shrewing daylong, and this twice before you, day upon day," he murmured. "No, Mok. The best painters are those plump-fed. The skin-and-bones have not the marrow to commit themselves. They paint with an eye on a full plate——"

"We paint because we must!" Mok whispered fiercely. "Eat or not——"

"We paint better fed," Tivi said. "Make me no hopping cats of this——"

"The good St. Francis starved himself," Simone began.

"The better to see out of this world into another." Tivi nodded. "But the work of painters is to see what more is in this world that most might never see unless we show them——"

The garden hushed, and all heads turned toward the middle table.

Il Cardinale listened, hand over ear, to Messer Dante speaking to the Count d'Orosa.

"It may be true, Signor Count, what you say, that many poor people have known greater suffering on earth, and not always of their making," he said in his fine voice, soft. "The Crusaders suffered many pains, yes. But did those warriors expect to be struck with canes of sugar?"

People laughed, but the Count leaned forward.

"They expected the help of heaven!" he shouted in his high voice. "How was it denied them? Why did no victory come to them? They carried the Cross——"

"But the Cross was not in them," Il Cardinale said quietly. "Help comes to those deserving and asking——"

"I spent a goodly fortune for my rigors, and the marks I shall ever carry," the Count said. "For what? Where is the help most powerful? Behind the Saracens? The victories went to them!"

"We must show ourselves the stronger," Il Cardinale smiled. "What use to complain? If we mock and take a name in vain, and in all things disprove belief and deny existence, why should we then expect help?"

"But the Cross was carried!" the Count said, hammering the table.

"Ah well," Il Cardinale said, holding up his hands, "because a sign is carried, what do we expect? That those behind believe on it? Or that others, seeing it, will take fright and run away?"

"The sign told all that the true host followed!" the Count said, forward in his chair. "The sign went before us, telling all that saw which men we were, which ideal was ours——"

"You believe that?" Il Cardinale asked with interest. "Anything carried before as a sign tells the beholder what to expect of the men who follow?"

"That is my belief," the Count said, striking the table and leaning forward.

"Very well," Il Cardinale smiled, leaning too. "Then could you tell me what a troop of yours was doing on the mountain

96

path today behind your banner when you were sitting at my table?"

Messer Gandolfi coughed into his wine and made haste to cover himself with the sleeve of his gown.

The Count sat straighter in his chair and moved his goblet to the side.

"My banner was not on the mountain," he said, barely heard. "Except that recruits were at drill and followed a marker, but no banner——"

"Eyes that I trust saw the D'Orosa banner," Il Cardinale said, smiling still. "In the time the town gave welcome to the most charming Princess, the troop rode beyond the further hill to the river. Is water so scarce at the castle that you must send in search of it?"

"As I have said, recruits, at proper drill——"

"Behind your banner," Il Cardinale said, and turned to Messer Dante. "Let us speak more of things concerning humbler men. When shall the copies of your *Comedy* be with us? It is long since I saw a page clean-wrote. Parchment is hard to come by and too costly for poor scholars."

"Perhaps your excellency will permit a gift of paper," Messer Polo said. "I have a selection——"

"What is this paper?" Il Cardinale asked.

"A substance made in the Khan's dominions, of secret process, sometimes of cloth, sometimes of certain grasses. It has a surface smoother than parchment, thinner, and a thousand pages would measure no more than a thumb in thickness——"

"Impossible!" Il Cardinale whispered, and looked at Messer Dante's surprise. "When shall we see this wonder?"

"I will make your excellency a visit tomorrow, and I am permitted. I shall also bring your excellency an ink, blacker than any——"

Count d'Orosa pushed back his chair and turned about to jingle and rattle through the house to the street. Nobody spoke as he went, and most pretended to drink or pour more in their beakers.

"Tell me, Messer Polo," Messer Giotto began, "what of the arts in the Khan's empire?"

"Far more of the brain than of the senses," Messer Polo said. "There is painting, though not of our style. Instead they profess as more important the art of writing with the brush instead of a quill or reed pen. They have no letters, but they draw pictures to the number of fifty thousand or more, and each picture is a word. They carve stone, though not as we do. They are engineers and alchemists and weavers. They are potters and shapers and painters of porcelain. They make an art of the sciences——"

"And for belief on this life and the next?" Il Cardinale asked.

"Little for the next that I know," Messer Polo said. "Their belief is to worship that which might bring perfection in this life——"

"And what is its secret?" Il Cardinale asked.

"Behavior, shall we say, of one to another."

"A start, at least. The Khan permits the teaching of Christian belief?"

"He permits all within the law. I am Christian, born so, but I was also governor."

"They have no scriptures bearing on heaven and hell?" Messer Dante asked.

"They have a full library, though not of scriptures as we know them," Messer Polo said. "My time was taken in business and affairs of government. I spent little with any but servants of the Khan and engineers——"

Franc nudged Mok.

"The time goes too soon, and I must go back to the owls," he whispered. "Take note of what is said and tell me tomorrow——"

"I will learn more about this paper and ink." Mok nodded.

98

"See how the Master slavers, waiting for a word with Messer Polo!"

"He feels himself in the use of it," Tivi said, using bread in gravy. "I stay on for a better reason. I am too stuffed to walk, and I wish I might marry a shrew!"

Franc pushed out through the back and into the serving room. Leda stood at the counter tapping flasks and adding and telling the serving wenches how much should be asked of each patron. She left all in the moment she saw him and ran.

"How, then?" she inquired. "I thought every man in town must have an ear to what went forward in there——"

"True," Franc said. "But I have a place above the town——"

"Shall you ever be there, a half bird?"

"Until there are feathers in some other nest——"

"Perhaps I know of one such——"

"I would still have to go back to the tower. Let me thank you for my feast at noon, and another now with my friends——"

"But the Mayor and Council are all inside. Who will see you? Or know if you went back or not?"

He looked at her eyes, thinking that Messer Giotto had copied them well enough, darkly smiling and peering.

"It's enough that I'll know," he said "and a lot needs watching——"

"At night?"

"I see well enough——"

She laughed, moving flagons for a wench to carry off, and took coins from another.

"The Count Schiavon came in by day with the D'Orosa troop and went out before noon and came in again tonight," she taunted. "You didn't see him!"

"How, did he come a-run to tell you?"

"They lodge here tonight against an early journey, and I was looking to their quarters and heard them speak——"

"Of me?"

"Of the blind Mayor and Council. No word of our blind Warden!"

"He is wakened enough, thanks to Leda's sharp ear. And happy of a midday meal, and another tonight, with hospitality for his friends——"

"Because they sat with you. When will you sit with me?"

"Let these Cathayans go. When we are quiet once more——"

"And Emantha is again in the kitchen and not out, beyond her place, in feathers and gold caps——"

"This was put upon her——"

"And she smiles under it and rides the air——"

"As a bird should——"

"Remember our wager. The time comes for payment!"

"Adio!"

He went through the back way to the inner courtyard and the stables. D'Orosa sentries stood guard at every gate below, and others snored in straw under the walls. The troop and its master very often slept in the town to save time on days when they guarded trains of D'Orosa produce going to outside markets. He stood in the shadow of an arch, aware of a new fear, seeing for the first time how it would suit the Perugians to have a strong ally within the gates, and how the fact might be bargained. He was far from proud that a squadron of horse had left the Rock Castle and had ridden all the way under the walls of the town to the end of the cliff without being seen from the watchtower. Nobody would blame the Warden, since his eyes could not reach through walls. But it showed weakness and need for some new place to keep watch, even to building another tower. It also showed need for more care from the Warden. The squadron should have been seen from the moment it left the castle arch until it rode under the town wall.

But his eyes had been wholly upon the Cathayans. The time had been well chosen, and that too seemed part of a plan.

Someone had relied upon the blindness of the Warden. Shame flew that the guess had been correct.

He went up the steps to the short cut back to the tower. All the doors of the lodgings were curtained with leather. Saddlery was piled outside every entrance, telling the rank of those within. The Count d'Orosa's room was marked by his esquire, asleep under a horse blanket. The curtain was drawn except for a crack, and he grasped at courage, and looked through.

Two pine torches lit the room. A bed was made against the far wall. A fire of twigs burned in the middle of the floor and a cauldron steamed over it. Count d'Orosa sat in a chair with his feet to the fire, and wearing the golden armor without helmet, so that the hood cast pale reflection on the breastplate. Beside him, Count Schiavon spoke in whispers, resting an elbow on the hilt of his sword. The weight of the curtain and the wind's breath hid all he said.

A stick flourished on the other side of the fire to prod flame, and a shoe moved on the hearthstone, of cured leather, long-toed, and belled, which only one man in all Assisi could afford to wear.

Councilor Corti, enemy of Messer Mayor and no friend of Il Cardinale, sat before the fire with Count d'Orosa.

Men-at-arms marched into the yard below and tramped up the steps. To be found there could have meant losing eyes and ears.

He stepped over the sleeper and slid back into the shadow, squeezing his shoulders into a drain from the roof, and the swinging arms almost brushed him. While a sentry was placed with shouting and pacing, he crept to the stair and down to the lane, and ran.

Chapter 7

Not for the first time, Franc thought he should have been keeping watch from the tower of the D'Orosa castle, which looked down on the town and the mountains on both sides, and over all the plain to the front, and across the valleys and mountains to mist-distance behind. The sentries in its keep had ample warning of all traffic from any point of the compass. The men-at-arms he talked to had contempt for his position as Warden in the watchtower, and the corporal said outright that any troops bent on taking and plundering could be at the walls and over long before an alarm would be of any use.

"I doubt they might," Franc said in the high wind, looking far over the plain. "Not many know the paths hereabout——"

The corporal laughed at his men-at-arms, and they all laughed back at him.

"No attacker comes the known way," he said. "What, are we farmers, to use tracks? Or farm wives, lifting skirts from mud or dust? Soldiers go the way they may, and that's the way that's best——"

"Which is?" Franc asked.

"Where least wounds come, and least trouble follows——"

"Let me ask a soldier of such known parts as yourself," Franc began, "where, in the attack, should we expect a thrust in Assisi?"

"Why, against the gate of the Little Brothers, open wide day and night, for one," the corporal said, something flattered, as Franc had meant. "And for another, at the back, see, where the wall is broken in. New walls at front, and broken behind? What is this but welcome and free entry?"

"We would hope to give steady account of ourselves," Franc said, looking over the battlements at the courtyard below. "We feel ourselves lucky to be in company of the D'Orosa troop."

"This will depend upon many things," the corporal grinned. "We are paid to do what we must——"

"True," Franc said. "As all of us. The Perugians, now. Could you withstand them, and they in attack?"

"On the plain, and thirty of them to one of us, no. But all of them, and any friends against us here in the castle, and we would rest tranquil upon our arms. But why should we fight them? I know a-many good lads new in garrison there——"

"They are, then, not all Perugians in that army?"

"Do you know so little? The most are got from Florence and Genoa and Venice, all homing from the Crusade and looking for hard money——"

"Soldiers all?"

"Some of horse, some of foot, and some of the sap."

"What is the sap?"

"Those digging beneath walls or driving tunnels to reach the sieged."

"But if the Perugian garrison fills, is this because they fear attack?"

The corporal shifted the spear and spat into the fire. His laughter went, and in his eyes came cunning, and he looked at the men-at-arms and blew out his cheeks.

"Here's a question," he said. "But what's for us lowly ones to say? Why, nothing. It's up top that gives word. And there's answer enough!"

Franc went down the keep stairway, wondering about the many items he had found, and ready to run on the instant to Mayor Gandolfi to tell all he knew. But Tivi and his company of apprentices were in the great hall, and Simone and his stone-cutters were about the walls and outer works, using plumb line and measure to find where other and nobler buildings might be raised, not least a chapel.

Simone greeted him, hot from a climb up the redoubt wall.

"Parts of this are the thickness of two men's height," he said behind his hand. "And at others a botch of rubble, pierced easy with a spike——"

"What is of interest here?" Franc asked, surprised. "Why, in thought of building a chapel, should you uncover thicknesses in a wall?"

"Why?" Simone looked at him and away, up at the height of the keep. "We who work among the gentler crafts must ever step one ahead of those whose business is destruction. Therefore, if the Count should cause us evil, or if his hand should tremble to grasp what is not his, what could we do to ruin his claw? Why, with a couple of my lads here, I would bring this mass waist-high within the space of half a night. Let him give us cause and see!"

They went together through the courtyard and into the entrance hall, stoned, barred, and with doors of iron, and into the great hall. Sentries stood at every door leading into the castle, but the long, high room was left to the painters.

Tivi stood on a scaffold, drawing a panel in charcoal upon the wall's squared blocks of stone. Mok and Laz rolled balls of string, knotted in their length with the various distances. Other apprentices bundled together planks and poles and coils of rope, and others stood with paint gourds, waiting to hand them up. Tivi jumped from the platform and caught the rope to slide down. He went to the far wall to view what he had drawn, a group, of men and women, and one apart, holding out his arms in appeal. He looked once and, satisfied, nodded to Mok and Laz, and all three went up on the scaffolding, and the paint gourds were handed up, and in a trice the busy brushes filled the figures with color, and all took shape, and the panel lived, so that the figure of St. Francis, him in appeal, might have stepped alive from the frame.

None stood near, and yet Franc felt driven to his knees and knelt for presence of a miracle.

"Well, good Franc, how think you?" Tivi asked from the platform.

"Words are gone," Franc said. "See me ready for prayer!"

"This, then, is the power of our gentle saint," Mok said. "Pray he may have some effect upon this D'Orosa monster!"

"Slow in this!" Tivi warned. "Let us see how one coat of paint pretends itself in this light. Lads, untie and carry away the standings. We have worked enough in the wilderness."

"It cries of blood and bones," Laz said, spitting. "See, Franc. Here, where no guards stand, come down——"

He went to a small door near the great fireplace and through and down a narrow stairway to an iron door just wide enough for one to pass at a time. A flight of steps against the wall went to the floor of a square chamber of unfaced stone, set at every few paces with iron rings. From the roof hung chains and pulleys. In a corner a bed of iron bars, with wheels at each end. In another, an iron frame, upright, with chains looped overhead. In the middle, a long firebox, and racks of strange tools, and a tub full of many kinds of whips, and a half circle of comfortable chairs, cushioned, with footrests.

"Here is the place of torture," Laz whispered. "See you the chairs for those looking on? They sup above at comfort and come down for entertainment by hours of screams and writhing. Fellows of happy conscience. The bed is a rack that stretches bones and muscle and presently tears them apart. The frame is to hold them steady while the tools are used. The firebox brings iron to white heat——"

Franc turned and ran up the stairway into the hall and sat on a coil of rope, trying to think happier. But he could see the Count sprawling down there in comfort, carousing with his guests, watching and listening and enjoying the agony of the helpless.

All the gear was taken away, and Franc stood so that the last coil might go, and they set out in a group, waving farewells to the men-at-arms on the walls and leaving the great gate by the postern in the archway.

"It is our good fortune that the Count's servants are all a-town while he is away from the castle," Mok said on the path down. "The place was ours except his own rooms. What I would give to see where he sheds his armor and becomes the soft thing we all are without it!"

"I went in all places outside, even to the armory," Franc said.

"With what profit?" Tivi asked.

"Much for the Mayor's ear. Eight armorers hard at work for a troop, in all, sixscore. Two would be plenty. All men draw extra pay. All weapons are sharp for war. Each has a shield of steel where before they had leathern bucklers. And fourscore of extra horses in the stalls."

"And this means?" Mok asked.

"Battle," Franc said. "All those men wore steel, ready. At other times they do their duty in tunics. They wait only for a note on the horn——"

"Which Count Schiavon wears at his saddle bow," said Tivi. "Ha, Simone, what then, stonecropper?"

Simone and his helpers got up from the rock at the side of

the path. They had the heaviest burdens of tools and balks, and they slowed the step.

"Enough," Simone laughed through sweat. "With no single arrow shot I could reduce that warren and all in it to a heap and a hole and a tomb, in one!"

"Fairly said," Tivi laughed. "How?"

"The keep wants only a pick in a certain place and it falls. The main wall is kept up by a keystone. Remove it. The redoubt rests upon an arch. Undo it!"

"This, then, is the truth beneath the threat." Tivi nodded and looked about at the bulk of the castle. "There sounds a marvel of ease in the doing."

"Say it so," Franc said. "And if we have as much in the wish as they in the threat, we are as soon to taste the mire as any!"

He left them at the top gate of the town with a whispered agreement that nothing be told in any quarter until he was given orders by Messer Gandolfi. He ran direct to the Mayor's house, seeing on the way that Stiro patrolled up in the town tower, and feeling a jealous twinge because of it.

Mayor Gandolfi waited in his parlor of green damask walls and furniture picked with gilt. He paced the floor, hands behind under his robe, and brushed his chest with his red beard, looking at the pattern in the carpet, a gift, he said, from Messer Polo.

"These Cathayan visitors bring us many pleasures," he rumbled when Franc had finished, "but more worry than we are ready to carry. Il Cardinale has set out inquiry to see what's afoot in Perugia. But I was made to die at that table last night. He knew of the troop at the river——"

"From Brother Egidio," Franc said. "If we mount a guard at the wall, and the Little Brothers' gate is shut by night, and Cathayans keep watch at the furnace, where can we be caught by surprise?"

"Wherever the evil-minded are pleased to plan," Mayor Gandolfi said. "We are in strange position, suspecting and yet unsure. The Count d'Orosa may be loyal to us and our town. The troop that crossed the mountain may be one that trains to put young soldiers into harder metal. The banner may not have been his. But the leader met Perugians. What says the Count to this? Nothing, with contempt, for such is his way. What are we to think?"

"That Crusade troops are in garrison at Perugia," Franc said. "That they have knowledge of the Princess Na-Nou and Messer Polo, and have the measure of their riches. That in all Italy no other place falls so soon to their attack as our Assisi, which has been theirs more than once——"

"To our disgrace!"

"And with them to attack from the front, and the Count from the rear, there is little to prevent them from conquering once again. A ransom each from the Princess and Messer Polo, robbery of all their treasures, and possession of all their animals, sale of all their servants——"

"A soldier's dream," Mayor Gandolfi said, and looked at him sideways. "You have spared some small thought to this, Franc?"

"There is time to spare for thinking in the tower, Messer Mayor!"

"That has often been my thought. I have often thought also that I have need of a right hand, one to follow my instruction and be my feet, which, though I have, I no longer see, or rarely have the breath to use. What do you say, Franc, that I promote you to be Esquire to the Mayor?"

Franc took quick thought of himself in a position not far removed from the Mayor's own, though without a councilor's responsibility or any civic power soever unless in the word of the Mayor, but for all that a heavy rank, one of privilege that would uplift him in the eyes of the town and bring no small honor to his mother.

"This is great promotion for a humble one, Messer Gandolfi," he said at last. "But the Warden has been our family honor for five generations——"

"Enough!" The Mayor raised his hand. "Let us say, then, Esquire to the Mayor, and Warden of the Smoke and Bells. Here is full title, wanting nothing. Find a man of family to take your place in the tower. Control him and supervise all. But work with me!"

"I must go first to my mother, Messer Mayor——"

"As a dutiful son," the Mayor said in kindly impatience. "Be back here ready for work within the chime!"

Franc ran, wondering if he should tell the Mayor he had seen Councilor Corti in Count d'Orosa's lodging. There could be no excuse, except that he had looked through a curtain where he had no right to be and had watched three men speaking among themselves. Councilor Corti could go where he wished. Count d'Orosa could invite his choice with no word from any. The more he thought, the less there seemed proper in his conduct and, rather than be thought a whisperer and peepholer, he made up his mind to be silent.

He went in his mother's house ready to shout, but he stood in the doorway abashed.

Il Cardinale rested on the stool with the woolsack under his feet, and his mother sat before the hearth skeining wool.

"Well then, Franc," Il Cardinale smiled. "Come, let us have a word in peace——"

"Franc!" his mother scolded. "To leap in so!"

"And why not?" Il Cardinale said. "When I was his age I flew, or I bounced, or I turned a saltimbank in every other pace!"

Franc kissed the old hand, and sat where he was put, beside the chair.

"We have set ourselves in fine ways of late," his mother said. "Roasts of poultry and silver dishes from the Three Silver Men. His own hearth is grown too small and pots fly from the window to feed the cats!"

"What says Franc?" Il Cardinale asked. "How was this roast? In better smack from silver, I'll warrant!"

"The better for the thought that sent it," Franc said.

"Well taken!" Il Cardinale laughed. "And Leda, there's a kindly one. Something lifted of her years, but of good heart——"

"And a good eye," his mother put in. "Her cap flies ever to his head!"

"He could do worse," Il Cardinale said. "But he has a thought of his own in this. Well, Franc?"

"Why am I argued in this manner as any lout one half my years?" Franc said angrily, wanting to speak of his promotion but finding no place for it. "If Leda is kind, why must she have words cast at her——"

"I cast no words," his mother said.

"The thought was in them," Franc told her, and stood. "I told Emantha I wanted no more at her hand or yours——"

"Ho, wait now!" Il Cardinale said. "Make no more in this. Recall the words, repel the thought, banish all memory. Amen. When did you last see Emantha?"

"Last night, Excellency."

"Did she speak of any traffic with these Cathayans?"

Franc looked at his mother, but she took the wool and bent aside to the loom.

"No word, except to quarrel over two of Messer Polo's household——"

Il Cardinale shook his head, and sunlight shone on the tonsure and froze the crop of white about his ears. His eyes, which always smiled deep blue, were paler, seeming to look through time and walls and far beyond in space.

"I speak of the Cathayans, not of their servitors and vassals," he said. "She was not at her sisters' house last night. Neither is she at work today——"

"If perhaps she is yet with the Princess Na-Nou——"

"It is one reason I am here to speak with your mother."

"Perhaps, Excellency, Messer Mayor will give me time to find her. He has promoted me to be his Esquire——"

"Why, then Franc, here is happier news and in good time!" Il Cardinale laughed and held out his arms in welcome. "I had often thought of you standing up in the clouds day after day, watching, a very crow a-pole. Messer Gandolfi has wisdom. In a little we shall see you wear the Mayor's seal. But not by quibbles with your mother. And tell Messer Mayor, with my compliments, that as your first duty you will find and bring back our Emantha, who is no white bird, but a little hen filled head and craw with Cathayan flattery. Go, bring her to me!"

Franc kissed the hand and ran out along the lane to the house of Emantha and her sisters. Two older girls, children of Hortensia, washed clothes in the yard, and a younger girl stretched wool for thread.

"Emantha is not home, nor any word," the oldest girl told him. "She went to the tents among the Cathayan women——"

"And what?" Franc frowned. "Who permits this?"

The girl shrugged.

"It is said the Princess desires her presence above any other," she said, blowing hair from her face. "If only it were me!"

St. Rufino's chimes struck the hour, and he shut his mouth to questions and ran down to the Mayor's parlor.

Messer Gandolfi allowed him no time to speak.

"Go first to Messer Polo and present my compliments," he said. "Say that Messer Dante will wait on him here at the second hour after noon. Go to the presence of the Princess Na-Nou and present my felicitations and say the same, having care for your address and grace of speech. Remember, no dawdles at wayside, or ogling of any wench. Hence, Esquire, and let us see your measure!"

Messer Polo's pavilion was largest in the Cathayan park. He gave name and rank to an officer of giants at the entrance and, at a sign, stood to wait.

The pavilion walls were of heavy white silk, and the hangings before the doorway were splendidly worked in scarlet and gold. Carpets stretched from the path's edge across the grass to the entrance in pattern of blue and white. In rough shoes and patched tunic he felt out of place and something mean as a messenger.

The hangings lifted, and Messer Polo stood between, laughing.

"What then, my friend of the hard words!" he said. "What mission have you with your victim? Come, enter!"

He stood aside, and Franc ventured in, to a gloom of rich tapestries hanging from the roof and lit by wicks burning a long flame in glass bowls, with heavy scent in smoke rising from metal dishes.

And among a mountain of cushions, in a Cathayan robe of white, there lay, chin in hand and smiling at him, Emantha.

Chapter 8

"I am come to present the compliments of Messer Mayor Gandolfi," Franc said steadily. "To say that he will attend at his parlor in the second hour after noon in company of the illustrious scholar, Messer Dante. Emantha, up, out of that silking, and outside within the minute. Or I will lay a belt about you!"

"A moment, and remember you are my guest," Messer Polo began.

"No moments, and I am not guest but messenger," Franc said. "Emantha!"

She got up, looking at Messer Polo, but she seemed to know what would happen if she stayed. Music began nearby, and from a curtain at the end Hsi-Soong came in with One-piece and Two-piece behind. Emantha ran, and a couple of Cathayan women met her and they went behind a screen.

"Hon'ble Flamp," Hsi-Soong said in the little voice. "How what you speak, do what, lo?"

Messer Polo spoke the Cathayan tongue, and Hsi-Soong nodded and clapped, and One-piece and Two-piece played, and she danced, on a foot, and the other foot, turning her hands this way and that. The music stopped, and she spoke, balanced on one foot, to Messer Polo. He bowed and turned to Franc.

"I am desired by the gracious Hsi-Soong to inquire what would be your pleasure in this house, either to eat or to drink?" he asked, as if no word had passed between them.

"My thanks, but nothing. I must go to the encampment of the Princess Na-Nou with a message——"

"Let me know and I will tell her——"

"That was not Messer Mayor's instruction——"

"It is not permissible for any to talk to her exalted highness. All messages are passed through a noble intermediary. Such is the custom."

"Then I shall go there and make my message known and receive a reply."

Messer Polo spoke again to Hsi-Soong. She laughed and clapped her hands, and again One-piece and Two-piece began playing, and she danced.

"The gracious Hsi-Soong wishes to know how you admire her dancing," Messer Polo said.

"It is not dancing to me."

"You do not observe the delicacy of balance?"

"Is not balance for acrobats?"

"But the refinement of the music, surely?"

"I have not a Cathayan ear or upbringing. I must be excused."

Messer Polo spoke again at length, and Hsi-Soong laughed the small, pretty laugh and spoke.

"The gracious Hsi-Soong requires to know what there is in all you have seen of this caravan that you admire?" Messer Polo translated.

"The silken walls and the carpets. And the horses!"

"I understand from the gracious Hsi-Soong that you live in the watchtower——"

"I worked there until today. I live in my mother's house."

"Your pardon. You are known as——?"

"Francesco, son of Caterina."

Messer Polo bowed his head and went to a table and wrote, though not with a pen, but holding a brush upright, making marks at the right-hand corner, up the page, and to a second column to the left, none of it to be read as letters, and Franc felt he could have given a world to discover their meaning.

Hsi-Soong took his hand and smiled up at him.

"You go one-piece Plinseps Na-Nou, make talk, lo?" she asked. "I come, Hon'ble Flamp, make speak?"

Emantha hurried from the end in her work dress of gray wool, and he saw why she would rather wear the silk. Her hair had been taken out of its Cathayan fashion, but the curls were still in the tails hanging over her shoulders. She looked mutinous and ready for tears, though no anger showed.

Franc made his bow to Messer Polo and got one in return and took Emantha's hand. Hsi-Soong took his other hand, and One-piece and Two-piece followed, playing softly, but not music. They blinked in sunshine when the hangings opened, and walked down the path toward the pavilion of the Princess Na-Nou. Cathayan women bowed low as they passed, and soldiers went to their knees and touched the ground with their heads. A tirewoman in splendid robes met them, and Hsi-Soong spoke and turned to Franc.

"You wait, I make speak one-piece Plinseps," she smiled. "So-so!"

Franc waited until the curtains fell behind her, and looked at Emantha.

"Fine worries you have raised," he began.

"My sisters knew where I went and all I did," she said. "Hsi-Soong asked their permission, and I stayed in company of her tirewoman. What is it to you?"

"I was told by Il Cardinale and Messer Mayor to find you——"

"Nothing more?"

"How, more?"

"You had to be asked. You never of your own will thought to find me?"

"Did I know you were gone?"

"Would you care? You have no thought beyond Leda!"

"She has no place with me——"

"She witches you with her finery and silver and a-many coins!"

"A dried bean for them all——"

"And her father's property——"

"No dream of mine——"

"The fat thing herself!"

"She is not fat——"

"As a butter keg!"

"Not she. You have more——"

"Solid! From work she never knew!"

"What is this new talk——"

"I am more graced by these Cathayans. They love me for myself——"

"As do we——"

"You hate me. You said so——"

"Never!"

"Last night. You threw the supper I had cooked——"

"You had cooked?"

"Who else? Your mother was with the nuns of the Poor Sisters of Clare. Could I refuse to cook your supper? Even if I lost the florin promised by the Three Silver Men? Even when I refused the gold pieces of Messer Polo? I cooked for you, and you threw it from the window!"

She bowed her head and shook in tears. He felt himself to be at least the lowest of all base dogs. He took her by the shoulders and shook her, though gently, and made her look at him. But the blue eyes, so sad, so weary, made him fall head-long, though yet upon his feet.

"Let me say this, that no man crawls nearer the mud than I," he whispered. "If I could find your supper, I would eat, though a-rot with mold and devoured of maggots. When will you cook more?"

A smile took her tears.

"Tonight," she whispered, "at your house, and I will bring it hot, before the chime——"

"No need. I shall be there——"

Hsi-Soong came, with music, and bowed, and he bowed in return.

"Plinseps Na-Nou speak one-piece, no want, no go," she smiled. "So. Plinseps no go. I go. So-so!"

"At the second hour——"

"Two-piece clock. This very good, I think?"

She began to dance to more music, and they left her and hurried to the Mayor's house. Emantha trembled to be going in, but Franc pushed her and stayed outside with the door shut, though not for long.

She ran out of the garden door and blew him a kiss and ran uphill toward the house of Il Cardinale. He went in at Messer Gandolfi's call. Four councilors were with him, and all seemed in high humor.

"You did well to find her," the Mayor said in a twinkle. "But let nothing of this bring tangles to your work. I know the ravages of love upon the young——"

"This is not love," Franc said, frying in a blush. "She is play-sister to me——"

"Well and good, and fish-a-dee!" Messer Gandolfi said, impatient, and putting a book here, and picking it up and slapping it down there. "Have a care of this play-sister. Go to the Little Brothers and warn them to lock the gate. Say that twelve of the town guard will stand watch until further notice. Go to Messer di Rovigo and ask him to survey the broken walls on the mountainside, and say I will speak with him in the matter of repair after I have seen Il Cardinale. Go!"

Franc ran down to the garden of the Little Brothers of St. Francis. Many of them dug among the plots, and others worked in the woodshed with adz and chisel. Brother Egidio listened to the message and nodded, looking out over the plain.

"The gate has been in much use lately," he said. "The men-at-arms of Count d'Orosa come in at any hour. Last night many went in and others went out, all a-horse."

"Are you sure?"

Brother Egidio smiled, and his dark eyes looked toward the church.

"They were not Cathayans and, from their loud mouthing, neither were they of the town."

Messer di Rovigo sat in a wooden shelter under shadow of the upper church, talking to a couple of his men over a long roll of parchment, and tracing lines with dividers. He listened to the message and got up.

"It wants little survey," he said in a big voice. "Rocks, and a mixture to hold them, and men to work. Tell Messer Gandolfi I want all the carts in the town, and four hours of work every day from every man able to turn a hand. With that granted, I will supervise, and finish in the week——"

"Too long by six days," Franc said. "If all worked with a will tonight and tomorrow, it would be finished——"

"And are you now become a surveyor in my stead?" Messer di Rovigo demanded angrily.

"A night of work would put the town safe from those who think to harm us. A broken wall invites a visit——"

Messer di Rovigo squinted down at the dividers, and his big fingers squeezed them shut. Franc watched and grinned to himself. Messer di Rovigo had much property and a large family, and any mention of danger was enough to make him think twice.

"Who is this seeking to harm us at Assisi?" he asked in milder voice. "Some whisper from Perugia——"

"Messer Gandolfi is not one to spend a copper penny in useless works. Fine harvest if we should wake one night and find blades at our throats, houses afire, and our women and children driven out to serve other masters——"

"Enough!" Messer di Rovigo whispered. "Tell Messer Gandolfi to rouse the town. We will work all tonight, and by light tomorrow we will be snug in a stone skin and forty feet beyond reach of blade or brand!"

Franc ran back and found the Mayor at midday table. He cleared his mouth to call the town crier, and gave order that all men able to fetch and carry, and all women not in care of children or the sick should on the instant go to Messer di Rovigo and, so that none might have excuse to stay away, all shops and marts must close until the rising bell on the following morning.

While the Mayor gave orders and men ran, Franc thought of Councilor Corti and wondered again whether he should say what he had seen. The house of Corti traded with the castle. There was reason for him to speak with the Count, although it was rare that a trader sat at the same hearth with noblemen. Yet there might have been reason, since the Count and his men were there to guard a wagon train of produce. If a word were said, and the word proved wrong, then the flaying knife would be the least to expect. Weighing all, he shook the thought away and said nothing.

"Heralds have gone from the castle to invite Count de Gubbio and his Perugian court to this jousting between the Cathayans and D'Orosa," Mayor Gandolfi said, munching at a rib of beef. "Here is excuse to bring a crowd of them into the town——"

121

"Perhaps this was reason behind the wagering——"

"Doubtless."

"If they all enter to find food and drink and lodging, they will take us without a blow. We must close the gate and fill the inns and stables. No man should leave the town——"

"You are in a sudden as easy with advice as Messer Polo with a gold piece," Messer Gandolfi said. "How fill the inns and stables?"

"With Messer Polo's troopers——"

"He could refuse——"

"If it should touch upon the safety of the Princess Na-Nou?"

"Then do you do the touching, with my sanction. But if the Count d'Orosa wished to come at us with help of the Perugians, why should he wait until now? What brings suspicion at this time?"

"His banner, meeting with one of Perugia. And why should the Count Schiavon play mouse-in-a-hole? If he must ride in and out, why not through the towngate?"

"Here is the end of it," Mayor Gandolfi rumbled. "If I go to the Count and ask a reason, he could run me through. Or he could make me prisoner, or any of the Council. While one of his men is in the town none of us are safe. But how shall we keep them out and remain at peace?"

"We could say a plague was in the town——"

"And send away the Cathayans? Over the complaints of the traders and all those having a profit? Where should we produce a corpse?"

"Then let us give thanks for the Cathayans. If we are attacked, they will help us——"

"Only fools put their noses into another's quarrel. This Messer Polo is no fool. Be at the town hall at the second hour——"

Franc ate his noon meal in the roof room and afterward sat in the sun with the birds to talk to him. A beat of Cathayan drums and notes on a horn came nearer and stopped in the lane outside the house. He heard his mother calling him and slid the ladder, seeing Cathayans coming in the yard carrying packs wrapped in cloth, and carpets long enough to want the shoulders of three men under them.

A Cathayan officer gave him a crackling scroll of white paper held by a seal and a black ribbon, and bowed low and went away. Opening it, he saw columns of marks made with a brush, but they said nothing. His mother stood, hands on hips, looking at a full yard and a full kitchen and a bedroom piled with bundles, with rolls of carpet poking out of the windows and doorways.

"What is this," she asked in fear, "some prank?"

"Leave it until I have spoken with Messer Polo," he said.

"Leave it!" She stamped. "How, leave it, and no space to put a foot in my own house?"

The chimes struck, and he went down to the town hall. All were gathering to hear Messer Dante read from his work. Mayor Gandolfi took the scholar to the podium, and the audience stood, except for Hsi-Soong, in scarlet, sitting on a white cushion with One-piece and Two-piece kneeling behind. Messer Polo stood in the front rank with many Cathayan officers and whispered a translation. Messer Dante's scholarly voice told of a region of the damned, chained together in flame. But if the new language was hard for most of the people to understand, the meaning was clear, and many went to their knees, praying for succor, and the uproar became such that Messer Dante's voice was lost, and Il Cardinale went in front to hold up his arms in appeal for silence.

"Be of good courage," he smiled. "I am here. Listen, and be warned!"

Franc caught Messer Polo's eye. Tall in black velvet, and black hair in a short plait from the crown of his head, and stroking the long ends of his mustache with the curved fingernail sheaths, he looked as much a Cathayan as his officers. He passed down the line without hurry, and Franc whispered his message, careful not to let any word escape to other ears. Messer Polo showed no surprise.

"At my pavilion," he said, "after this reading is done——"

For more than an hour Franc listened to a recital of torments and terrors which made him think that Messer Dante must have known of attack by Perugians. He left before it was over and went to find Ubaldo, son of Emantha's sister, at the senior school of the Poor Clares. The Abbess gave permission for him to do duty and at the same time to practice his studies in the tower, but she insisted that at least one other must help because the boy was young.

Up in the watchtower, Stiro saw them come through the trap and raised a sigh that might have burst his belt.

"Ah, the lonely hours wished upon me!" he fretted. "The cold o' nights, and the sweats o' the day, and no blessed draught to loosen the stretch o' my gizzard. For a hundred times the pay, I'll sooner guard the streets and know a passing word——"

He went down, falling a flight at a time in his eagerness. Step by step Franc went over the duties with Ubaldo and showed him the bell ropes, and the water bags, and the flame, and where to apply it in the stack of twigs. But with equal care he showed the places across the plain and toward the mountain and up at the castle where surprise might come.

"So think many others I have heard," Ubaldo said. "There has been much galloping, they say, on both sides of the river during the nights——"

"They practice to find their way along the paths in darkness. But you will have warning from our scouts on the plain. Two others will come up at night to help with the watch until sunrise——"

"Let one be Toma, the ironsmith," Ubaldo pleaded. "He practices his studies and I am his teacher."

"So be it," Franc said. "The other shall be Paolo, son of

Corti. A night watch or two up here and he might grow into something better than the frip-sop he is."

"He will run many a league before you catch him——"

"Toward Perugia?"

"So goes the talk. That his father and others believe we should sign accord with them, and so save ourselves——"

"But where is the threat to us, if all they want is ransom for the Cathayans?"

"Most fear it is war with us of the town," he said. "My mother is afraid of the night in case the morning brings the shields arrayed against us——"

"Perhaps those of Perugia would wish us all to dream in such a way. This is weakness, and you must say so!"

Franc went down, seeing the crowd in the streets all going toward the broken walls, and made way through cheerful smiles and many a compliment on his promotion to the pavilion of Messer Polo.

A Cathayan officer took him in. But he entered a place much changed, and in stricter way than that of the morning. Gone were the hangings, and the scents, and the glimmering lamps. Messer Polo stood at the head of a long table. Cathayan officers in many different uniforms ranged about, silent, hands clasped on the crowns of short bows. No eye lifted to look at him coming in, and none watched him while he explained the reason for the Mayor's request. Messer Polo translated what he had said, and the officers spoke among themselves and to Messer Polo.

"Here is the way of our thought in this, Messer Esquire," he began. "We are in a town walled about, but without soldiers except for its citizenry, and no commander except a mayor. These are good in their way, but not good enough. Further, there is above the city a notorious freebooter, of experience in the stratagems of war, armed, trooped, and horsed among the best. He is until now supposed a friendly man, gentle in his

125

purpose, and peaceful in his ways. Suspicion grows that he has some design to attack this caravan and extort ransom of its members. You say he plots with the Perugians——"

"That is our belief," Franc said. "Lacking word from Perugia, we have no proof——"

"Which could come something late on the edge of their blades," Messer Polo smiled. "I agree with Messer Mayor Gandolfi. Fortunately, these officers of her exalted highness's bodyguard have long set their plan. Our mounted patrols have scoured in all directions since the day we arrived, but so far without incident——"

"If they were attacked, suspicion would fall in its true place," Franc said. "The Perugian is a wily animal, sly——"

"I am not concerned for the outcome, tell Messer Mayor——"

"But as father of the Council he is concerned for the town first," Franc reminded him. "What is to be the Cathayan plan?"

"How is an esquire caught in this?" Messer Polo asked, not with patience. "I will speak with Messer Mayor——"

"My father was chief sergeant-at-arms at Jerusalem," Franc said. "He taught me the planning of action. This, of patrols, is well. But if we fight, where and how, and in what manner shall it be done? Divided command is death to all——"

"Learning is not by words alone," Messer Polo said. "True learning is in the deed. What deeds have you in war?"

Franc opened his mouth to reply. But sudden clangor and shouts that grew shrill brought him about in a run for the entrance. He tore the hangings apart and stared into the sun.

Smoke of alarm burst blue and black from the top of the watchtower. Tiny against the light, three figures leaped among the bell ropes, imps at riot, thundering peal on peal in clamorous echo.

"An alarm!" he almost wept. "Smoke is up and bells toll, and I, Esquire, rot here, niddering!"

Chapter 9

The smoke took only a few moments to stifle, but much as he had wanted to peal the alarm bells at any time before, there was little enough contentment in swinging Big William. That great clear-mouth tolled out a single voice to warn all of false alarm, and so stop the runners, allay their fears, and send them back to work. When he had rung enough, he piled fresh twigs from the store below, and filled the goatskin water bags, and afterward swept the platform clean. By that time, with a few people gathered in the forum, the Mayor and Council were waiting for him. He said no word to Ubaldo, standing shamed and stricken in a corner, and went down.

He looked Mayor Gandolfi in the eye and had to say that Ubaldo had been bribed out of his place for no longer than it took to go to the Cathayan encampment for gifts of paper, ink, and wax. In his absence, Hsi-Soong, the briber, and One-piece and Two-piece had lit the fire and rung the bells and then had scampered off, laughing and dancing and playing music.

He heard his excuse speaking back to him from the forum echoes. The town was quiet, except that the voices of townspeople at work sounded from the back wall as a great sigh.

"It seems you chose poor substitutes," Mayor Gandolfi said. "Assisi cannot afford aberration in her servants——"

"This one will make no more," Franc said, looking up at Ubaldo's woebegone face leaning out of the tower. "He was made mad by thought of this paper, for he is first a scholar——"

"Some more practical one is needed," Councilor Corti said. "We are made fools by a student——"

"By one offering gifts that blind," Franc said. "These Cathayans believe that all may be done by a gift. Ubaldo has learned his lesson. Let him stay, and I will be responsible——"

Mayor Gandolfi shrugged.

"Once, then," he agreed. "But in bad grace. Remember, no public servant should take a gift. What said Messer Polo of his plan?"

Franc told what had passed, and saw the faces of the councilors change again, and knew himself with few friends.

"He is too young to treat with soldiers," Councilor Corti said angrily. "Are we come to such that we send as our general one, a stripling?"

"He is my mouth and eyes," Messer Gandolfi said. "Mine is the knowledge and authority. Come, Franc. Let us together see these Cathayans. We will also word them in the matter of this dancing wench and her two black sheep——"

They were met with all courtesy in the same pavilion, and with the same corps of officers. Messer Polo listened to the complaints about Cathayan tricks with gunpowder and Hsi-Soong's escapade.

"Messer Mayor"—he bowed when Messer Gandolfi had finished—"this matter of the gracious Hsi-Soong is small, of no import, and easily remedied. It shall not happen again, and no fire sticks shall be used or gifted except for the procession of the White Bird, which, you agree, we shall hold on the day after tomorrow——"

"Agreed, all being in order, and the repairs to the walls of

128

the town finished," Messer Gandolfi said. "Let us come to the plan for defense——"

"It is this. Think not for one moment that we are come half the world around by sea, and something of the rest by land, enduring every hardship of weather, vagary of evil-tempered men, and misfortune of terrain, only to perish here at Assisi——"

"Such is not our desire——"

"Be it so. We have known that many have a mind to attack us for abundant prizes. We shipped from Jaffa to Brindisi, and debarked there, preferring to fight robbers ashore, as a troop, rather than the pirates at sea, all separated into our several ships. Our arrival caused comment. Our appearance created respect. We were unharmed to this point. But we have several powerful lords between us and our destination, which is my birthplace, Venice. My charge is her exalted highness. These officers command troops by order of the Grand Khan solely for her protection. This town, or surrounding property, or its people are alike of no concern to us——"

"Then why should we not ask you to remove yourselves, as a menace to our peace?" Messer Gandolfi asked bad-temperedly. "Here we thought we had a duty toward guests——"

"A moment," Messer Polo smiled. "I explained the attitude of the Cathayan soldiers. I am between you, as spokesman for her exalted highness. It is her wish that we should stand together. Here, then, is the plan."

He gestured, and an officer took a silken cover off the table. Messer Polo pointed a wand at an open scroll of paper covered with lines and black marks.

"This is the map, and a plan of the town and the surrounding country," he said. "This line is the wall enclosing the town. These crosses are the towers. These rings are the churches. The arches are gates——"

"By the sons of Danae!" Messer Gandolfi marveled. "And where is the town hall and mayoral court?"

"Not in——"

"Not? The most important of all?"

"Very well. It shall be put there——"

"And where do we now stand?"

"Here." Messer Polo pointed to a shape. "This is my head-quarter——"

"Then when mine is also in I will speak further of your plan!" Messer Gandolfi said in a rage. "What, you are in, and I not? Where is Assisi honored in this? When we are shown in fitting style, Messer Polo, then you may bring your underlings to me in my parlor, and we will talk. Come, Franc!"

He clapped on his hat, and there was nothing for it except to follow through the hangings and on to the road. Franc listened to the Mayor's rumblings all the way to the site of repairs on the town wall, and thereafter to repeats of the story to each councilor and any who would stand to listen. He tired of nodding to every "Hey, Franc?" and "Was it not as I say, Franc?" and went instead to lend a hand where Emantha and her sisters worked, carrying stones from the pile up to the workmen. Even in so short a time much had been done, and it was plain that the work would be finished long before dawn and the town made doubly safe.

Emantha carried stones as easily as any man, and rested less, with less to say. When she sat, he sat beside her.

"What said Il Cardinale?" he inquired.

"Little, except to keep away from the dancer——"

"Hsi-Soong?"

"The same, and the two in black——"

"One-piece and Two-piece——"

"Them. But what? All I did was to teach her certain child songs——"

"For which reason?"

"That she wished to learn the child talk of other languages. In this way she begins to speak. We were late abed in the women's quarter——"

"But in the morning you dressed for Messer Polo!"

"Not so. Hsi-Soong came into our pavilion with handmaids. They took away my dress and made me follow the Cathayan style of bathing and dressing, and thereafter brought me before Messer Polo. These things I told Il Cardinale. Also that the Princess Na-Nou would like me joined to her Court in the sum of many gold pieces——"

"Il Cardinale said no?"

"He said he must have serious talk with my sisters. Fortunes do not fall every day, he also said."

She got up and stretched her arms. He noticed, not for the first time, the wondrous blue light in her eyes, the length of lash, the smooth gloss of the wheat-tip hair, and the pocket beside her mouth when she smiled. Emantha, herself, was simply Emantha. But once the boys got scent of a fortune, they would be about her, bees after the sweet. She, with many gold pieces, was a prize, far more to be desired than any of the Mayor's daughters. Even, he admitted, much more than the hostess of the Three Silver Men.

"I see no mark of Leda," he said, pretending to have heard nothing of fortune. "Is she taken of a fever?"

"Of learning, yes," Emantha smiled, picking up a rock of size that he might have passed over. "She kneels at the feet of Messer Dante."

"She chooses brave teachers!"

"Indeed. She became pale as a scholar in the moment the town crier called us all to work at the wall. Messer Dante pleaded for her. She will fold the paper for him which Messer Polo sent as gift——"

"I, too, had many gifts, though no time to order them returned——"

131

"Returned?" Emantha paused, with the rock half lifted. "Your mother has gifted most away to her neighbors. No mouse could squeak in any room——"

Franc saw that the Mayor's walking pace to the furthest stretch of wall would give enough time to get home and back without being missed. He ran down the side lane and along to his mother's house, wondering what he might say to the Mayor, or how excuse himself.

But he could barely believe that this was the house he had always known. The walls were hung with worked silks, carpets covered the floors, and tables and chairs of Cathayan style furnished every room, even his own. Up there, a long Cathayan vase held roses, and he stood openmouthed before a thick wallet, full of crackling paper, and an ink bar of solid black, and a small white dish with ink mixed ready, and a pot of brushes and reed pens.

And two armfuls of books, new, ranking along the top of the table and on the shelf. There was no time to stand, and he ran down bawling for his mother. She came, all smiles, from the house of Emantha's sisters, and waved him to silence.

"We are all become as great ones," she laughed. "What gifts are these! How happily they sit! That small dancer, with two men playing music, came here. She called out all the elderly ones left in the houses, and sent them into everybody else's to hang silks or lay carpets or carry furniture. Every house is now a dream, though better than in sleep——"

Franc held out his arms and let them fall.

"What will Messer Mayor say?" he whispered. "I cannot take a gift——"

His mother clasped her hands in her lap with laughter.

"Go, ask him," she said when she could. "He has taken more than all of us together!"

Franc ran back to the walls and found the Mayor and his councilors watching a horseman in D'Orosa livery leaping the rocks on his way from the castle. All stopped work to watch and listen, and the man slid off his mount and made a low bow.

"With the compliments of my lord, the Count Althasar d'Orosa," he shouted. "Please to tell what goes forward in this work upon the walls, and to remember that his land abuts and the stones a-quarry shall be paid for!"

"Render my compliments also," Messer Gandolfi said, as loud. "And in return, say that the walls are in repair against attack, that all stones are taken from the town side, and no foot has been set on lands that abut!"

Messer Gandolfi watched the messenger go, and turned to look up at the castle.

"We are this much more out of your reach," he growled. "By dawn no town will be safer than ours of Assisi. Franc, invite Messer Polo and his timber-polls into my parlor to discuss the plan, if his map is properly courteous, but not unless!"

"I have a certain confession," Franc began. "I said that Ubaldo had taken gifts and would return them for his error. But I should tell you that I too have had gifts of these Cathayans——"

"As have I," said Messer Gandolfi, rubbing his paunch. "But these are not gifts for favors sought. They are gestures in kind. Therefore we may accept them with no straining of conscience or slip of duty. When they want something we say no. And there's an end to it, and nobody in the wrong——"

Franc trotted down to the Cathayan encampment, and the officer showed him to the same pavilion. But the hangings were up, and the light bowls swung, and the metal dishes burned the same sweet smoke. Messer Polo, in Cathayan robes, listened and nodded and said he would wait upon the Mayor within the chime.

"One thing," he added, before Franc turned to go. "This girl, Emantha. How may I send her a message? The tirewoman of her exalted highness searched the town but failed to find her——"

"She works with all others in repair of the walls——"

"Emantha? That darling creature?"

"The same——"

"Monstrous! She should reign in ivory and gold——"

"She sweats in wool, among rocks——"

"I shall complain to Messer Mayor——"

"His own daughters sweat as much——"

"Disgraceful!"

"Speak for these do-nothings you have about you that climb towers and create mischief and push honest youths into a pie of trouble——"

"I shall speak also of you!"

"I shall be present to hear——"

He made his bow and ran back to the Mayor.

"Stand beside me," Messer Gandolfi said, pointing to the mayoral chair. "He'll make nothing in his search for our girls, of that, be sure!"

True to his word, Messer Polo and a score of Cathayan officers arrived on the stroke of the chime. A page unrolled the white oblong upon the mayoral table and pointed out the position of Assisi, Perugia, and the points between and about, where attacks might be launched, or where trouble could be looked for.

"Our plan is to keep a main body of troops within the gated town," he said. "Our cavalry will disrupt any troops of theirs in passage over the plain——"

"And if they are outnumbered?" Messer Gandolfi asked.

"They will kill at least their own number of the enemy, and our main force is still behind the walls of the town, to say nothing of the citizenry of Assisi. They cannot bring enough, though they are fifty times our number, to defeat us. And once they are defeated, remember that Perugia itself is at our mercy——"

"I will count my eggs in the nest," Messer Gandolfi growled. "Are you sure, in this, of the Count d'Orosa?"

"I am sure of little, him least of any," Messer Polo said soberly. "But if he turns upon us, he signs away his neck!"

"I would give much to cover the seat of our mayoral curulis with his banner," Messer Gandolfi sighed, waving at the chair of worn bronze that some said had once been part of Roman justice, with a place in the forum. "With my seat upon it I would know us safe from carrion——"

"Would not the Count bend every effort to regain it?"

Mayor Gandolfi shook his head, and his beard brushed the seal from side to side.

"The banner could only rest upon the curulis if D'Orosa were no more," he said, soft. "I spoke of that time when Assisi will rest at peace. And what a dream is this!"

"D'Orosa, you believe, is your enemy?"

"Wanting only a proper time to strike——"

"Would it not be better to put him into the open?"

Mayor Gandolfi nodded.

"I have split my skull to think how, without bringing harm to the town," he rumbled. "How?"

"And if he were shown so, how then would you engage him?"

"I would bar him the town. Bar his produce from our markets. Bar his labor from lodging. Bar townspeople from working his lands——"

"And if he came against you with the sword?"

"Outlast him in siege and beat him down on the walls——"

"But still he would sit at the castle, ever in threat——"

"His father and grandfather did so. We would have to get into the castle to beat him. But how?"

Messer Polo spoke with his officers, and Mayor Gandolfi looked at Franc.

"Here, you see the way of it," he sighed. "We twitter and

135

we gossip, and we propose this plan and that. But remember, Franc, the sword decides!"

"This may be so in certain places," Messer Polo said, ringed about by his officers. "In other lands, no. There the brain rules——"

"Where does a brain win against the swung sword?" Messer Gandolfi asked.

"In the manner of its usage, as I shall show you——"

"Until that time is come and past, I shall wear my helmet!"

"One question, Messer Mayor. In this matter of Assisi and Perugia, what says the church and its servants?"

"No word. The churches will burn as easily as the hut or the barn. Her servants are men of peace. We shall defend them."

"Then you must defend the town within the wall, and also the part outside where the churches stand?"

"That is so——"

"With how many citizens?"

The Mayor took off his hat and raised his arms to the sky.

"As many as there are," he whispered. "Gentle St. Francis, we look to you!"

Chapter 10

"One matter remains," Messer Polo said when his officers had saluted and gone. "That of Emantha——"

"Seek not to turn the heads of these maidens with fine words and gifts that cause them to think contempt for their fathers," Messer Gandolfi warned. "You have women to spare."

"Understand me!" Messer Polo said, sharp, and looking less Cathayan than usual. "This is not spoken for myself, but for the Princess. Remember, I chose Emantha as the White Bird. This ceremony, of a few words indifferently spoken and a bouquet of flowers, touched the heart of her exalted highness, herself young. She requires the companionship of those of her own age——"

Franc remembered the withered face of the crone in the palanquin and almost trembled to ask a question.

"—and though this Emantha is of common stock, she has a beauty of face and figure and a temperament transcending any claim of those presumably of greater name and better family. The Grand Khan is himself of humble breed——"

"What is this you wish to say?" Messer Gandolfi asked impatiently. "Stocks and breeds?"

"That her exalted highness is prepared to set aside a sum in gold for Emantha's companionship during the time the Court remains in Italy——"

"With what safeguards?"

"Those that pertain to all women of the Cathayan Court. Complete privacy——"

"But would she, as this morning, be found in your pavilion?"

"Only in company of the gracious Hsi-Soong——"

"That one who rang the bells? Tchah!"

"She has particular privilege. A sum shall be paid for her misdemeanor——"

"Why is she permitted privilege?"

"By order of her exalted highness——"

"And supposing Emantha comes under the same influence?"

Messer Polo shrugged and opened the golden claws of his hands.

"Do you not think that one as wise as Emantha might have beneficial advantages? Could it not be that her exalted highness is rich in her choice for exactly that purpose?"

Messer Gandolfi sniffed and pinched his nose.

"Il Cardinale will have to decide," he said. "All things equal, there is no doubt her family will welcome a gold piece or two——"

"If the Count d'Orosa accepts our invitation to a tournament, and we win our twenty thousand gold pieces, it is her exalted highness's intention to double them and present them to Emantha," Messer Polo smiled. "If we should lose, she shall have triple the stake——"

"This is strange reckoning," Messer Gandolfi said in surprise.

"Not. For the entire sum will come from the pay of the losers. Therefore they will be at proper heat to win. This is Cathayan reasoning——"

"It has merit," Mayor Gandolfi said, impressed. "And for the rest?"

Messer Polo pointed to Franc.

"This youth. I find him stubborn——"

"That is our way, here in Assisi——"

"And having a tongue he is in no ways shy to use——"

"Having his instructions from me——"

"And a particular curiosity——"

"My own, instilled——"

"And a manner more fitting to the stables than to the Court——"

Messer Gandolfi removed his hat and smoothed his bald head, shutting his eyes.

"All my life I have spent as a buyer of horses and cattle," he whispered, opening one eye. "After those years in stalls and stables, let me say I have met better men among the bales of clover than any in the castles and palaces whither I have been. Any man fitted to pass his time with horses is more than fit to enter any court. Speak at all times to Franc, my Esquire, or never speak to me!"

Messer Polo bowed and gathered his cloak and went out.

"Stables!" Messer Gandolfi rumbled. "No man names any name to me for breed. One look at a fetlock and I will tell you far more. Listen to me, Franc. If the goodwife Gandolfi should make inquiry after me, say that I look to the work on the walls. If she make a move to go there, then come to the Three Silver Men and give me notice."

"Taken," said Franc. "And where shall I wait?"

"Here in this room, and no move till I return," the Mayor whispered. "An error in this and you go back to the tower. For no other reason than to swing in place of a bell!"

He went, and Franc sat, impatient. There were many things he wanted to do, most to go to the walls to work near Emantha. He tried to tell himself that this was not because of the gold pieces she might harvest. But he could find no other reason as good, and he felt dissatisfied to think of himself as little more than one of the bees after the sweets of gold.

The door creaked, and the youngest Gandolfi daughter put her face in the room and sniggered down her nose and withdrew. The second Gandolfi peeped and ran. The third and fattest put her head in.

"Is all well?" she asked in a whisper.

"All, thank you."

"Would you drink a stoup of the cellar's best?"

"Bring it and see!"

But misfortune ruled. A door swung near to, and it seemed that everybody fell down the stairs in a crashing and shrieking, which brought the servants on the run, shouting robbers and murder. But Goodwife Gandolfi had the loudest voice and, from the sound, the heaviest slap, and between slaps and shrieks and the clatter of broken glass there presently came silence.

The door swung open and the goodwife walked in, linen-and-laced about the face, ruffed about throat and wrists, and belted in the middle with cords of silver heavy with keys that rang together as she walked.

Her cheeks were red and her eyes stared half out of their pouches, and she carried a leathern flask and pewter beaker.

"Well then, Messer Esquire, let us meet!" she said, breathless and ill-willed, as if she would rather use a knife. "A-thirst I'm told, as many another, for the best in the cellar——"

"Water from the well will do——"

"You asked for wine!"

"I said, 'Bring it and see!'"

"You argue?"

"I say what I said——"

"You contradict?"

"I state the fact——"

"Where is my husband?"

"He has duties at the town walls——"

"My daughters are returned. Why is he yet there?"

"A mayor has something more to do than any helper——"

"You are glib in defense——"

"Go there and see——"

"Discourteous!"

"With reason!"

"Rude!"

"In kind!"

"You say I am rude?"

"More. Unjust!"

"I shall call my husband!"

"Be off!"

"Ah! Such lack of manners——"

"Equaling a lack of grace——"

"I'll have no more!"

"Go, and take less!"

She shrieked and threw down flask and beaker and ran howling from the room. He let her reach the street by the garden gate, and went over the wall and down the back lane to the steps behind the Three Silver Men, and in along the passage to the inner room and tapped on the door.

The Mayor opened it a crack. Several of the councilors sat about the table with playing cards, and a flask and beaker stood at each elbow. Franc had no need to say a word. Messer Gandolfi came out straightway and hurried up the hill toward the wall.

"Go home, or do as I and stay out," he breathed in a hurry. "I will now so heavily use her that she will clip her mouth for a full moon or more. I'll meet her on the topmost stone of the wall and the town shall hear what I have to say. She's a good woman and puts up with much, though in the doing, so do I.

If alarms are toward between now and dawnlight, look for me in the same place. Sleep well!"

Franc went first to the tower and saw that Toma, the iron-smith, was at his post and happy in his honor, though Paolo Corti had not obeyed the order and Ubaldo went to fetch him. The little white city of tents on the wall showed bright lights, and all the shadows danced to Cathayan music. Toma swore he made better noise in the smithy and set to work with his lute to pluck out the tunes his mother had taught him, if the words he sang were his father's. Franc waited a verse or two below, listening if they might offend some delicate ear. But distance and a friendly wind drew their teeth and, satisfied, he went along to the Three Silver Men.

Emantha had been sent home, Soffolo told him above the noise of a full tavern, by order of Il Cardinale, and the house suffered the loss of a pair of hands worth any six. Leda was hostess in the inner room, where Messer Dante and Messer Polo and Messer Giotto and others of the great met to talk about a table, or game as they wished, beyond the noise of the general room.

"Happy am I that the Count d'Orosa is not here tonight," Soffolo said behind his hand. "If he tried for entrance, he might find himself barred. Then would come blood!"

"And who would offer him a bar?" Franc asked in surprise.

"All in there," Soffolo grinned. "Messer Giotto first. The word is out about the jaunt with the Perugians——"

"There is no proof," Franc began.

"Proof!" Soffolo spat through the window grille. "The word will do. As with his father, he is traitor to us. Should we wonder that he is ever in armor? Without it, how would he escape the knife?"

Franc went to the house of Emantha's sisters and found Hortensia at the hearth, watching the night meal, and Emantha outside, singing at the loom with the daughters. The house was changed with silks and carpets, but work went on as before.

"His excellency leaves it to us," Hortensia said. "He told Maldina it were better that Emantha stayed close to the house until the procession of the White Bird, to be out of the run and away from long noses. These things make the mind soft——"

"Which things?" Franc asked.

"Chatter and too many questions and many giving advice. Better to be silent for a space and then, with the mind at peace, come at it again——"

"This, whether or not she shall join the Princess's Court?"

"That. Why should we stand before her, if by going she brings herself an estate and, who knows, a blessed marriage? Many a noble looks for a wealthy wife——"

"Is this where things have gone?" Franc whispered. "Money first and, after, a noble marriage?"

"Why not?" Hortensia demanded. "She is more beautiful than any between here and Rome, or in Rome itself. Given the gold, who would not marry her?"

"You are cut from the same piece as the Mayor Gandolfi! He would sell his daughters——"

"And who should stop him? A man of noble name, is he not better to marry than some fool from the fields knowing nothing except the vines or the stalks and, away from them, the taverns and the inside of a flask? Is it not better to live in a house and mistress, than in a hovel and drudge?"

"Since when do you think on this?"

"Since there was sense in my head the size of a pip of barley. Emantha is not born to this small activity of ours, with an hour at a tavern to earn a silver piece, or a day at the washtub for some other to gather copper pence, remember. She is herself of family. This do not forget. Il Cardinale knows her parents better than all of us——"

"She is your sister——"

"We call her so. She is not. My mother nursed her. Nothing more——"

"These are strange news to me——"

"Sleep on them and, waking, let them sharp your wits. We make little of those we know best. As we wear our shoes, forgetting them, so we use those near——"

Franc looked at her, big and black-haired with a line of white across the top of her head and black eyebrows and angry gray eyes, and he wondered why he had never before seen that Maldina and the youngest, Rosina, two of a piece with Hortensia, were as much like sisters to Emantha as any three pumpkins were like an apple.

"She was to cook for me tonight," he began.

"She is bound to the house until we are all of a mind. Your mother has cooked and waits you——"

Franc went out and along to his mother's house, barely seeing which was his way, or caring where he set foot. It seemed to him that the sisters had made up their minds that Emantha must go with the Princess and earn the gold. If Ubaldo became scholar and Emantha was bent under moneybags, then the family would indeed rise high, certainly beyond the reach of any warden or esquire.

The silked room and the feel of carpets underfoot did nothing to relieve his mind, and neither could he enjoy them. His mother surprised him by agreeing that Emantha would be better off. She put the trencher before him and went back to the hearth, sitting on the stool to work a hem in a length of loomed wool.

"Why should she slave here for pence when she might live easily and garner gold for her share?" she asked the back of his head. "How is it that men may earn and all will call them clever ones and deserving, though if a girl should gain equally she is something less than she was thought, and all evils attend her?"

"That was not in my mind," Franc said, impatient. "But if she gain, why then should she seek to marry a noble one?"

"Why should she marry a beggar?"

"Plenty of good ones are not beggars!"

"Well? Why should she not marry one of her choice?"

"Why not?"

"And if he should be noble?"

"Plenty of good ones are not noble——"

"Well? If they are not of her choice?"

Franc found his appetite gone. He made excuse of tiredness and an early morning in his new duties, and kissed her cheek and went outside and up the ladder to the roof room. The birds wakened for him and he fed them tidbits, taking small comfort from the grateful tweaking of his fingers.

The new books at another time would have occupied him through the hours, rapt. But he sat, by rushlight, and though they were ranged within reach, he sought not to open one, even by a page. He put down the pine branches and laid the wool-sack over and undressed, thinking while he took off patched and darned shirt, hosen, and tunic that Messer Polo's simkins might have given Emantha notions of a fine marriage by flaunt of their silks and laces.

Steps in the yard were plain enough, and a man's voice, and so were the raps on the kitchen beams that his mother made with the soup ladle when she wanted him below.

He threw on his cloak and ran down.

Ciro, purser to Il Cardinale, put a finger over his mouth and signed to him to shut the door.

"I have searched the town for Messer Gandolfi," he whispered. "Find him, and tell him to go on the instant to the house of Il Cardinale, with no word to any——"

"What if he refuse, saying the morning is soon enough?" Franc said. "We know Messer Mayor after a fat flask or more——"

"Say then that tonight his excellency is warned that the Count de Gubbio, commander at Perugia, has sounded to arms and the land about streams with the banners of those joining him——"

Franc looked at his mother. She sat with the wool over her knees and looked away from the fire and threaded the bodkin.

"Go, do your part," she said. "There is time enough for mine."

Chapter 11

"I want to know nothing about your military plans," Il Cardinale said gently. "I propose to place the children of Assisi beyond reach of any soldier——"

"We have not such omnipotent patrons, Excellency," Messer Polo said, calm too, but without patience. "If we are defeated, how shall you, with priests, monks, and nuns at command, prevent a horde from sacking the town and doing as they will?"

"Though not with the children," Il Cardinale smiled, and turned to his chaplain. "Set forth our tactic and hear their opinion."

The little room in Il Cardinale's house was full to the door, and well Franc knew it, because his back was jammed against the iron bolts by the press in front. Messer Polo and all the Cathayan officers were in with Messer Gandolfi and the Council and all the high officers of the churches. Everybody had something to say and it had all been said, but the facts stayed as they had been. Singly or together they meant that the Perugians were gathering for war, which might come on the morrow, though how or when made no matter, for it would come.

Franc had been late by reason of running to the tower to make sure that the watchmen were alive to their duties and to strengthen them with two of the town guard. Thereafter a visit to the gate of the Little Brothers to count that twelve men were on watch, and last to the sergeant of the town guard to see that all men slept with arms at hand in event of alarm. On the way back he called on Messer di Rovigo and saw by torch that the last pointing of stones was almost done, and the town was beyond reach of any seeking to gain entrance by a gap.

Between the heads in front Franc saw the chaplain draw certain marks with chalk.

"Illustrious and most excellent Prince, and distinguished gentry, all," the chaplain began. "It is our purpose to place the children of Assisi beyond reach of those who threaten us——"

"How are you sure that Assisi will be attacked?" Messer Polo asked.

"Our source had no doubt and left no doubt in the mind of any who heard," the chaplain said. "Much planning has gone into it——"

"For what reason?" Messer Polo stamped a foot to each word. "This is, forgive me, a poor town. There is no single thing here worth any effort or, being got, worth any coin. You have no ornaments, no valuables, no works that might be judged rare. I place apart, naturally, those works of Messer Giotto's——"

"My thanks in this," Messer Giotto smiled. "But since they are painted direct to the wall, those wanting them must take the building!"

"You have my meaning." Messer Polo bowed. "Then, considering these things, what is their object? Her exalted highness, the Princess Na-Nou, and my most unworthy self? I cannot believe it——"

"You are prizes rich enough!" Messer Gandolfi rumbled. "Where in a lifetime would they get such yield for so little of a journey?"

"Again I deny you, or I believe the Perugians more stupid than their animals," Messer Polo replied. "For consider. If we of the Princess's caravan are their prize, why should they attack us here within walls? Why do they not allow us to reach the hills to the north and there make ambush with most advantage to themselves?"

No voice came to answer him, but Il Cardinale settled deeper in the chair and tipped his hat further over his eyes and smiled wider.

"Perhaps they have a thought to take all in one," he said. "However it may be, my thought is for the helpless. If we can take from the town the children and the infirm, shall we not strengthen the defense?"

"I had been told that you were men of peace and not given to acts of war," Messer Polo said in surprise.

"Is it an act of war to protect the helpless?" Il Cardinale laughed and nodded at the chaplain. "Explain our thought!"

"There is tomorrow a tournament of arms between the Cathayans and the Count d'Orosa," the chaplain said nervously. "The children of this city will make procession to the church of St. Rufino during the afternoon, but instead of finishing at the forum, they will go down to the furnace and on across the plain to Perugia in the Cathayan wagons——"

Il Cardinale smiled at the astonishment in Messer Polo's face.

"I have already made this plan known to the Archbishop in Perugia," he said softly. "He, naturally, wishes to prevent war, but the noblemen of that city are not of his mind. We must therefore take our children out of the sphere of battle——"

149

"And place them in the hands of the enemy?" Messer Polo said helplessly. "I do not share your belief, Excellency. With the children in their grasp they may then make what terms they will, and succeed without sharpening an edge or fastening a buckle——"

"That is not my opinion, Messer Polo. Will you first lend us the wains?"

Messer Polo spoke to the officers. One after another, they spoke in turn.

"They are Assisi's children, Excellency," he said. "The wains, animals, and drivers are yours. But I cannot explain to them why you should venture your weakest citizens into Perugian hands. They do not know why you make gifts to an enemy. If we were responsible, they would not venture beyond the gates!"

"Give me the wains and the responsibility," Il Cardinale said. "A five-hour journey and they will be safe——"

Messer Polo bowed, and his officers saluted and followed him out, pushing Franc behind the opened door. But when the door shut, with the freer space, he was surprised to see Hsi-Soong with One-piece and Two-piece sitting on cushions at Il Cardinale's feet.

"What think you, Messer Mayor?" Il Cardinale asked.

"Our faith must rest in your excellency's judgment," Messer Gandolfi said, each word dragging. "Are the mothers to be asked?"

"Could any take the children without permission?"

"And if some begin a wailing?"

"Let them take their children home——"

"I fear not many shall join the procession, Excellency. The fathers will be worse than the mothers in this——"

"Let them think of their children, safe from harm——"

"They will rather think of them taken directly into it!"

"I shall speak to them. Is there more you have to say to me?"

"Only that the walls are repaired and we are beyond reach of any attacker——"

"Would we might proclaim it of our spirits! Pax!"

Messer Mayor had much to say in the dark lane going back to the Three Silver Men, but nothing in favor of Il Cardinale's plan. None of the councilors offered a word for or against, but from their silence it could be told that they were only waiting to get home to tell their wives, and afterward their neighbors.

"What say you, then?" Messer Gandolfi asked them all before the fountain outside the Three Silver Men. "Shall we now warn the town of what is to come, or wait until morning?"

The councilors shuffled feet in the darkness and scratched and thought.

"Better the morning," one said. "By light we shall have a hold that darkness takes away."

"And between now and then you'll spread word? Tell all in secrecy. I want no night alarms of screaming women!"

The councilors hurried off, and Messer Gandolfi looked after them.

"There will be no procession of children to Perugia," he said. "No child leaves those gates while I am Mayor!"

"But if Il Cardinale leads them?" Franc asked.

"He grows old and a warp is in his thought. Tonight he babbled and I was silent. Tomorrow the town will know and I will give speech. To bed, Franc!"

He went toward his mother's house, thinking of the width of the dark plain that might even then be a-crawl with Perugians and their allies, and listening to the night's silence, which only a little way further out might be burdened with the sounds of an army on the move. He thought again of his father's stories of war with Perugia, and of his mother's grief on a day in the year when she took flowers to the church in memory of his three elder brothers and a sister, killed in war with Perugia during the time he was an infant. He could remember as a small boy the burning of the town and the screams of women, and the cold and hungry days of waiting in the cellars of St. Rufino until the last Perugian had gone. There was terror in thought of those days returning, but there was also desire to fight and win.

A gentle touch on his sleeve brought him to a halt, but tiny laughter reassured.

"Hon'ble Flamp!" the little voice whispered in the darkness. "You come, make one-piece joy, dance, lo, yes?"

"It is late," he started to say.

"Late, no late! Music, dance, all time, late, no late. You come one-piece clock, chu, then go, yes?"

Her hands took his right hand, and One-piece and Two-piece pushed gently from behind, but, even so, each found time and space to play or sing. He felt it foolish to resist and a few minutes, he thought, would harm none, and there was chance of seeing Emantha.

They passed through the garden behind the Mayor's house and beyond a guard of Cathayan giants to the tents and pavilions. Hsi-Soong went to the largest, and all the women covered their faces and bowed low, and servitors lifted the hangings for them to enter.

Messer Polo's rich pavilion compared as a stables to this, in white silk walls, and a stretch of carpets, and golden furniture, and a pile of crimson cushions that made a bed waist-high and a whole room in length and breadth, covered in part with the white pelt of some snarling animal staring dead eyes from the footrest.

Hsi-Soong clapped her hands, and women entered with bowls and beakers and flasks in gold, and a line of dancers in strange costumes came from another entrance and among them, four giants carried a chair on their shoulders.

Emantha, in the robe of white feathers, laughed at his astonishment and sat back, stretching out her feet in white Cathayan shoes with thick soles and showing her hands bright with rings and brilliant with bracelets.

"How are you here?" he demanded.

"Il Cardinale said I was to come," she smiled. "I was brought by his Purser not an hour ago. I shall stay as long as the Princess wills——"

"Hon'ble Flamp, you sit, please, eat, drink, many-piece food very good, yes? Sit 'Mantha, sit Flamp, sit Hsi-Soong, all sit, eat, this very good, I think?"

Franc sat beside Emantha and found his appetite returning with every mouthful, even though food was far from what he wanted. His main desire was to mope, to starve, to show himself cut to the heart. But the food was too good. From the way she ate, Emantha had no other thought in her head than to satisfy hunger, and not only that, but to put herself far beyond its reach for as long as she might. Hsi-Soong, for all her tininess, appeared to want little encouragement to eat as much as Emantha. But One-piece and Two-piece ate their food behind a screen with the musicians.

A tirewoman came in to bow and kneel, and Hsi-Soong nodded and clapped her hands. The hangings opened and Messer Polo entered and bowed and approached, bowing at every pace. Franc would have got up and bowed in return, but Hsi-Soong put him gently back, chattering in Cathayan.

"I am asked by the gracious Hsi-Soong to say that I am here to make her wishes plain to you," Messer Polo said. "She regrets her inability to speak the language intelligibly. She says that I speak the same sort of Cathayan, and thus we are equals in foolishness——"

"I would like to know what is to become of Emantha," Franc said outright.

"I will let you know, good Franc," Emantha said. "Seek not to know too much in my affairs——"

"All that happens to her will be within the beneficence of

her exalted highness," Messer Polo smiled. "Little enough of harm——"

"But how long shall this be?" Franc asked.

"Perhaps a year. Perhaps two, or more. It will depend upon the desire of her exalted highness to study the daily scene in this and other lands in Europe."

Franc remembered the withered face of the Princess and Messer Polo's remark about her youth. A desire came to ask a question, but there was no grace in such curiosity. He knew of women in the town aged long before their time by some lack in their bones or blood. The Princess might be another such.

Hsi-Soong spoke at length, and Messer Polo listened, barely looking at the dancers and never turning toward Emantha.

"The gracious Hsi-Soong wishes to know if you have any knowledge of music," Messer Polo said.

"None."

"You play no lute or pipe, or sing?"

"Never. A chorus with a crowd, no more."

Messer Polo spoke at length to Hsi-Soong and turned again.

"I am asked to say that you cannot be offered a place with the Court musicians. It is felt that an apology should be made to you, since it might perhaps injure your feelings to learn that you were considered unfit."

"I feel no injury——"

"A musician is held in high repute, as scholars are with us," Emantha whispered. "I am joined to the Court as dancer and companion, but much thought was given before I could enter. Her exalted highness may not speak to any except the gracious Hsi-Soong, and she may speak only to dancers or musicians or to those given to the arts. I may speak to musicians and dancers and my own tirewomen, but nobody else. Nobody may speak to me unless I command——"

"And a day ago you worked upon the wall!"

"And happier. I would run away, but there are guards at the door——"

"Then come home with me——"

"Would you live past this curtain?"

Hsi-Soong got up to dance, and Messer Polo waited for a servant to straighten the cushions and arrange the robe, and sat.

"I am instructed to offer you a place in the caravan," he said, clasping his hands, leaning on an elbow, and stretching to find comfort. "You will take immediate service as chamberlain. Nobody else among us speaks any language but Cathayan or the Mongol dialects. The valets and housemen we engaged in Brindisi and Rome suffer the defects of their kind. You, at least, have letters and small learning and are honest, of severe approach, and of appearance not wanting in a certain handsomeness——"

"If Leda could hear!" Emantha laughed, licking her fingers.

"—which is also in your favor, since Cathayan philosophy teaches that the exterior reflects what is within," Messer Polo said, taking no notice. "Your uniforms, valets, and horses will be provided, with payment of one thousand gold pieces in a month, and you should prepare to travel immediately. What shall you say?"

The dancers spun in a golden cloud. The pavilion wall melted. His mother sat at the loom, and in velvets and gold chains he stood before her and took her hand and led her forth to the bows of her neighbors and down to the house he had built for her. One month's pay alone, and the thousand gold pieces would make him as wealthy as any man in Assisi. More, he might seek out Emantha, not as a bee after the sweets of gold, but as one of substance.

The gold coins vanished and his mother went back to her loom. The pavilion walls came silken in the light and the dancers stepped and turned. Time hung, and yes or no sat in balance.

Chapter 12

"Others must first be spoken to," Franc said.

"But, Franc," Emantha begged, "you would be with me!"

"He will join my personal staff," Messer Polo said. "The women of the Court are kept apart!"

"But in the same caravan," Franc said. "That would be enough to know——"

"Are you, now, trothed?" Messer Polo asked.

Franc looked at Emantha, but she turned away her head with the great gold beak for cap, and took an apple and bit, and juice burst in bright drops from her teeth.

"There are minds," he said. "But none made up——"

"This caravan is bridal," Messer Polo said, lying back, looking up at the roof. "Her exalted highness was to have married a king of Persia, but he died before we arrived. We shall travel until the Grand Khan answers our request for instruction, to return unwed or to marry another of his choice——"

"Not of hers?" Franc inquired.

"Cathayan women do as they are told," Messer Polo said.

Franc looked at Hsi-Soong dancing a pattern of her own among the troupe.

"This one does as she pleases," he said.

"Her exalted highness permits her——"

"Would she also permit Emantha?"

"This, we have said before, has no answer from me. I am a servant of the Grand Khan, chancelor to her exalted highness, and commander of the caravan. I use no mind but my own. I shall look for your decision in the morning."

"Shall you come home with me, Emantha?" Franc asked.

"I stay with Hsi-Soong, and together we go to the Princess," she smiled. "I am moved from my sisters' house——"

"Moved!"

"My place is with the Princess until my service is finished——"

"You are given?"

"So Il Cardinale advised my sisters——"

Hsi-Soong left the dance and took Emantha's hand, leading her in steps with drumbeat and piping from One-piece and Two-piece as if no other person were in the world.

Messer Polo bowed to her, but she took no notice. Franc wanted to give her thanks and waited, trying to draw her smile, but she turned the other way, intent upon showing Emantha how to place her feet.

"Our audience is at end," Messer Polo said. "I shall accompany you beyond the sentries——"

With great desire to stay, Franc was led to go. Outside in the darkness Messer Polo drew a deep breath and walked in long strides.

"What think you of this plan of Il Cardinale's?" he asked in a sudden. "What thinks Assisi?"

"I believe, knowing us, that we should feel more comfort if each child were ten men accoutered for war——"

Messer Polo clapped him on the back.

"After our own heart!" he whispered. "What shall happen?"

"Some mothers and fathers will not resist Il Cardinale. He

158

is much loved. Therefore, some of the children will be captured——"

"You place no confidence in the Perugians' kind hearts?"

"As much as in wolves admitted to the sheepfold——"

"And concerning attack? What do they gain by taking this community, so poor, so undistinguished in anything except the name of a saint?"

Franc heard the question with scorch to his feeling of pride in the town. But he realized that Assisi might look poor after so great a city as Rome, or by comparison with nearby Spoleto. He found only one answer, which had always been his father's.

"It is the sport of nobles to ride out with banners and trumpets and the panoply of war," he said. "If others are to be attacked, let it be with as little hurt to themselves as possible. For that reason they recruit foreigners for their men-at-arms. Those do the fighting, and the nobles ride in when all is over. In that way, with victory won, they return brave to the cheers of their citizens and the smiles of their noble ladies——"

"This has happened before in Assisi, I am told——"

"Many times."

"The Perugians have a wealthy city and many lords. What profit comes in the capture of a poor community?"

"Butchery, burning, and prisoners, slaves and profit, with little loss to themselves——"

"They should be taught the dangers——"

"Only show us how!"

Messer Polo gave him farewell and strode back with the torchbearers. Franc wondered if he should go first to Il Cardinale to tell of his good fortune, or to his mother, or to Messer Gandolfi. The latter, he thought, would be snoring, and the first might be with his advisers. His mother, at least, would be at home.

She was still before the hearth, sewing, when he went in. He took a stool and went over the happenings of the night, but she put aside her work only after she heard of the offer.

"You will need Il Cardinale's advice," she said with no surprise. "For me, you are grown to proper years. You will do as you will. You have been twice your age since you could walk. You need no word from me."

"Other mothers are more concerned with their sons," he said. "Why are you always far away? Neither glad nor sorry, or any word except to speak to Il Cardinale?"

"You have been the man since your father went," she whispered. "Should I treat you as a babe and so weaken myself?"

He knelt before her and took her hand.

"Let it be so," he said, and kissed her cheek. "With my gold you will have a happier life——"

"No happier than I have known," she smiled. "And no different, because I have what I want. But I will be happy to hear you shaking the rafters on your way to bed. You are blue about the eyes with want of sleep. Good night, and angels stand near you!"

The rising bell was in his ears almost before he felt he had slept. But his mother moved below, and hot broth waited for him after he had almost frozen his head under the pump.

He went to the tower and found all well and Paolo Corti asleep in the twigs. The sentries at the gate of the Little Brothers had passed the night with no callers in or out. At the Mayor's house, Messer Gandolfi lay abed, but wakeful. His councilors were in with him, and his goodwife ran to serve this one with a hot posset and that one with buttered milk, another with thin soup and others with a potage, or a bowl of whey, and all the time she gabbled of the poorness of her house and how unfit she was to serve such distinguished company, until the Mayor threw down the bedcovers and held his fists to the ceiling and roared command to shut her mouth, the door, and the kitchen, and all else that might offend his sight or hearing until the town's business was finished.

"Well," he said, "what do our people think of Il Cardinale's plan?"

The councilors babbled, but there came one opinion, of denial, and a common prediction that if anything were to happen to a single child, Messer Mayor would hang from the tower gate.

"So I have told myself in and out of dreams all night." Messer Mayor nodded. "What shall we do?"

"Go to him now, and forbid it," Councilor Corti said with a red nose in pink splotch on a flashing steel breastplate. "And while we speak, let me say that my son, Paolo, is not at the beck of any esquire——"

"He is at my beck," said Mayor Gandolfi. "He will do his duty in the tower——"

"The steps make his heart trip——"

"At least we find he has one. Enough. And let this be said once for all, that Esquire Franc is my mouth and legs. Well, Franc? Why do you raise a hand?"

"I am offered a thousand gold pieces a month, with uniforms, valets, and horses, to accompany the caravan of her exalted highness——"

All eyes turned upon him and all mouths were open.

"He casts his gold as I cast stones before my feet!" Messer Gandolfi groaned. "You won't leave me, Franc?"

"I shall take opinion, Messer Mayor——"

"But what is gold to your sense of duty?" Councilor Corti pleaded.

"With half a month's pay in his pouch, he'd buy you out of the ground," Messer Gandolfi laughed. "Sense of duty? If it were offered to you, you'd be smoke across the plain!"

"This is an insult to a councilor——"

"Insult? If he should go and returns here, who's to stop him buying the town and all about? Who becomes Mayor? And who will wait upon him hand and foot? You, you rogue!"

"I'll have none of this!" Councilor Corti shouted.

"No? Why do you think I chose the boy? Because he's a fool? Which of you, in my stead, could be Mayor and survive the week?"

"You put weight upon him," Councilor Forra said, pulling gray whiskers. "His father was sound metal, though——"

"Never mind his father!" the Mayor rumbled, impatient. "The boy has an offer. Very well, he'll see Il Cardinale. Next business? The children. I'll speak against it. Next business? Who goes to Perugia with Il Cardinale?"

"Why should any go?" Councilor Corti demanded.

"Because we must be represented. We are the Council——"

"We are against it——"

"But if children are going, some of us must also——"

"I have much to do," Councilor Starace said. "My animals are all driven in today——"

"I am chained to the shop," Councilor Corti said. "All stocks go below floors to be bricked in. If they attack, they'll find nothing——"

"We all have boarding and bricking to do," Councilor Forra said. "What should we do in Perugia except lose our eyes or our tongues or both, and by all odds, our lives?"

"Then, for the honor of Assisi, I will go," Messer Gandolfi said. "Franc, I will leave you here, in command of the town——"

"Messer Mayor, with all respect to your seal," Franc began, "if you were put upon with indignity, this would be hurt to you and to the civic pride. But if I go, Assisi is properly represented, and at the same time no man of affairs suffers loss in pride or business. I, having none, can afford it——"

The eldest Gandolfi daughter filled the doorway.

"Il Cardinale desires Esquire Franc's presence in the instant." She giggled, pulling at her apron. "At the lower church, in the south transept——"

At a nod from the Mayor, Franc squeezed by the giggler and took the side door and the path through the garden and leaped the wall. A short run brought him to the work yard and the long face of Messer di Rovigo.

"First to hear of trouble are the workmen!" he shouted. "The moment my back was turned, most left. They don't want any fighting——"

Franc waved and went on down the steps, among all the rock and cut stone and shaped lumber, to the door of the lower church, and knocked.

A Brother of the Order let him in. Others inside waxed the tiles or dusted the walls and ornaments. Up on the scaffolding Messer Giotto's apprentices were working almost in darkness. At the wall, by candlelight, Laz brushed color into figures, and Messer Giotto watched from the floor, with Tivi at his right hand.

Franc went on to the south transept and found Il Cardinale sitting in his chair with his retinue about him. A choir behind the altar began to chant, and some of the priests went away.

"I hear this morning that you are tempted from us," Il Cardinale said without greeting. "This is severe loss, Franc!"

"I am of little moment, Excellency——"

"A knock on the head too hard, or a fever too high, and which of us is of moment? Will you, then, join Messer Polo?"

"It was my duty to ask you——"

"I shall say go. With the money, you will build a house and buy farms and vineyards. In that way the town is made wealthier, with work for more, and bread for more mouths."

"Excellency, a word, please, about Emantha——"

Il Cardinale rested his chin on the little and third fingers, and the other two went beside his right ear. His eyes were pale in the darkness, and candlelight shone gold in their moisture, and the wrinkles about his mouth and nose were dark and deep.

"What, then, of Emantha?" he asked gently.

"Of which family is she, and what should I know, if I am to ask for her in marriage?"

"She is of good family, as you know who are grown together with her, and of that, an end," he said with no smile or move. "If you are to ask for her in marriage, then ask and, having got your answer, be satisfied, and an end to that!"

"But she is not of Hortensia's family. The mother nursed her, no more——"

"When Emantha says yes, then be about your business. And if she says no, then give thanks that she is not already sworn, so that you have yet time to prevail upon her to change her mind——"

"But if she dreams of a noble marriage?"

Il Cardinale smiled and moved and opened the book on his knee.

"Which girl does not? Have you thought of a wife with riches?"

Franc looked down at Il Cardinale's thin sandals and found himself happy to be in the darkness.

"This was a dream," he said unwillingly.

"Others may also dream. But all must waken too. Shall you be with us to Perugia?"

"It is my hope, Excellency——"

"And mine. Tell Messer Mayor Gandolfi that the Sisters of Poor Clare have already found those mothers willing to bring me their children. For the rest, let them stay at home."

Franc went through the church, halting for a procession of chanting Brothers, and out across the grassy space and over the wall, into the Mayor's parlor.

Several townsmen were there, wanting the Mayor's judgment in matters of their business. Mayor Gandolfi could be heard shouting as he dressed.

"What ails our first man this morning?" a stall-keeper whispered.

"The wine of last night," another said. "His head is not his own, wanting a nail or two to keep it in place——"

"How shall we have balance in our affairs?" one grumbled. "We speak and he hears nothing——"

"Only as much as he wants," said another, grinning. "And that's enough to give him the right and wrong of it——"

"Let nothing happen to him, wine or not," prayed another. "Where should we look beyond him? Which of his councilors would give us poor ones proper hearing in a cause where he had other interest?"

"And if that one up at the castle chose a favorite, then think of our grief!"

"A Corti, let us say?"

"Ai!"

"A Forra?"

"O!"

"Then who?"

Mayor Gandolfi pushed the door open and went to sit in the curulis, red of face and eye, shoes undone, with both hands holding a loaf with strips of ham hanging from it, and tearing out chunks by pulling away from his teeth.

Everybody shouted at once, wanting first hearing. But a trumpet call outside brought silence, and at a nod from the Mayor, all left the parlor except Franc, and he obeyed the gesture to stand at the right of the curulis.

Messer Polo came in with three Cathayan officers and made a bow. Messer Gandolfi gave the loaf to Franc and beat the crumbs from his beard and tunic and nodded greeting.

"Messer Mayor, I recall to your mind a word said last night, in jest or not," Messer Polo began. "You said that you would prize the Count d'Orosa's banner——"

"With all that it would mean——"

165

Messer Polo took a package from an officer and held it out in a bow.

"Be pleased to achieve your desire. This banner was taken from the castle during the night by a patrol of ours——"

"And the Count?"

"At last hearing, deep in his feather bed——"

Messer Gandolfi looked at the package and leaned back, pounding his knee in openmouthed laughter.

"Under their snouts!" he bellowed. "Franc, take this to my goodwife and say it needs a stuffing and a needle. Within the hour we'll sit upon that viper, with all his lowborn fathers——"

Ciro tapped his staff three times to warn of an important arrival. The Abbess of the Sisters of Poor Clare came in with a group of her nuns, and the Mayor stood to receive them.

"Messer Gandolfi, we are here on a happy errand," she smiled. "We wish to make it known that the Count d'Orosa has gifted us full title to his building, lying beyond the wall from our cloister. We will use it for the children's school we so badly need. But we require to cut a door through the town wall so that the children may enter through our premises instead of having to go back and forth through the towngate——"

"This is generous in the Count," Mayor Gandolfi said, staring at the package in his hands. "He is not noted for these broad acts of charity——"

The Abbess held out a scroll, sealed and ribboned.

"This is the deed," she said. "We come for permission to open a door——"

"We must be no less generous than the Count," Mayor Gandolfi said, and put the package on a ledge behind the curulis. "Permission is granted. Franc, let this gift of Messer Polo's rest here. Can we think harm to those who bless our town with charity?"

166

Chapter 13

Just after the noon meal, Ob came into the yard, holding the reins of a white mare saddled in silver and scarlet. Cathayan cavalrymen in the lane held three ponies, packsaddled and loaded.

"She is sent to you for your personal use by command of Messer Polo, and no youngster is luckier," Ob said. "The pack ponies are also yours. Will you keep them at my stables?"

Franc nodded, stroking a warm pelt, with no word left and a tightened throat.

"Then tell him I obeyed his instruction," Ob said. "What of this madness to Perugia? I told my woman I will hang her from the gatepost if she let any of our children go!"

"Let Il Cardinale decide," Franc's mother said, sharp, from the open door. "Should we ruin the day so, with talk of hangings?"

Ob winked and turned back to his mount.

"There will be ruin before the day is out, be sure," he said, vaulting into the saddle. "The word is gone about that D'Orosa's banner is under the Mayor. How long shall he squat in comfort?"

Franc watched the party clatter down the hill and looked up at the castle. Flags and pennons flew from every pole and banners hung from the windows of the great hall, with chains of leaves hung between.

"They expect visitors up there," he said, "though not the visitors from Cathay!"

"How was it wise to affront the Count at such a time?" his mother whispered, washing the crocks at the well. "Shall he not be down here with men-at-arms? And with that, the loss of the only force we had to save us?"

"He was never the one to save us," Franc said.

"His strength kept many away——"

"Only until he chose the time."

"He gave the Clares their school."

"A broken building on the other side of the walls from their cloister? How else could he knock a hole in the town wall, except under guise of a door for the nuns' school? What gift is this?"

"You look for evil where none is——"

"I look for the animal under golden armor——"

"There, perhaps. Franc, take care in what you do. You are come to a great place in short time. Will you join the caravan?"

"Why should I not?"

"I think of us left in Assisi. The Cathayans will soon be gone. What after?"

She went inside and sat at the hearth with a length of loomed wool.

"We shall be as strong as before the Cathayans came," he said from the doorway.

"With you gone from the tower? And Emantha gone from her sisters?"

"Little enough loss——"

She put the wool down and bent her head in tears.

"I fear for us all," she whispered. "The Mayor has few

friends. Il Cardinale is soon to go back to the Order of the Little Brothers of St. Francis. Who shall take his place? Who shall strengthen the Mayor? One we know? Or one given to thinking as the Perugians?"

"How is this, he becomes a Brother?"

"He is Il Cardinale only in our hearts. He is Brother, as all the others. When his time of authority is past, he goes back to the Order. Franc, in many things are grown, in height, and breadth, and strength. In other things you are yet ungrown, with much to learn——"

"Then a year or two in company of Messer Polo cannot come amiss. Will you go to Perugia?"

"If the Abbess needs me, yes. And you?"

He nodded.

"Save us both!" she whispered, and her clasped hands were black against the firelight.

Franc went down the hill with plenty to think about. For all the years he could remember, Il Cardinale had been the strength of the town. The notion had never come close that his excellency was no more than one with Brother Egidio or any of the others.

The tailor called from his bench that the Esquire's uniform was ready to be worn. Franc looked at the rich plum of the tunic and at the dark blue shirt and breeches. Next door, the shoemaker held up knee boots of soft black leather with silver straps and buckles.

"I join the Cathayan caravan," Franc said. "These will be for another——"

"Who else in this town is fit to wear them?" the tailor asked. "We have youths a-plenty. Which?"

"One will come to hand——"

"Easier to the toe of a boot!" the tailor grunted. "Who takes blame for the banner of D'Orosa?"

"It was a gift to the Mayor——"

"He may earn one that sits not so happily. See, D'Orosa's fugelman sets out——"

Many people in the street were looking up at the castle. The gates had opened, and a fugelman rode in front of a strong troop, though without a banner at their head, and neither was the sun as usual busy in golden armor.

"The Count is palsied of his loss," the shoemaker called out.

"These are like to palsy us," the tailor whispered, taking the shutters out of his shop. "I will lock and bar till they are gone——"

Franc ran down to the Mayor's court, and the shouts began to race him, and the streets and lanes were full of people running, and the sounds of shutters going up and bars falling echoed all about.

Mayor Gandolfi sat in the curulis under the archway, and the Council stood in a half circle, though they, too, looked ready to run.

"Go to the gate and tell Keeper Mozo not to open without my order," he said quietly. "See that the Little Brothers' gate is shut and guarded——"

"And the school," Franc reminded.

Messer Gandolfi nodded.

"There, too. For how long are you Esquire?"

"For today, and until we return from Perugia——"

"At least one of us has faith in a home-coming. Hasten, Franc, and tell me the town is safe!"

Franc ran to the stables and took the white Cathayan mare without saddling her, and called a soothing word to the angry groom. He rode first to the gatehouse and shouted to Keeper Mozo. He waited until he heard the drawbridge raised, and then rode to the Clares' school and got off at the cloister gate. A nun admitted him, and he found a gang plastering the arch they had knocked in the wall leading to the Count's stables. It took little time to haul beams and logs into a cross-works that blocked the arch on the cloister side, and by the time the Abbess had come out the masons were dry-walling stones into a barrier.

"We have need of this entry!" the Abbess started to say. "I have permission from the Count, from the Mayor——"

Franc explained quietly what was toward. But the Abbess was impatient.

"These things have no interest!" she said firmly. "Pull all this down at once. You have no right to give orders here——"

"Any man setting hand to pull down any splinter or crumb of earth I will set in the dungeon," Franc warned the workmen. "Permit any soft point of entry and you will find enemies here in the town——"

"My school!" the Abbess wept. "After all this work!"

"Good lady, allow a day or two," Franc pleaded. "Let this alarm pass——"

"I shall go to the Mayor!"

"That is best. You men, make all safe. I shall return to make sure!"

He ran out and mounted the mare and trotted her down to the tower. His days away had made a difference, and he found his legs ailing at the window platform and he was glad to grasp the wooden ladder to climb the rest. Ubaldo sat under the parapet, teaching Toma the run of the alphabet.

"These things are well," Franc said. "But what of the watch and ward?"

"Nothing moves." Toma shrugged, sweeping a hand across the distance. "See for yourself——"

"Except these men-at-arms from the castle." Franc pointed to the troop. "If they require to enter?"

"The Count will give the word——"

"And if the Mayor has refused it?"

Toma stared.

"Refuse the Count?" he whispered.

"Messer Mozo raised the drawbridge minutes ago. You, happy with your letters, saw nothing, heard less. Of what use are you as wardens? Ubaldo, you are a second time at fault——"

"There shall be no third, I swear it!" Ubaldo pleaded.

"And leave me!" Toma begged, almost on his knees. "All my life I have wanted place as Warden, and secondly a hold on letters——"

"Both are in your reach, but earn them," Franc said. "I will send up Paolo Corti——"

"Him?"

"And you shall twig-and-muscle his hide into exact obedience——"

"It shall be done!"

"And Sesto, son of the coppersmith, shall help you here. What of traffic on the plain?"

"A crowd of pilgrims to the chapel of St. Francis. A troop of Cathayan cavalry comes back from the river. No sign of any from Perugia——"

"It is well——"

He ran down the stairs and mounted the mare, turning her toward the shop of Councilor Corti. The shopmen and carpenters were busy with boards and timber outside, and masons and laborers worked between the ground floor and the cellar. Councilor Corti came up at his call, but he refused to send for Paolo.

"My son works at his proper trade!" he shouted. "He is below, putting all in order against attack——"

"Who says there will be attack?" Franc demanded.

"Who says? Am I lived to this age, and knowing nothing of signs? Will the Count stay in his castle, and this insult made to his banner? Are we madmen to believe that all goes peacefully? Before nightfall there will be a new mayor. Yes, and a new esquire, take heed!"

Franc led the mare down to the stables and gave her to the groom.

"Shall you name this one?" the groom inquired. "Remembering three pack ponies, also unnamed? You have the finest of any horseflesh beyond the Cathayans' own——"

"I will name them after we are returned from Perugia——"

The groom turned down his mouth and shrugged.

"They will stay nameless," he said. "I had as soon thought you would cast yourself from the tower——"

"The pride of Assisi demands it——"

"A dead one on the cobbles of Perugia? Would your father go? Would you not better serve us by using your head as he might, and the right arm as he taught you? Who is pride? A dead one?"

Franc went down to the court. Messer Gandolfi talked in his garden with the men he employed on his farms. They and their families were all in, and their carts and wains filled the space beyond the Cathayan encampment.

"Well then, Franc," he said when the men had gone. "We are left to look to the town. What of the walls?"

"All well, Messer Mayor. Councilor Corti refuses his son Paolo for service in the tower——"

"He shall now take a brush into the sewers and help to cleanse them. Four prisoners are in the dungeon, and with him as fifth, they shall end their sentence——"

"And if he will not work?"

The Mayor pulled his beard and grinned.

"If those four are told that the sooner they are done the sooner they may go to their families, will he not be made to?"

He called the Wand Bearer and gave order, and the man went off at a trot.

"The Count's men-at-arms are by now at the drawbridge," Franc said.

"They have good sun and the grass is plentiful——"

"If they complain to come in?"

"We shall listen to their complaint. We have one weakness. We cannot bar Messer Polo and his men, and when they enter or depart the gate is open——"

He stared at shouts from uphill, toward the towngate. A troop of Cathayans rode four abreast. Behind them, D'Orosa's men-at-arms came at a trot, and people ran screaming in and slammed doors.

"Well," the Mayor sighed, "let us see what is toward——"

"You knew how it would fall, Messer Mayor, when you took the banner?" Franc said in surprise. "How could you then not return it? Or a hole in the earth, or a fire had been better——"

Mayor Gandolfi rested a hand on his shoulder.

"Franc," he said with an eye on the men-at-arms, "I had no son to sweeten my potch of daughters. But if I had been so blessed, I would have had one such as yourself. Make no disappointment in me by speaking as these councilors of mine. Know this, that D'Orosa must be shown for what he is. Better he appear as himself while we have Cathayans to help us——"

"But did you think him traitor before this?"

"Since first I saw the eye behind the hood. His mark is Assisi, and all in it——"

"So Messer Polo delights to ask, why?"

Mayor Gandolfi rasped his beard and showed yellow tusks.

"That we shall discover, perhaps? And perhaps it is already known——"

The men-at-arms turned and formed ranks with much pulling and curvetting outside the arcade before the Mayor's court. The sergeant gave the Mayor no civil greeting. Messer Gandolfi looked at none and walked under the arcade toward the curulis. The sergeant rode his horse under the vault and blocked the way.

"Foolish gestures," Messer Gandolfi rumbled. "I will indite a word to the Count d'Orosa——"

"He sends word to you," the sergeant grinned. "It is a question, stuck upon the point of a lance!"

"These are not for us," Mayor Gandolfi said quietly. "And how are you so blown up, a mercenary, coming before me covered and a-horse? Get down, take off your helmet, and know that I am Mayor——"

The sergeant spat at his feet.

"So much for your mercenary!" he shouted. "Where is the banner of the Count d'Orosa?"

Messer Gandolfi nodded to the package in a ledge behind the curulis.

"This, it is said by some, contains a banner," he said. "It has not been opened, and therefore nobody knows. Take it, with my permission——"

"With or without," the sergeant grinned, and leaned from his saddle to pick it up. "Think fortune it was never flown——"

He lifted the package high and wheeled about, trotting to a place at head of the troop, and led them in a turn toward the gate.

Mayor Gandolfi showed no sign of bad temper. Instead he went up the three steps and sat back in the curulis and crossed his knees and laughed into his beard.

"You think me put upon, Franc?" he asked.

"I had expected more in defense," Franc said. "Where is Assisi's pride in this?"

"Resting on its own honest flesh. Consider, was this not better done? Before, he could choose his time. Now, he is known. By his order, a mercenary flouted my authority——"

"Where is this an advantage to us?"

"We shall now destroy the path from the castle. He shall not enter the town. He cannot draw water from our wells. His workmen shall not lodge with us. For what were they, except men-at-arms within our gates?"

"These things are strange to me, Messer Mayor——"

175

"They have been strange to me since he came to frown upon us from up there. His father was king of terror in my youth. Then the son returns in my mid-age. He is last of the family and I have ambition to end the line. Go, find Simone!"

Franc went to the stonecutters' bay in search. Messer di Rovigo told him they were all working on the tower outside the lower church. Franc climbed down into the dip where the churches were built, one over the other, and through the timber supports, and called Simone off the ladder.

"No man went happier to work!" he laughed, and shouted to his gang and sent them for tools. "Next, we shall see the castle fall!"

"You take pride in destruction——"

"My father died up there. Nobody has raised a hand for us. Who will, in this town of traders and fieldmen? They suffer to be governed by any, so long as they live and do not die, or eat enough not to starve. So are we placed lifelong——"

"We have a good mayor——"

"That, yes. But he is one——"

"A strong town guard——"

Simone put his head back and laughed as a mewing cat.

"A shout from the right throats and they would all run for the drains, as many a time before!"

"This is why Messer Mayor ordered the sewers cleansed!"

"For what other reason? He knows their bolthole. Why should you look askance here?"

"I think Assisi better manned——"

"You stayed in the tower too long, good Franc. You dreamed windy dreams, at far distance from all of us. If these traders can save their trade and their hides by lowering their heads, think you they will raise them at risk of losing both? These things Mayor Gandolfi knows and we know. How are you so slow?"

Franc shook his head, wordless.

176

Simone clapped his shoulder.

"Come! You are well out of it, high or low. You will grow rich with these Cathayans and buy a palace in Rome. Who, then, shall threaten you? If you need one versed in stone, think of Simone!"

Franc climbed the cleft by the rough steps and stood to watch the Brothers sing their way into the upper church. The more he thought of what Simone had said, the more he saw its truth. There were numbers in the town guard, but few fighters. Fat Gil was good as any. But to think of him in hard press of steel and hoofs was plainly foolish.

He was tapped on the shoulder and he turned, looking into the eyes of one of the tiptrots so free with Emantha's blushes.

"Messer Polo presents his compliments to the Messer Esquire of Assisi," he said with a bow and a juggle of his cap. "He wishes it known that if, by fortune, your honor has a moment not engaged, he will deem it greatest pleasure to entertain in his pavilion——"

"Wait," Franc said. "I had meant to inquire of you and the other. Let me make known, now, that I felt regret to have caused trouble between yourselves and your master——"

The face was empty. The eyes stared.

"Remember that I set upon Messer Polo while he spoke with a maid, Emantha——"

"That?" the youth laughed and snapped his fingers. "He rewarded us——"

"Rewarded?"

"Certainly. He it was who put us to follow her and find out where she lived and who she was, how named. In such manner he found his White Bird——"

"Then what was this of blushes?"

"Blushes?"

"That you spoke to her and she blushed for shame——"

"Of this I know nothing. But I would feel grief for any who said more than was proper to her——"

"How is this?"

"She has the muscles of a bullock——"

"Aha!"

"And she makes no wait in using them. The apprentice painters know it well——"

"Which are these?"

"Those in Messer Giotto's studio. One took his place to pinch her while we escorted her, and with no effort, she tripped him flat——"

"And this I taught her!"

"You had a good pupil, Messer Esquire. For blushes, I will take another. Be pleased to bend your step this way!"

Chapter 14

"I would be greatly pleased if you could join us soon, though if
you ask why we tarried so long in this poor community, I will
tell you," Messer Polo said easily. "Our animals required shoe-
ing and our people needed rest. Of more importance, her exalted highness found an expression of faith here. This St.
Francis has much in common with a holy man of Cathay, by
name Lao-tse. Even the erudite Messer Dante had never heard
of him. His excellency, Il Cardinale, blessed scholar, was one
more reason. The Princess has enjoyed many an hour in his
company."

Franc listened, but although a vision of the Princess's face
came plain, he forbore to ask a question. Curiosity, his mother
had taught, was sly work for crows.

"I cannot give you answer until Messer Mayor has less work
for an esquire," he said at last. "Not, certainly, until we return from Perugia——"

"You will be absent from our tourney with the Count
d'Orosa?"

"My only grief!"

"We meet beyond the walls in the flat space between the furnace and the chapel of St. Francis——"

"Chosen by D'Orosa?"

"By his heralds." Messer Polo nodded.

"They made good choice. It is near enough to bring every man outside the walls——"

"But why would anybody want the town of Assisi?" Messer Polo asked impatiently. "Why should D'Orosa try to take it by stealth when he could take it at will? Why? What is here?"

"Assisi is a town older than the Romans!" Franc said, hot.

"Of what value?"

Franc looked through the pavilion doorway. He could find no answer. The land, certainly, was worth little. The houses were nothing. The few shops could not be compared with Perugia's. There were no fine palaces, or monuments, or any park or garden. Even the stones of a Roman theater rolled in ruin.

"Only to us," he said dismally.

Messer Polo nodded.

"Every man fights for his own," he said. "But why does a man of Count d'Orosa's rank and power want something that would bring so little? Why do the nobles of Perugia make constant war? A few houses, a tavern or two, churches of bare walls now taking paint, and a country market. What is this to desire? Being got, of what use?"

A gong struck, and drumming and piping came clear, and the hangings were lifted and Hsi-Soong danced in, one foot raised now, and the other then, and hands lifted and put down, and One-piece and Two-piece dancing in the same way with her and turning about each other. Behind them Emantha stood smiling.

But a changed Emantha.

She wore a white Cathayan dress that held her body with nothing spare, and jewels were clustered in the Cathayan set of her hair piled up with combs. Blue spread glistening above her eyes, and her mouth shone crimson, and her cheeks were pink as the peach.

Hsi-Soong took Messer Polo aside, and Franc went to Emantha.

"You are something different from the one I have known," he said.

"Colors from pots and a silk or two. Little. Do you like me?"

"Yes."

"So much, no more?"

"What shall I say more than pretty?"

"Messer Polo makes more with words——"

"And what with blushes?"

"I don't blush!"

"Under that red ruddle, who could tell?"

"You speak as one from the fields!"

"How else? Are you of the palace?"

"I like the gentler way——"

"You'll have good practice——"

"Messer Polo speaks to me as to the Princess——"

"Have you seen her?"

"Heard her——"

"You serve her, but without seeing her?"

"She is not allowed to be seen——"

"But Messer Dante has seen her and spoken to her——"

"Him I have seen, but only in the Three Silver Men. But I am not allowed to enter in the Princess's pavilion. Nor is any other except Hsi-Soong and the Princess's tirewomen. Franc, do you join us? I would give much to know that you are near to me. I grow lonely in this gibber. I think sometimes of a tub of clothes and I could run to them!"

He looked at the flash of tears in her eyes and swift put out a hand to pull her close.

"I must make up my mind between now and tomorrow," he

whispered. "Messer Polo gives me so much time. Think of the gold that is ours at the end and what it will do!"

Emantha nodded, but the tears ran, and the lower lip trembled, and some of the blue of her eyes streaked the red of her cheeks.

"My sisters and their children will have better lives," she whispered, shaking. "We shall have a great house and fine clothes to wear and filled tables. But how shall I stand the hours without a word from them?"

Hsi-Soong and One-piece and Two-piece danced, piped, and drummed down to them. Hsi-Soong took his hand and led him to the end of the pavilion, and Messer Polo joined them.

"The gracious Hsi-Soong wishes to know which clothes you will wear and how you prefer the arrangement of your pavilion," Messer Polo said.

"I shall be grateful for what I get," Franc said.

"She wishes to know why you wear old clothes——"

"Because they are all I have——"

"Cathayans believe it proper to keep fine clothing for special occasions——"

"As do we. But where shall poor people have fine clothes?"

Messer Polo spoke in Cathayan, and Hsi-Soong answered.

"You are to take one thousand gold pieces immediately and buy yourself clothes of every kind, by order of the gracious Hsi-Soong," Messer Polo said.

"Half of a single gold piece will buy me the best wardrobe in all of Umbria," Franc laughed. "She is ready with her gold——"

"Which comes to her as sand upon the shore," Messer Polo said. "Take your thousand pieces and dress!"

"Keep your gold and know me as I am, and good day!"

Franc went out in a rage and ran himself breathless down toward Il Cardinale's house. Tivi came out of the upper church carrying trays of color gourds and pots.

"Ha, Franc!" he shouted. "Where, in such a reckneck?"

"To help you, if a hand is needed."

"Take the top two trays, if you will. They slip. Ah, what a day!"

"Tragedies?"

"Of many kinds. Most, that we lack certain colors. The church is dark. Red in any tint goes on the wall and dries out near to black. Reds, that is, such as we have——"

"Are there others?"

"The one we need is made with the ruby. Who, in this poor town, has a ruby? And Messer Giotto curses and, remembering where he is, goes outside the better to rid himself of bile. And the work suffers——"

"A ruby, now——"

"A stone from the Orient. Red as blood. That one, worn on the fourth finger of the right hand by this little Cathayan, she with the drummer and piper——"

Franc piled the trays back on top of Tivi's armful and turned away.

"I will meet you in the paint shop before the chime," he called, and ran toward the Cathayan encampment.

But nobody was there. Cathayan guards tried to stop him, but he understood nothing, and they prevented him from going inside to search. He called out for Emantha, walking between the pavilions, and she came running from one at the end. He told her of Tivi's worry and the disgrace that Assisi had no single citizen able to supply a ruby.

"What is this ruby?" She frowned.

"Hsi-Soong wears one in a ring upon her little finger. Go to her and say that I will give her my gold for the first month for it——"

"You will join us!"

"If I have the ruby and the walls have the true color!"

She flung her arms about his neck and soundly kissed his cheek, and he stood as a block, watching her running to the pavilion at the end.

"What then, Franc? Are you now of another mind?"

Messer Polo stood in a pavilion entrance not far away, looking at the nail sheaths.

"No," Franc said, hoping the blush would be taken for a touch of the sun. "But I am ready to join your service——"

"Then remember what I said of the separation of men and women. There can be no meetings between yourself and Emantha. And no speaking, or so much as a look——"

"That, too. There will be time——"

"What are these runnings to and fro?" Messer Polo asked, watching Emantha hurrying toward them. "Some private alarm——"

"Here!" Emantha laughed, holding out a hand, cupped. "Rubies that I had worn in my hair without knowing!"

Franc took the few red pebbles that flashed deep flame and kissed the hand that gave them.

"That, for Assisi!" he whispered.

"Nothing from you?"

He would go close to kiss her cheek, but Messer Polo came to them.

"Who speaks of rubies?" he demanded.

"They are wanted to make color for the walls of the church," Franc said, turning to go. "A bright red, got in no other way——"

"Ask Messer Giotto what other stones he requires," Messer Polo said. "They shall be provided as mark of devotion by her exalted highness. Here, rubies, emeralds, and sapphires. And here a necklet of lapis lazuli——"

He took off the sheaths from his fingernails, and the nails were naked, curved as claws, and those of the little fingers were longer than all. The necklet dropped heavy from under the lace collar, with a fastener of pearls each the size of an eye.

"Approach the gracious Hsi-Soong's tirewoman to replace the rubies you gave away," he told Emantha. "You, Franc, take these gold pieces and find your dress for the moment——"

Franc took the gold pieces and, with his double handful, managed an awkward bow. Emantha caught his arm.

"Remember to say the stones were my gift!" she whispered.

"By permission of the gracious Hsi-Soong," Messer Polo cautioned.

"She gave them to me!" Emantha stamped. "Is a gift with permission?"

"Will Messer Giotto care, so long as there is powder to be painted on the walls?" Franc laughed. "Let us all give thanks. The red is found!"

He ran down to the paint room and through the watchmen and the mixing bay and the sound of pestling and chanting into the studio. Messer Giotto sat in a carved chair, listening to Messer Dante reading from a great book, too large to hold upon his knees, and balanced on the head of a marble cherub.

Tivi held his hands to his head in horror of disturbance, but Franc knelt before Messer Giotto and offered his gifts, saying where they were from and what they were for.

Messer Giotto's face of bones and tight flesh took color with pleasure and he shouted aloud, running into the paint room, calling on Tivi and Mok and Laz. The four gathered about the largest mortars, and pestles were chosen, and each apprentice called seniors from the lines of those busy on the floor, and the groups went to places apart to begin work.

Messer Giotto came back to the door and put his hand on Franc's shoulder.

"So, Esquire, you are now come to help me," he smiled. "What shall I do for you?"

"A sketch, in any size, of Emantha," Franc begged.

"Emantha?" Messer Giotto frowned. "Our angel has a-many admirers. The Count d'Orosa, malediction upon him, bought all I had done——"

"Count d'Orosa?"

"That one in the rocks up there. But I will paint another for you. Have you met Messer Dante?"

"Only by whisper of his work."

"Now hear the true voice. Messer Dante, permit me to bring before you an esquire of Assisi, by name Franc——"

Franc bowed and looked into the sharp and yet kindly eyes. Messer Dante wore a cap of blue and a gown of samite with a crisp white shirt, and a gold chain about his neck held an ink-pot and a gold quill.

"Are you the same whose name I heard spoken by the splendid Leda?" Messer Dante asked. "Truly a fortunate esquire!"

"But with Leda in your thrall, good Franc, how do you then keep the lovely Emantha a-hook?" Messer Giotto inquired.

"I do not keep. I have fortune in knowing both from a time we were babes——"

"Leda, from all she told me, expects to be prisoned in wedlock in the twelvemonth," Messer Dante said. "Fortune, indeed!"

"But not mine," Franc said firmly. "I have time to fill with these Cathayans——"

"Many a woman half as alive as Leda has done the thinking for two," Messer Giotto laughed. "You want no sketch of her?"

"To make Emantha jealous," Franc said.

"A flight with fire," Messer Dante smiled. "And how shall Emantha be robed for this painting?"

"As a Cathayan," Franc began, "with jewels in her hair——"

"Ah, no!" Messer Giotto said, shocked. "In her plain glory

of Assisi homespun, and wooden shoes, and that mountain light in her eyes——"

"Pure, and made apt for mounting to the stars," Messer Dante said gently. "These have no need of jewels——"

Knocks came on the door, and Tivi opened it and bowed low, and Il Cardinale hurried in with no more than a nod for all.

"Permit me this intrusion, Messer Dante," he said. "A word, here——"

"At your excellency's disposition." Messer Giotto bowed. "If it is in the matter of the drawing of bishops instead of Brothers, let me say that I find the gray habit more lively to paint than any cope——"

"Matters are more serious than habits and copes," Il Cardinale began worriedly. "This clash between the Cathayans and the D'Orosa men-at-arms threatens our peace. You must warn all in your employ to keep within the town walls. I have news of a Perugian advance to the river, an exodus of metal——"

Messer Dante and Il Cardinale and Messer Giotto spoke together in whispers and, at Tivi's nod, Franc went next door.

Mok showed them a spoonful of red crystals in one mortar, and in the next a glinting greenish powder, and a pale blue glitter in another. Laz lifted the pestle from a pile of deep blue sift and touched it with his finger.

"How many men have died for rubies, sapphires, and emeralds, to say little of lapis lazuli, that we now dab upon a wall," he grinned. "These rubies, which could buy this town and all in it——"

"Rubies?" Franc stared. "Have they, then, a true worth?"

Tivi's gray eyes stared back, looking to see if there was a joke at hand. But then he laughed, careful to turn his head from the dust in the mortar.

"These few colors in the mortars are greater fortune than all of us shall ever know! Were you not told the worth of what you gave? Poor Franc!" ·

"Poor Emantha!" Franc whispered. "If she knew!"

Il Cardinale came out of the studio and called him, and together they hurried outside.

"Messer di Rovigo will use force on his wooden-pates to keep them in," Il Cardinale breathed. "Messer Giotto is now warned. The women we may safely leave to the Sisters of Poor Clare. There remain the market men and shopsters. The town crier must warn them. The Perugians come in three columns——"

"To witness the tourney——"

"If I could think so. More likely they use it as excuse to come close for attack——"

"Which Messer Polo thinks not possible. Or, if possible, lacking all sense, for there is nothing in Assisi worth any effort——"

Il Cardinale stopped, hands behind his back, with the threadbare red hat over his eyes and the tassels making bars of shadow over his face. But his eyes glittered as the sapphire dust.

"Nothing?" he whispered. "You, of Assisi, say so?"

"But, Excellency, a few poor houses, no monuments, or works of art, or fine palaces——"

"Have I nursed a witless one these years? What are houses, or palaces, or monuments soever, against the sanctity of our holy St. Francis?"

"But him they will never find——"

"They will try, with murder and destruction. Have they not made effort time on time?"

"But where is this an honor to them?"

Il Cardinale turned full upon him, and suddenly his eyes were smiling, aged of wisdom, and pitying.

"For then, good Franc, with their victory they would move the tomb to rest at Perugia. To Perugia the pilgrims would go. And where now we in Assisi permit them all freedom in the sanctuary and in the chapel and in his churches, can you not see what fortune would come to the lords of Perugia? A charge of one gold piece a head or even more for each faithful pilgrim, and what riches would mount for these nobles. And what shame to us!"

Chapter 15

Mayor Gandolfi gave order that all men known to have any link with the castle were to be thrown into the dungeon. He next called out all the yeomen and walked about the walls placing men, a strong one with weaklings, and the best men at the points weakest to attack. All gates were closed until he gave further order.

During that time he said nothing of any help, and when all was ready and the last arrowhead had been emptied from the town stores, they turned for the mayoral court.

"If evil should befall me this day or tomorrow, do you take charge as Mayor in my place," he said cheerfully. "None will gainsay you, except the battle go hard against us——"

"I am something young for this——"

"You have promise of one thousand pieces of Cathayan gold a month," Messer Gandolfi grinned. "These are credentials enough. You have the young men with you. They know you to be trained in weapons of war. This, too, is enough——"

"Let us hope it will weigh against Perugia——"

Messer Gandolfi nodded and walked on. Shopmen and jackso'-trade watched them pass. Some called out, but Messer Mayor waved them to silence. Women's heads came out of windows, and many a whispered prayer floated as soft rain.

"Here is our problem, Franc," Messer Gandolfi said in a low voice that none might hear. "We are a small town, given almost all to the Holy Brothers of St. Francis and the Sisters of Poor Clare. They first created the peace that brought poor people about them to live. The tomb of our saint is buried, none knows where, but certainly in the rock near the church. This was done long before my birth. Perhaps Il Cardinale knows where it may be found——"

"We shall defend both——"

"We have not the men of war. In my father's time we were beaten. In my babyhood we were beaten. In my boyhood. As a grown man——"

"When I was crawling——"

"Then. Now they are at our throats once more——"

"Have others known torture to find the tomb?"

Messer Gandolfi turned about to look up at the castle.

"How many have you heard of, even in your time, that were spirited to Perugia, or who entered in up there and never came forth?" he asked. "What, do you think they sit to play gammon and drink the D'Orosa wine?"

"But why comes the attack now? Why, with Messer Polo here?"

"I believe they distrust the new work on the churches. They suspect something is being done to recover the tomb. That is their greatest prize. Second, the riches of the caravan. Even if the Cathayans are not taken and beaten here, they will be weakened, and easier to attack and swallow later when they move——"

"What think you of our chance?"

"The Perugians and their allies are at least twenty to one, and hardened in war. What think you?"

"Little."

"As do I!"

Franc found many a small matter made plainer in those moments. He had always known that the tomb of St. Francis was unmarked. Others in an olden time hid the saintly remains and left no record. Through many years the Perugians had tried to force the secret, but the grave was yet in the rock, though none could guess where at any point, even to fifty paces. Among all the women and children, his mother made pilgrimage once a year down to the saint's little chapel to pick the bracken roses that flourished about its walls. Other roses of the same kind flowered nearby, but they were all a-prickle with thorns. Those the saint had blessed grew smooth of stalk and leaf, and they were gathered on a day in the year and taken up to the cleft in the rock where his churches had been built, and flung down into all the space around so that a petal, if no more, might rest near the tomb of one whose memory was loved. Only in that way, and unknowing, could the grave be marked.

Instead of the hatred he had always felt for the Perugians, he began to feel pity. It seemed that not force of arms could save the town, but only, as before, a faith, and almost a laughing faith, that the strength of the gentle Francis was with their spirits, and the rest would follow, evenly, to victory.

He said so to Messer Gandolfi, hardly knowing that he spoke.

"In this you have the right of it, Franc," Messer Mayor said quietly. "Only those blessed thoughts may save us. Listen well to me——"

Mayor Gandolfi stood in the mid-lane, fists on hips.

"A man must always think of his family at these times," he said. "How would you savor thought of marriage with a daughter of mine? Any of them. Choose. I will settle gold and silver and properties upon you. Ask so you will and it is yours. Well?"

"I am promised to serve with the Cathayans——"

"At a thousand o' gold a month? For how long? Who warrants time or place? Or your life? If dislike came, could you defend yourself?"

"I had not thought so far——"

"Think more. Marriage with a Gandolfi might also carry itch of fear. They are spinshift wenches, and as thick in the ankle as they are in temper. But good. Dear and sweet, yes, so well I hold them, puddings every one. What say you?"

"The Cathayans——"

"A house near the gate I will build you, of eight rooms, or more if you wish, with a dairy room to itself and a loom room to itself, so that you shall not be wakened, as I in my early days, with thumps and knockings and clashes and scrapings. You shall live quietly in damasked rooms with apple-wood raftering——"

"I have a promise——"

"Carpets shall spread your floors and silver shall adorn your table, with a crystal goblet——"

"Messer Polo——"

"A garden, a green pleasance, shall be built to your largest liking, under my own eye, for nothing so cools and charms as the green in early morning, or in wash of evening's breeze——"

"Messer Mayor——"

"The house, then, and any artly contriving, with the fat Gandolfi of your choice. Come, Franc. My affairs must be ordered!"

"None of your daughters are for me, Messer Mayor. Besides, I have a promise to serve the Princess Na-Nou——"

Messer Mayor took off his hat and beat the knees of his breeches. The look of misery in his face almost forced an agreement. But the will for Emantha held, even against the Mayor's heavy sigh.

"Never thought you would," he grunted. "But I promised the goodwife——"

"She spoke for me?"

"Warmly. A brain and a tongue, said she, and both needed with any of ours. We are done with it. To work!"

For an hour the Mayor rumbled at his duties with his Purser. He paid the street sweepers, the turnkeys of the dungeon, all the town guard, Mozo and the other gatekeepers, the officers of his court, the gardeners, the water carriers, the stablemen and coachmen, the Purser, the Wand Bearer, and himself, and turned to Franc.

"Three silver florins, less fourpence," he called. "This is for duty not done over three days as Warden in the tower, and one florin in that time as Esquire. Shall you be in this duty tomorrow, or gone to the Cathayans?"

Franc tried to make up his mind. He felt all eying him and heard their thoughts. Five generations of wardenship were gone at a word. And the esquireship given up after less than a week. Great questions were there. But the Mayor waited.

"I shall be here till this storm from Perugia has become a balmy whiff," he said.

"Then take your three florins less fourpence," Messer Gandolfi said. "Give to Toma your workday tunic and that for festals. Shall you wear uniform of Esquire?"

"If we join battle——"

"And so spoil new clothes? Wear your own!"

Franc took the coins, and the Mayor tapped his wooden hammer to let all know he was finished. Fine smells came from his kitchen, and Franc thought of the days of loaded tables and filled beakers that would be his with marriage to a Gandolfi daughter. But he assured himself that after service with the Princess, his life with Emantha would be as rich, if not richer, by experience of foreign places and life in the Cathayan Court.

He grinned, thinking that never before had he thought of keeping house with Emantha, or of sitting at the same table as husband and lord of the hearth.

He went to his mother's house and found hot soup in the pot and cold meats, bread, buttermilk, cheese, and fruit set out on the table. Her loom seemed not to have moved since the day before. He wondered if she worked at the convent of the Poor Clares, or if she tended the sick or those unable to cook for themselves, as she often did.

After he had eaten, it wanted something more than an hour to the time of the tourney. He thought that the watchtower would be a better place than any on the wall to see the jousting, for there would be no more than Toma, Ubaldo, and himself, and perhaps the Mayor and a couple of councilors if they could breathe themselves up all the steps.

He went out, nodding to see the empty streets and lanes. All the women and children were indoors by order of the Abbess, and all the men, plainly, were on the walls, waiting.

The forum was empty. Even the scripmen had left their desk boxes. But he saw in passing that Minerva's altar was heaped with laurel garlands, perhaps to plead with the goddess to give wisdom to those in charge of the town.

He climbed the steps slowly, for his repast had been of the best and he was heavy, with thought of a wink or two in shadow of the twigs. All was quiet above. On the window platform he paused to look out. As he had guessed, the walls were crowded with the men of the town watching the columns approaching from the river and Perugia.

He gulped to see their number. Knights and their companies rode in formation, those of equal rank abreast and the lesser following behind. The heads of each column were long over the river, but the rear guards were not across the far bank. The great flag of Perugia waved in front of a gallant cohort flashing in ranks of gold and raising a dust that covered the men-at-arms behind. After came the companies of foreign knights, each with his retinue and all led by banners. Spear tips and lance shafts flashed long furrows of silver, tricky as sunlight on water, and, in between, the pennons streamed and the dust puffed, though no sound came but only the sighing of ripening wheat before the walls.

Franc went up the ladder, trying to think what might happen if that mass came on in attack, but, in a memory of Fat Gil and Councilor Corti and a few more, made up his mind not to think. He pulled himself through the trap door and stood, unbelieving.

His mother sat on a pile of sacks, hemming the wool blanket over her knees.

"Well?" she smiled. "Did you eat all I set for you? It should have been hot——"

"What is this you are doing, or am I taken in sleep?" Franc whispered. "Never have you been here——"

"Except when I was a girl and your father did his duty——"

"But why are you here today? Where is Toma?"

"Sent away. What, did you think I would let the Warden go from our family? After the men of your name gave their lives, birth to death, through five spans? Not for as much gold as there is in all Cathay!"

"If this is how you thought, why did you say nothing to me?"

"It was not as you thought."

"But if there was disgrace in this, how could you keep silent?"

"It was no disgrace to you, or how could you become Esquire, much less serve the Cathayans?"

"But you were proud I was Esquire!"

"I had been prouder if you had kept this wardenship, and not so easily passed it to another——"

"You should have told me!"

"Why should I tell what is not plain to you? Should I stand in your way? Should you in later years tell me I was to blame for your poor estate——"

"Never!"

197

"That you could have earned more than two florins of sil-ver——"

"Twelve, as Esquire!"

"What matter? Not as many as the Cathayans will give you. No properties or great houses, no vineyards or fields, or cat-tle——"

"I am your son. Tell me what to do!"

"You are a man of proper years. You should know!"

Franc shut his mouth and leaned on the parapet.

"This, at any rate, I know," he said slowly. "You have no place here and I am not yet gone as Warden. There, take your hemming and go below. The duty is mine. See, you could not with a finger tip so much as touch a bell rope!"

"Neither shall I try," she said, getting up and folding the blanket. "In truth, I feared those bats hanging up there——"

"Then begone, and let my supper be hot!"

She went to the trap and looked down and stood back.

"I fear this!" she whispered. "Coming up, I almost fell with every step. I faint at heights——"

"Come," he said tenderly. "I will go first——"

He helped her down the ladder and on to the window plat-form and picked her up, shocked at her lightness, which seemed almost as a dried leaf, to begin, but further down came weight, and more weight, and at the foot she was heavy as any Gandolfi.

She opened her eyes when he put her down, and leaned against the wall.

"How the years have gone!" she breathed. "It was so the last time and your father carried me. Did you never think why Emantha brought your meals? It was because I have always been afraid of these steps. And Emantha had twice the fear——"

"She made no complaint——"

"Or would she be Emantha? How should you know? Did you ask?"

"I never thought——"

Trumpets fanfared out on the plain. Franc saw his mother's eyes fill bright and brim, and she held her heart. He kissed her cheek and put her gently through the archway.

"If I am not a-house for supper, find one to bring a basket, and I will lower a rope," he said. "Have no worry. A warden is yet of our family!"

He ran up the steps and made no pause till he reached the top. The D'Orosa gates were open, and a long troop of men-at-arms reached down beyond the town walls. But the head had stopped, and Franc guessed at a barrier of stones where Simone had destroyed the path. The head of the troop was hidden, but even as he watched, the banner was brought up and the Count appeared, and the men-at-arms followed, and they all turned and rode up again and then across the space between the back wall of the town and the castle front.

Count d'Orosa spoke to his sergeant-at-arms riding beside, and his golden gauntlet struck the saddlebow as though in anger.

Franc grinned to think of what he might be saying. The short path had been easy, despite its steepness, for the slabs were well laid and rough to the hoof. But the rocky ground behind the town walls made the war horses step up and down, and jump here and slide there, and the riders were hard put with shields and lances to make much of the reins. Horse after horse fell and threw its rider. Other riders fell off. Some turned back to fetch runaways, and some became runaway in the chase. Instead of a long troop, four abreast and brave in steel behind a banner, the company became a rout of men trying to sit a prancer.

Franc watched until the leading riders passed beyond the cliff. He reckoned it would take the troop at least a broad hour to put itself together, and two sets of chimes to ride down to the jousting place.

The tournament would be late.

He had begun to think about Emantha and her fear of the steps and the height and her silence over the years of running up every day, morning and night.

Blast of Cathayan horns and thunder of drums burst loud in the narrow streets below, and he ran to the parapet, looking toward the pavilions near the churches.

He drew breath of amazement, and the cold flew in his blood.

Perhaps the daily come-and-go of Cathayans from the camp at the furnace and the gatherings in the wineshops and taverns had served to hide their number, but the troops a-horse and marching seemed as many as the Perugians. They stretched from the forum all the way down the hill and beyond the Mayor's court. Cavalry in scarlet came first, and then cavalry in blue, and a troop in yellow, and one in black, with soldiers in furs marching in rear. Between each corps a Cathayan band played, and after the band, a great emblem of some animal with bared teeth that floated from poles each held by a horseman. More emblems floated and more bands drummed and clashed cymbals and more horsemen came behind, and at their head, Messer Polo in black, with the feathered hat, and behind him, Hsi-Soong on a white pony, and after her, One-piece and Two-piece on blacks.

And on a gray palfrey, a-sidesaddle and dressed in red with a skirt that billowed over withers and crupper, Emantha.

"Franc! Franc! Ho, Franc!"

Messer Gandolfi and a couple of councilors were below, faces up, shouting over the noise of the band.

"Get to the tailor and wear the Esquire's livery!" Messer Mayor bawled, pointing. "Get a-horse! Go with Emantha!"

Chapter 16

Franc found the Esquire's uniform hot after the race down the
tower steps, and the sweat of getting into new white hosen and
a heavy blue shirt and the plum velvet tunic, and pulling on the
black leather boots, and leaping on the white mare for a head-
long gallop to the forum, and a pacing down the steps, and
another gallop to catch up with the cavalcade. But he felt none
the worse to be carrying arms beside Emantha.

Messer Polo made no turn, and neither did Hsi-Soong or One-
piece and Two-piece, though Emantha's open hand and glad
smile were more than enough of welcome.

Four corps of Cathayan cavalry went down the furnace road.
The rest stayed within the walls, and all those a-foot, unseen.

"This will be sharp surprise for those Perugians!" Franc whispered. "Where they expected a handful, they find a tight-pack
army. See their faces!"

It was plain from the way the Perugians looked that the
number and fine discipline of the Cathayans had an effect far
from pleasing. The Perugian ranks had halted, and the leaders
were taking positions under the various banners. The great flag

of Perugia was brought up with much flourish of heralds and trumpets, and the Perugian commander, the Count de Gubbio, rode forward in black armor touched in gold, and black feathers in his helm, and mounted on a black stallion, to present himself to Messer Polo.

With fanfares, the heralds moved in front to proffer compliments and effect the courtesies. Cathayan heralds blew long silver horns, and the Perugians blew golden trumpets. The Perugians made long declarations, one after another, of their lords' names and the riches of their families, and when the houses had been raised, and how many battles had been fought by each, and where. The Cathayans replied for twice as long, and as loud, but none among the Perugians knew what was said, and most stared at their horses' bridles, or talked from the sides of their mouths, or picked teeth.

The Count de Gubbio and his staff went to Messer Polo, and he was introduced to Count this and Count that, and in turn he introduced his own officers, though the sounds meant little enough and as easily slipped from mind. Everyone nodded, bowed in their saddles, and talked of something else.

But all in the Perugian cohort made great bones of Hsi-Soong and Emantha when they caught sight of them, and they, not loth, rode in among them, laughing their prettiest, and causing such a backing and hind-legging that Count de Gubbio begged Messer Polo to bring them back, and was told on the spot that the gracious Hsi-Soong did as she pleased, when and how and where she wanted, and none could say her nay by order of her exalted highness, the Princess Na-Nou.

"This royal lady, where is her imperial presence?" Count de Gubbio asked in his throaty voice. "We are come some distance to bend a head over that regal hand——"

"She is not with our cavalcade," Messer Polo said. "She is something young for this show of gallantry and not yet trained to the sports of the joust——"

Franc looked at Emantha, but she had eyes only for the knights of Perugia. He wanted to ask a question, remembering the withered face of the Princess, but again he forbore. There would be time enough, and in any event, it had little to do with him.

Knights and their esquires mixed with the Cathayans on the outside without once breaking their ranks. A horn blast drew them off, and the Cathayans wheeled to the side and made a long line, and the Perugians wheeled to the other side, with a space of two bowshots between. A flag was placed at either end and a party of Perugian and Cathayan officers gathered under each.

"So is the field set," Messer Polo said over his shoulder. "Where do you see the Count d'Orosa?"

"Behind, and coming on to the plain," Franc said, looking toward the mountain. "They will be a chime or more. And their horses will be lathered——"

"So much the better. Attend me, Franc. Your duty is not only to show the device of Assisi, but to watch at all times for the safety of the gracious Hsi-Soong and her musicians, and Emantha, whom we now call Nanou——"

"Nanou?"

"Nanou, by desire of her exalted highness, who gives her own name, altered to suit. It has the meaning of womanly beauty——"

Franc looked at Emantha sitting her palfrey a short distance away, beside Hsi-Soong and in front of One-piece and Two-piece. He wondered why, in all the days he had known her grown to a woman, no thought of her beauty had ever come to him, beyond little flights that her lashes were long, or her eyes were a certain color, or her hair another. Watching her, he was smote of her loveliness, which he seemed to be seeing as if they had never met before that day.

A thought of his mother came, gray, to worry. He must make

up his mind whether to be Warden and please her and have her smile, or to give the honor into the keeping of another and endure her displeasure. There were two silver pieces as Warden and twelve as Esquire to be earned in a month, or there were one thousand pieces of gold. At face, only a fool could balance one with another. A wise one would take the gold and the travel and the luxury and all that came after. An idiot would stay his days in the tower, or running errands for the Mayor, and, in his old age, warm his bones with saved pence in a hovel under the walls. Different then, the one who had saved the gold and bought properties and cattle and had fruit of every harvest, and no lack of comfort for a weary soul case.

And Emantha for wife, lifelong.

Trumpets sounded, and the throng set up a cheer of welcome for the D'Orosa troop, riding hard and, as Franc had thought, slashed with the foam of their beaten horses.

Count de Gubbio gave the Count d'Orosa welcome, and Messer Polo went forward with Cathayan officers to hear the terms of the joust. Franc drew in between Emantha and Hsi-Soong, and the heralds rode down the ranks, calling out the names of the contestants. Some of the Perugians lent spare mounts to the D'Orosa men, but none of the Cathayans offered so much as a side glance.

"To the north, the jousters of the most noble and gallant Count d'Orosa!" a herald called. "To the south, the jousters of her most exalted highness, the Princess Na-Nou. First, the tourney by lance and shield, armored, a-horse!"

The six-man team of D'Orosa men-at-arms brought their mounts into line. At the other end, the Cathayans, in scarlet and armor like bars of gold and tall helmets with dangling ear flaps, walked their mounts to the start line, and the crowd sent up a howl to see that none was larger than a pony, shaggy of mane and tail. Esquires gave each rider a tilt-lance, but the points were of steel and sharpened, and not of wood, rounded, as in other times of tourney.

A trumpeter sounded the prepare. The D'Orosa team listened to the advice of the Count and took hold of their lances and set their shields. The Cathayans stood at their ponies' heads, without shields, lance a-hand, idle.

All the trumpeters sounded the Charge.

In a roar of voices the D'Orosa team struck spurs and went off at standing gallop, lances at point, knee to knee. The Cathayans threw the reins over their ponies' necks and leaped upon their backs, and yet the animals had started and were already in gallop before the riders were in the saddle. Their lances came down as one, and they crouched lower than the D'Orosa team and rode further apart. But as they neared, they crouched lower still, almost down at the stirrups, and not one D'Orosa lance found any target, although every Cathayan hit, and as the lances struck, each pony set its fores and slid to a stop, pushing over the D'Orosa team, men and horses, all, and when the lances were withdrawn, they stood and wheeled and trotted back where they had started.

No sound came from the Perugians, but Count d'Orosa made noise enough for three, complaining that the Cathayans were riding in strange style, unjoustlike and therefore improper. Messer Polo called out that the D'Orosa team had been strapped to their saddles, which was a ruse and according to ordinary usage, cheating.

Count d'Orosa rode headlong to the Count de Gubbio and reined, screaming his anger at an insult. But while he spoke, D'Orosa men-at-arms were unstrapping their comrades from kicking horses.

"Perhaps your sergeant-at-arms had little knowledge of the strict rules of the joust," the Count de Gubbio said. "Undoubtedly, the use of straps is forbidden. But the language of Messer Polo is harsh, and that, let us suppose, is fault of his travels and a lack of that society given to a more elegant turn of speech——"

"Count de Gubbio," Messer Polo called from his place among the Cathayan officers. "Be good enough, I pray you, to understand that contrary to your suggestion, my travels brought me to the most civilized court on earth, where behavior is considered an art, and to a country where elegance of speech marks not merely the nobleman but also the beggar, and a judicial system where dishonesty of thought, much less of deed, is in itself a crime!"

"A fair place, but far distant," Count de Gubbio said, and nodded to the heralds. "The second event is called——"

"Instant apology, or satisfaction!" Count d'Orosa shouted.

"Satisfaction on the instant," Messer Polo called, walking his horse. "Shall it be with lance——"

"Lance uncovered, and sword a-foot!" Count d'Orosa shouted, as if his armor would never contain him. "No grace, no quarter!"

Messer Polo spoke to his officers, but before any could reply, Hsi-Soong rode into the middle and seemed to be asking questions. Messer Polo answered, and some of the officers, but Hsi-Soong raised her hand, small, white, and jeweled, and spoke, and all bowed their heads and were silent.

"I am informed, Count d'Orosa, that feats of arms are a military perquisite," Messer Polo said. "I, as civil governor of a province of Cathay, cannot therefore engage you——"

"Frightened cur!"

"You may take as your opponent any of these——"

"None! I fight those of name and birth——"

"My name is Polo. My father was a merchant——"

"You are sprung some distance——"

"Indeed. Many a long league from Cathay——"

"Is there any, higher than a fardel, in this motley of yours whose hide I might brand without suffering some contagion?"

Messer Polo looked at the Cathayan officers.

"There are here several of the most noble houses of Ca-thay——"

"I fight no infidel dog!"

Messer Polo shrugged.

"I am the only Christian," he said. "Except for Franc, an esquire of Assisi, all here are infidels——"

The eyeholes in the white hood turned to look at Emantha.

"And this mopkin," Count d'Orosa said.

"This is the lady Nanou, ennobled by her exalted highness," Messer Polo warned.

"This is a town serving wench! How is such ennobled?"

Franc spurred forward.

"By thought of those who respect her!" he said. "Get you prepared to ride!"

"I'll have the men-at-arms attend to you!"

"Let you, or any one, or a dozen, for a thousand pieces of gold!"

"Upstart! Pence are beyond your lot!"

"Here you are mistaken," Messer Polo smiled. "He has six thousand pieces at this present, and I wager ten thousand upon his prowess——"

He spoke in Cathayan, and all the officers laughed, calling out and Hsi-Soong clapped her hands and chattered. But a whisper grew to loud uproar among the Perugians.

"Each officer here wagers one thousand pieces, and the gra-cious Hsi-Soong wagers twice my total, which is, in all, sixty thousand pieces of gold," Messer Polo said. "Are you able to cover——"

"Sixty thousand pieces to spit a churl?" Count d'Orosa laughed. "Where is your gold?"

"On this, I raise the wager to one hundred thousand," Mes-ser Polo said, and gestured to an officer, and he forthwith turned and rode split-gallop toward the furnace. "Where is your stake, coin by coin? Mine will be here in some few minutes——"

"I will first dispose of this offal," Count d'Orosa said. "Thus, I shall save time in the opening of my strong room——"

Franc turned and rode down to the far end. Two Cathayan officers rode beside him, and Messer Polo rode behind to the mark.

"Put on one of these officer's corslets," he said. "Take a helmet and that Cathayan saber if you should fight a-foot——"

"The saber, yes," Franc said. "But the corslet, no, with thanks. I will fight in the colors of Assisi, and our device shall be armor enough——"

"Why, then, Franc," Messer Polo said, holding out his hand, "God a-mercy, and strength come true to you!"

Franc watched him ride back, touching his broad-brimmed hat in taking the wagers of the Perugian nobles. Count d'Orosa chose his lance from a nest stuck in the ground, and his Esquire tied the D'Orosa color to its head and handed it up. One-piece and Two-piece galloped down on their ponies and pulled up in a roll of dust. They held out, One-piece a scarf of Hsi-Soong's, and Two-piece a strip of scarlet that came from Emantha. Franc lowered the lance point for them to tie on the talismans and took his place at the starting mark.

One-piece and Two-piece began a drumming and piping and the heralds raised their trumpets.

But the Count d'Orosa waited for no call or signal. He set lance and knees and rode, shouting to the Count de Gubbio that he made no joust, but skewered foul meat.

Franc heard the Cathayans call as if in warning, but he was ready. He had long learned that most jousters made the mistake of marking the rider instead of the horse. Low in the saddle, and keep point on the animal, and just before impact raise point to the rider and take him low, sitting back and reining hard. The hours of practice paid well.

Almost as if the words were spoken for what he did, he found

208

the golden armor at lance point and struck, and his mare sat, and the lance broke at the tip, and the hand guard slipped up the shaft. But the Count d'Orosa was on the ground and rolling, trying to get up. Franc dismounted and went to the scrambler and took him by the helm feathers and lifted him to his feet.

D'Orosa cursed and swung his armored fist. Franc pushed to turn him about and knocked him over on his back. Again the Count tried, screaming in rage, to get on his knees, trying to clamber up. Franc footed him flat. A couple of D'Orosa men-at-arms ran to help, but a group of Cathayan officers made a move, and the Count de Gubbio ordered them all back. The crowd was laughing and some had begun to jeer.

D'Orosa drew his sword and, kneeling, leaned upon it to stand upright. Franc slid the curved Cathayan blade from its sheath, singing thin like the razor knives of the town barber. D'Orosa made a cut. Franc stepped aside. A second cut whipped over his head. A third cut he caught in mid-air with the back of his own blade, which must have numbed D'Orosa's hand, for he dropped his sword and threw off the gauntlet and cursed. He stooped, reaching for the hilt, and Franc footed him flat once more and kicked away the blade. D'Orosa crawled toward it, stretching out the ungauntleted hand.

The golden armor, the badge upon the shield, the colors on the lance, and the hooded face all proclaimed the Count d'Orosa.

But the knuckles of the right hand were clear of any scar.

Franc ran forward and trod upon the left wrist and in a quick pull, took off the gauntlet. The left hand was unmarked.

D'Orosa caught him about the legs and kicked up with the armored heels and spurs. Franc dropped, and the legs went over his back. He turned and took the helmet in his hands and twisted hard to the left. D'Orosa thrashed, kicked, swung the steel arms, but nothing broke the hold. Franc started to drag him, little by little, and, once the weight began to move, he turned in circles, faster and faster, until D'Orosa's feet were off the ground. He put his weight into an even heavier swing, until D'Orosa was spinning and screaming waist-high, and higher, and ever higher, and Franc let him go, and he curved and turned and hit the ground in a cloud of dust and a clatter and lay with no breath in him.

Laughter and jeers moaned to silence. Franc's eye caught movement toward sword hilts and a tightening of reins among the Perugian ranks. Count de Gubbio rode forward and bent over the saddle arch.

No surprise was in his face, but only disdain.

"Count d'Orosa, how are you brought so low, and by such unworthy means?" he said with a look at the Cathayans. "You are many thousands of gold pieces in debt. And we, who were your friends, are also something at loss."

He looked down at Franc and smiled, though high in patronage.

"I had not known Assisi could produce such a gamecock," he said. "You joust as a veteran. But you fight as a Berber, lacking polish or finesse, and all except savagery. What then, would you join my banner as Esquire and learn your business?"

"I am Esquire to the Mayor of Assisi and I know my business well enough," Franc said in dislike of the tone. "And how could I join Perugia, that would war upon us?"

Count de Gubbio drew back his steel flail to strike. But Messer Polo had ridden up with his Cathayan officers, and their restive horses had effect upon the Count's great black, so that for moments he must forget his flail and cling, cursing, to a neighing monster that would have thrown him except he was helped by men hanging on to the bridle.

"Well fought, Franc!" Messer Polo laughed. "Here, see, you are become wealthy when these debts are paid, and if they are not, still there will be plenty. Do you now command these troops in my place and watch them in the next events and lead them when we return——"

"Ho there fellow, you, Polo!" the Count de Gubbio shouted. "Do you set a joust, or are you ended with tumbled dolts?"

Messer Polo took off his hat and indicated Franc.

"Here is the commander of the day," he called. "I return to my charge——"

With no other word he rode toward Hsi-Soong. Franc felt the chill of pride in his blood, but he tried to let nothing show in his face and pretended much care in climbing into his saddle.

"We are at end after another five events," he said, seated and reins a-hand. "Each to cost the Count d'Orosa one thousand pieces——"

"Of this, I know nothing! Joust then, or be done——"

Franc nodded and the Cathayans parted their ranks to allow a saber team to enter the space. Each man was naked to the waist. All were bald-cut except for a long tail of hair growing from the crown of the head, and all wore mustaches in the Cathayan manner, with long scrimps of beard under the bottom lip. Each rode a stallion, yet the giant size of the men made the mounts look like ponies.

From the corner of his eye Franc watched the man all knew as Count d'Orosa lifted and carried to a ditchbank. He was in two minds whether to go over and tear the hood off an impostor. But he thought that much might come in letting the hood remain and of telling Messer Gandolfi what he had found out. Certainly the Count de Gubbio might not have dealt quietly with one presuming to wear the D'Orosa badge and so usurping those honors and dignities.

He saw Emantha's wave, and himself waved the ribboned lance, and Hsi-Soong clapped her hands, and One-piece and Two-piece piped and drummed and clashed the little cymbals, and all the Perugians whistled or jeered, trying to make the same sounds.

Men of the D'Orosa team had set up poles in a long line, with thirty paces between each. At the top was tied a crossbow and from that swung a string. On the end of each string there hung a lemon or a melon, one and one, at about a horseman's shoulder height.

The sergeant-at-arms of the D'Orosa team gave his signal. The heralds fanfared to clear the field and called the names of those riding in the Point and Cut event, and gave first run to D'Orosa.

Six men galloped, cutting at the lemons, and trying to stab the points of their swords into the melons without breaking any string. Of the six, only the sergeant-at-arms scored a full mark for each point and cut. The rest of his team showed enough prowess to warrant a great cheer and more wagers were called among the Perugians.

Franc felt that in this, perhaps, the Cathayans had met their masters, for he knew well enough that little else was done by men-at-arms except practice of their skills, and the hours showed in the precision of their movements.

The lemons and melons were replaced, and the Cathayans went down with the sun bronze on their knotted back muscles. But where the D'Orosa team had slashed chunks out of the lemons, the Cathayans cut thin peels, and where the D'Orosa men had stuck points into melons or missed altogether, the Cathayans first pointed, and entered, and sliced down, so that when the six had finished the course, three neat slices were gone from each melon and six thin rounds from each lemon, and all the strings were intact.

"This is like to cost D'Orosa his property," Count de Gubbio throated. "Why did he not choose events where his men might have chance?"

A herald called out a Lance and Peg event, and D'Orosa's men went down a straight course, setting wooden pegs at every twenty feet. The D'Orosa team galloped first, each picking up three wooden pegs on the lance tip. The Cathayans not only picked up their pegs, but tossed wooden balls and stabbed them through while they rolled, though no D'Orosa man could do more than glance off, no matter how they tried. While the Perugians catcalled, and the last D'Orosa man was making a clown of himself, the D'Orosa sergeant-at-arms approached Count de Gubbio and took off his helmet in salute.

"The heart is out of us, Lord Count," he said into his teeth. "We are not on our day and our commander is not with us——"

"I make you no blame," Count de Gubbio said. "Bring your troop to join mine in rear. Where is the Count d'Orosa?"

"Ridden to the castle, Lord Count——"

Count de Gubbio turned to look at the Cathayans and spoke to the distant walls of Assisi.

"Well then, Esquire. A victory of some fortune and matter for congratulation. We must make a match if these barbarians stay further time——"

"Now, if you have the patience——"

"We ride to Assisi. Do you accompany us?"

"I must also be here when the Count returns with his gold——"

"You will have a stretch of waiting, today and tomorrow and into winter. What, do you think he will pay his wealth to some nameless one? Remove yourself!"

"Do you move me!"

Count de Gubbio turned to a lieutenant.

"Rope him to a tree and let my troop use their reins upon him," he ordered. "He shall be taught how to use his mouth——"

Franc raised the lance.

"Let no other man do your work," he said. "The field is ours. You and your friends are much in our debt. Will you pay?"

Count de Gubbio looked between his lieutenants and esquires as if he doubted his presence, or their appearance. Certainly he made no doubt that he had never before been spoken to in such manner, or in such tone.

In a sudden, up went the steel flail again. But a Cathayan arrow hit him in the fist and the feathers struck him in the face, and again he had to fight his mount, and once more his men-at-arms had to hang on to the bridle, but this time he had only one good hand. His right arm hung useless at his side and, if his face told truth, he sat in pain.

Franc saw the Perugian ranks close in. But the Cathayans were lighter on their mounts and with the exception of the knights and some of the esquires, far better horsed. A quick skirmish and a retreat by gallop back to the towngate seemed the best tactic. A Cathayan troop guarded Hsi-Soong and others rode out in a double rank in front.

"Well then, Franc," Messer Polo called, "the Khan of our troops wants to attack. What say you?"

"Let us put the women into the town," Franc said. "Let us then be together with a complete army——"

Trumpets and a noise of singing brought them to look about, and men called out in wonder. A long procession of gay Cathayan carts and streamered horses filled the path leading from the town to St. Francis' chapel and the river ford on the Perugian highway.

Il Cardinale rode in front upon a gray mule and waved the red hat at the massed troops. They, to a man, dismounted and knelt, and he blessed them as he passed. Each cart held a dozen or more singing children in the care of nuns of the Poor Clares.

But the barrel of a man wearing the mayoral robes of Assisi on a strawberry roan brought Franc at a gallop to meet him.

"Good Messer Gandolfi, why is this?" he called. "Are you then leaving Assisi to a Corti and a Fat Gil?"

"I leave it, instead, to good St. Francis!" Messer Gandolfi shouted. "We shall go to Perugia and sing in their cathedral.

We shall return tomorrow, with help of the saint and his Master——"

"Then I shall follow," Franc said. "Let me only make my farewells——"

"Stay in Assisi," Messer Gandolfi commanded. "What use when there is reason for no more than two, his excellency and myself? Are you so ready to die?"

"Where would I find better company?"

Franc rode closer and, behind his hand, told what he had seen under the golden gauntlet. Almost immediately he was following the Mayor stretch-necked down to Il Cardinale.

For a few moments Messer Mayor whispered in the dust, but Il Cardinale's face showed not even the politest disbelief and his sneeze blew away all except his patience.

"Say nothing of this to any other, Franc," he said. "Do you join us to Perugia?"

"That was my hope, Excellency——"

"Then ride behind me and in front of Messer Polo and his party——"

"Are they, too, with us?" Messer Gandolfi asked, amazed.

"That this pretty creature Hsi-Soong may learn more of our country and some little extra of our churches," Il Cardinale said. "You shall find them lodging this night, Messer Mayor."

"That will I. And the Khan's troops guard Assisi?"

"The great part remains. A few cavalry, Messer Polo says, will ride on our flanks. I shall speak to the Count de Gubbio and discover his intention. At least our children are safe for the moment. The journey will do them little harm. Your good mother, Franc, stayed with the Abbess——"

He rode off toward the group of knights and the great flag of Perugia. Messer Gandolfi wiped the inside of his hat.

"He saw a way that was no dreamer's jaunt," he said quietly. "If there is to be fighting, the children are spared. Not, as in other years, burned, or slaughtered among the houses. For this, at any rate, let us give thanks!"

"And how shall we feel, absent?" Franc asked.

"We shall ride back tonight," Messer Gandolfi said. "Once the children are settled, we have lifted grievous doubt from our minds. We shall all fight the better for it."

Il Cardinale managed to get a canter out of the gray mule and he waved his hat to the cheers of the troops making way for him. He showed no feeling, and his smile was as gay for any Perugian as it was for any of the children.

"Let us go on," he called. "These, the Count tells me, are military exercises. He has no intention of harming our city, or any of its people."

"If these are in exercise, I am spent my life a sailor," Messer Gandolfi said, looking at the troops forming to march. "See the quantity of provisions packed in their sutler trains. See also their bombards. These are for breaking walls. We did well to close the city gates!"

"You do not believe them?" Il Cardinale asked.

"No, Excellency!"

"Distrustful man. Nor I. Ride on!"

Chapter 17

Except for halts at both sides of the ford and a pause at the top of the longest hill, nothing slowed the march, and neither was there any report, except that Cathayans told of a band of horsemen, which must also have crossed the river, riding hard toward Perugia and passing in the darkness with no hail or any salute.

Franc rode for the longest part beside Emantha, made happy by her praise for the way of events during the afternoon, though she feared that D'Orosa's vengeance would come upon him.

"He has every chance to take you, either in the town or beyond," she whispered. "Let us hope that when we return he will be gone, or put with the worms——"

"Return? When?"

"After we have served the Princess——"

"I think I shall not——"

"But you made a promise——"

"True. I shall ask her pardon, and freedom. As one of good heart, she cannot deny me——"

"And I shall be alone? Ah, Franc. I had so rested on thought of you!"

He heard the little voice blown by the night breeze and sad though she might be, yet he was glad because the sadness was for him.

"Has it not passed to you that I am one with a store of gold all my own?" he whispered. "Why should you go off to serve the Princess? I have all we shall want——"

"But I have promised. And Il Cardinale has made an agreement with Messer Polo——"

"Both may be gainsaid, with apology——"

"But what is your gold to me?"

"Could we not share?"

"How, share?"

He had a feeling she was dense with a purpose.

"It is usual in marriage to share," he said clearly, even to hear it himself. "And not usual for a wife to be away from her husband——"

"But I am no wife——"

He had no chance to reply. They were reaching the crest of the last hill before the road curved up to Perugia's gate. But at the top, torches flared and voices called welcome and a chant began, and dozens of Perugian women and older children came running to meet them, kneeling to Il Cardinale, and going back to the wains to claim a child to lodge and board. Messer Gandolfi called Franc to ride with him in front of the procession to make themselves known to the gatekeeper and claim entry.

Emantha's face glowed in the torch flares, and her soft-eyed smile sent him off barely able to see his way. He had small regret not to have finished what he had begun to say, but he swore to catch her ear at some soon moment and then make good end of it.

"We will first happily settle the children and know them cared for," Messer Gandolfi said. "After, we will lodge the Cathayans. We will then return and reach the gates before the first of dawn——"

Franc looked back to Assisi on the far hill, seeing the glow of many a campfire outside the walls, and thinking of his mother and wondering if she sewed at the hearth or wrung her hands in a sigh.

"All seems set at peace," he said.

"They will arraign themselves in good time," Messer Gandolfi rumbled. "The time will be well chosen. What need have they to trip themselves of hurry?"

"I am come to think as Messer Polo," Franc said. "For what reason is this shock made now, with the Khan's strength on our side?"

Messer Mayor gave greeting to other women hurrying to meet them and shook his horse to a smarter walk.

"Franc, I will here give you the weight of it," he said in a low voice. "We had a plan with Master Builder di Rovigo to build a chapel under the lower church and there establish the tomb of our saint. From what we hear, it seems that the Count d'Orosa had pairs of ears among us——"

"Why does this cause attack?"

"They believe we have uncovered the tomb——"

"Is its place known to any of us?"

"Nothing of this is known to me. It is matter for the Brothers. But I believe the Count de Gubbio will make every urgent effort to take the town and dig into all the cliff and even uproot the churches, stone by stone, to find what they seek——"

"Again, I find no reason——"

"Think of a certain Count de Gubbio, Defender of St. Francis. Think of his banner, of his badges, of his retinue of knights and esquires. Think, then, of his dreams. He could be foremost Knight of Christendom. Think of the glory. Wealth and pomp, Franc, they are root of all war——"

"It goes hard that Assisi must suffer——"

"We have suffered many an accursed year. These few past have been the most peaceful of my life. For this reason our women are harsh-tempered. They fear the times of war——"

"Little of war appears here——"

"In good sunshine that will ripen wheat, it is enough that one fool raise his sword. Then the arrows fly and the spears advance and flame falls. Within the chime we are gone from peace that was to death and wounds——"

Messer Gandolfi reined under the gate arch and pulled at the bell. Women and children ran out from the postern to give welcome, and a clamor inside told of many more. The gatekeeper put his head over the wall and waved a lanthorn.

"Ho! Who comes?" he shouted.

"Small citizens of Assisi, hoping for hot food and shelter!" Mayor Gandolfi shouted up. "Together with sundry persons of the Grand Khan's suite——"

"Have the walls yet taken a breach over there, or do they wait till morning to plant their ladders?"

"In this, I know nothing——"

"What, did you see no army? Which way did you travel?"

"An army we saw. But at peace."

The gatekeeper laughed.

"As to that, let us talk tomorrow," he said.

Mayor Gandolfi said nothing while the gate screeched open, but he sighed his heaviest when they trotted their horses through, and his greeting to all the women was not as hearty as it had been to the others.

"This is the substance of it, Franc," he said at last. "They used the jousting as excuse to gather before our walls. This, not to alarm us. How long shall we stand in siege? We have food for a month, no more. And the wheat is not cut, nor any grape in a basket——"

"Let us finish here and ride——"

"Do you wait with Messer Polo in the square. Keep ears and eyes open."

Franc waited for Il Cardinale to pass in with the wains and the crowds of Perugian women and children. Messer Polo rode up with Hsi-Soong, and Emantha came between One-piece and Two-piece. They reached the great square and dismounted near the hostelry of the Golden Comb, and the host bowed them inside to a fire and cushioned benches.

"You are lost for custom tonight," Franc said in the empty tavern.

"Not a man of any size left in the town or country about," the host grinned. "But we shall have good profit of it——"

"How profit, if here is loss?"

"Why, when our men return," the host said, eyebrows up. "They are promised all they can carry. The harvest stands ripe to the scythe and the vineyards are dark with grapes. A week before the walls, and a couple more to gather their shares and march back. You have looked your last upon Assisi. Not a rock will be left on another——"

"For what reason? What has Assisi done to you?"

"We have battled them ever. Now we battle for the last time. Would I had my youthful years again!"

He went off to draw wine, but Franc put on his cap and took his saddlebags.

"Here is not the house for me, or any in these walls," he told Messer Polo. "A drink, and I would die a-retch. I won't stain my mouth with anything of this accursed town!"

"And if they think as you?" Messer Polo asked.

"We shall settle it on edge of steel. As for me, the open air——"

"I will join you."

Messer Polo and his Cathayan officers left with him. Other Cathayans were riding about, watched by townspeople open-mouthed as if they saw miracles.

"So we looked at you when you first came," Franc said. "You are about to regret your visit——"

"As to this, I doubt it," Messer Polo said, strolling. "We are now shod, every animal, and there are extra shoes against the future. We are well rested and all in good health——"

"But will you remain with us, or will you ask passage of the Perugians?"

Messer Polo spoke to the Cathayans and they all laughed together.

"We shall ask nothing, but we shall take," he said. "We had good chance of seeing their worth today. They are many in number, and that is all. Tomorrow we shall go to the castle of D'Orosa and demand payment of our debt——"

"This, indeed, will provoke war!"

"And we shall not sleep the less. Remember that much of the gold is yours. The rest, Emantha's. Shall you, then, ride out with us in service of her exalted highness?"

The question came soft. Franc knew that now was the only time he would have to answer. There must be yes or no.

"Much as I would serve her highness and earn so great a sum, I cannot, and there is an end to argument," he said. "My mother would keep our family honor. It would be no gain to displease her. Money is good, but smiles are better."

"Think well, Franc! You are young——"

"My mind is finished with thought on this. I cannot serve the Princess and Assisi. Therefore I serve Assisi and I shall seek pardon of her exalted highness——"

"Which I will ask for. What sum of gold, think you, is yours from today's wagers?"

"I will be happy to have what I get. Or, if I am luckier, what I am owed——"

Messer Polo laughed aloud.

"There is a soldier in your right arm and a little of the merchant in the other!" he said. "We shall see how we count it. Is it true that you will wed the beauteous Leda?"

"Emantha, or nobody!"

"But Emantha shall come with the gracious Hsi-Soong——"

"If I can say a word against, no!"

"She is pledged, and the gold is paid——"

"It can be paid back——"

"This is not the agreement. Or do those of Assisi keep no bargain or mean any word?"

Franc found nothing to say. His own fine-weather conduct came before him.

"I do not speak for Emantha," he acknowledged. "But I shall try to keep her in Assisi, depend upon it!"

He saw Messer Gandolfi and Il Cardinale enter the square, and excused himself and ran over to them. Women crowded about and knelt, making a press that he had to climb over.

"We are all lodged, warm and safe," Messer Gandolfi said, aside. "There is no fighting man left in the town——"

"So I am told——"

"His excellency will stay here in sanctuary. He will also take these women in safeguard. We shall ride free and, if we run foul of their patrols, we shall fight the better. Say your farewells and let us go——"

But if Messer Polo was willing to stay, Hsi-Soong was not. Her little voice chattered in the hostelry and echoed in the square and her little feet stamped and pattered.

"To make a plan is one side, but the gracious Hsi-Soong sees no side but her own," Messer Polo said. "We shall return to Assisi immediately——"

"But there is great danger," Mayor Gandolfi rumbled. "It is no staging for women——"

"Ride on," Messer Polo invited him. "We shall ride in our own manner. The wains are gone——"

"The wains?" Mayor Gandolfi frowned. "They were to stay——"

"They are needed on the morrow. We too are leaving!"

Mayor Gandolfi shrugged.

"Then let us ride together," he said. "The more blades, the more cuts!"

Franc went to bend a knee before Il Cardinale sitting on the cathedral steps and ringed about by the Perugian women.

"Age keeps me here, but my heart is with you all, Franc," he said. "Use your head in this Cathayan matter and remember I had no greater pride in any scholar of mine. Do your duty!"

"Poor lad!" a woman called from the crowd. "I have two gone in the Count's own troop. And the fields cry out for their hands——"

"Make no mourn!" another called. "I have two and a husband out. What shall our babes do if none come back?"

"Our fields are full of summer's promise," another voice wept, "but there are few to gather——"

"Who is the Count to order them out in battle?" a woman cried. "Why should they go? Which in Assisi has done harm to us?"

"Enough!" Il Cardinale stood, raising his hand. "Let none hear your plaints, lest you should be taken away and chained. Franc, tell all in Assisi how think the women of Perugia——"

He ran back to his mount and had to ride hard to catch the others. Hsi-Soong and Emantha waved as he passed, both sitting in comfort in a wain. The caravan surprised him by its length. But more surprise was in the strength of Cathayan cavalry riding all about, and yet more in the speed of their going. He saw, on closer look, that all the wains' horses were of blood stock, and the drivers sat the leaders instead of riding on the shafts.

Messer Gandolfi remarked upon it and seemed in deep thought. He pointed to the wheels and bodies, which were un-

224

like those on ordinary wains. They were steel-banded and the wheels were steel-pegged. The difference could be told once they reached the flat land, for then, on a whistle of many notes, the caravan went into a gallop and cavalry and wains went neck and neck for short periods and fell back to a trot and then a gallop, and a trot, and so to the ford and over in a walk, and gallop and trot again.

"My horse is blown, and he is best in all Assisi," Messer Gandolfi complained. "These of the Cathayans have two lives!"

"They are trained," Franc said. "See, mine is yet fresh."

"We are home in half the time, and this is pleasing. What shall we find?"

"A town asleep. There is no move, see, on the plain."

"Ride forward and find Messer Polo, and lead the way up the chapel path to the gate of the Little Brothers. But have care, thinking of their patrols!"

Franc had to ride the entire length of the column to find Messer Polo, sitting in the wain with Emantha and Hsi-Soong, wrapped in furs and drinking from a hot jar.

"I am in no doubt of reaching any gate and entering in," Messer Polo said impatiently. "Go fast or slow as you will and meet which one or several, and it will be the same. We have already dealt with two of their patrols. Did you hear any sound?"

"None!"

"In this way we fight in darkness. By day, something different. That, too, you shall see. This is the helm of the leader of the last patrol, and there is his banner——"

By light of the lanthorn, he held up a steel helm a-cock with pheasant's tail feathers, and threw a lance-pennon over the end-board.

"These are the Count Schiavon's, second man to Count d'Orosa," Franc marveled. "Where is he?"

"Tied to a saddle with the rest," Messer Polo said, indifferent, and throwing them behind among a pile of other trophies. "He made attack on the wrong enemy, at the wrong time, in the wrong way. Three chances are long odds!"

Franc went to the front before the first troop of Cathayans. Signs were not wanting that alarm was abroad. Huts and houses were dark and the doors of all the barns hung open. They went up the path through the wheat, and he reined often to listen. Songs came on the breeze from the plain, but there was no movement, nor any sound nearby except the breathing of the wheat.

Not much further on, in approach to the town, the noise of wains bouncing over rocks must reach the ears of those guarding the walls, and remembering a welcome of red-hot arrowheads sent without warning, he left the troopers behind and rode forward. He followed the outer wall of the garden of the Little Brothers and around, through the flower garden, to the towngate, and reined, unbelieving.

An arch in the solid wall told where the gate had been, and its shape was plain in new-cut blocks of stone.

But no gate.

Chapter 18

"The Count de Gubbio and his knights all came bugling up and rode about the walls, but well beyond our bowshot," Keeper Mozo called down from above the raised and battened drawbridge. "If you could see the gatehouse you might count the arrows their men-at-arms flighted at us. Toma sent out the alarm just before sunset, though some were against it. Everybody got in, with loss of nothing except a roof and land——"

"Who spoke against sending out the alarm?" Mayor Gandolfi whispered.

"Councilor Corti, for one. He said the Perugians would leave after the joust. But they were up here not an hour after you had crossed the river. Before night came down, their bombards had been pulled to the furnace. Tomorrow they will haul them before the walls. When the rocks are piled ready to throw, they will attack——"

A thunderclap shook the ground, and sent the horses on their hinds. Mayor Gandolfi blessed his tired mount and pulled him under control. Franc's mare made no move. Down on the breeze floated the same smell of fire sticks, and the strange

Cathayan whistle of many notes piped out, bringing the cavalry to move on.

"They have fire-sticked a way through the dry wall at the Clares' school," Franc called up, to hold Keeper Mozo's fear. "Easier to tear down than these of Simone's!"

"He built up this gate and the one at the Little Brothers' at order of the Cathayans," Keeper Mozo said in a tremble. "We thought you would not survive the journey back——"

"Is Councilor Corti within the walls?"

"The Cathayans allowed none to leave, or to keep sentry. Our men stand guard in the streets——"

"If De Gubbio lays hands on those fire sticks, how long shall we hold the town?" Mayor Gandolfi rumbled, spurring on. "Let us give thanks the Cathayans stayed here and not in Perugia!"

Cathayan horsemen tied ropes to the timbers of the old D'Orosa stable that leaned against the town wall, and rode off, and the building spread flat. Wains bumped through a gap into the Poor Clares' cloister on the other side. Some of the nuns stood among the columns and wept to see the garden trampled, and Mayor Gandolfi ordered them to the churches, promising all help to restore their flowers in the moment the town was out of danger.

Cathayans tore the posts out of the convent gateway so that the column might pass into the town, and Franc rode through with Messer Polo beside the wain carrying Emantha and Hsi-Soong.

"Our new encampment is on the rock above the churches," Messer Polo said. "If you have need of our counsel, find me under my battle flag, a golden carp on a field of scarlet."

"Should we look for Cathayan help?"

"We shall help ourselves in all ways," Messer Polo said. "We have no thought above the safety of her exalted highness——"

"In this, I am assured of Emantha's safety at least——"

228

"Where it does not touch upon the well-being of the Princess——"

"Then if disaster comes to the Cathayans, I shall ride only for Emantha——"

Messer Polo put up his head and laughed, and the plumed hat was black against the sky and the white feathers glowed in darkness.

"Yes, I have a fondness for you Assisians," he said, as if thinking of something else. "If you have nothing of a town and nothing for comfort, at least you have honesty——"

Hsi-Soong slept covered with furs, but Emantha sat looking over the tailboard and answered his wave.

"Tell my sisters to visit me!" she whispered. "And come soon to the encampment. I hunger to talk——"

"Be of good heart!" Franc called. "I shall plead for you——"

"Remember," Messer Polo warned, "speech with women is a privilege——"

"Speech is ours to take," Franc said. "Expect me at a proper time, and know my gratitude for safekeeping to Perugia and out——"

He turned off in the forum and tethered the mare behind the temple. Scabbard and Spada were both in their stalls and nickered at his pat and an armful of feed. He went up the flights and stood for a moment on the window platform, looking at all the campfires on the plain, and thinking of the number of those snoring with their feet to them. He called up to Toma, and his voice flew and came back two or three times, but without reply. He ran up through the open trap and stood in a stare.

The middle of the floor was empty where it should have been piled high with twigs. The water bags were gone. His woolsack and leathern blanket were neatly folded in a corner, and the packages of fire sticks were heaped on top. Nothing of

Toma's was there, and neither was there mark of him or Ubaldo or any other.

But a look up at the belfry brought a dry mouth and feeling that his eyes played tricks.

All the bells were gone.

The bars and the wheels had been taken away. The belfry was empty. He kicked the parapet and by the pain knew himself wide awake. He climbed up a pillar and crawled over the beams. Ropes, bars, weights, and wheels, all were gone with the bells, and the bats flew, seeking a perch.

He ran down to the stable and got up on the mare and rode for Messer Gandolfi's parlor. Torches were burning, and a large shadow moved over the courtyard.

"Which fool plays tricks?" Messer Gandolfi shouted at silent councilors and town guards. "Where are my robes? My seal? The key of the towngate? Where is the flag? Who has stolen the curulis?"

Franc edged nearer and stood in the light. In a voice he could barely hear for himself, he told of the town's further loss.

Messer Gandolfi stood with his eyes tight shut and his hands hanging.

"Who seeks to destroy us as a town?" he whispered. "Which is our enemy?"

He opened his eyes and flung up his fists.

"Search every house and cellar, stone to rafter!" he bellowed. "Find them all, every item, and put them before me, and drag in the criminals behind——"

Town guards and yeomen ran in squads, taking both sides of the street. Most doors were not wide enough to pass the smallest bell, much less the heavy curulis. Searchers went to the largest houses and, although most knew that they passed in a fool's errand, none said so above a whisper because of the Mayor's rage. Street by street the search went on, all about the churches and the forum, and behind the temple, and around

St. Rufino and the building of the Poor Clares, and all down the street leading back to the Mayor's parlor. Nothing was found, and nothing told of their passing, and nobody had seen their going.

"Six bells, tons of twigs, and thrones of bronze cannot be took a-wing!" Mayor Gandolfi whispered in great rage. "I demand every man in Assisi show himself worthy of his name by going into every crack and cranny. Bring them forth!"

Everybody was of good heart, and all scrambled in eagerness. Franc ran with everyone else up the streets and into houses, but with no result. Fat Gil came with Sesto, holding the end of a charred torch, and stopped to wipe his head on a soaked sleeve.

"Here's a feast!" he groaned. "The town robbed and not a trace. But all should help. None should slam a door, councilor or not——"

"Which councilor slammed a door?" Franc asked.

"That one, Corti," Sesto said. "If we had made him open, he said we'd never know another day's work——"

"Tell Messer Gandolfi!"

Fat Gil shook his head.

"I say nothing, having a family. That Corti would keep his word. Sesto and his father would earn no more——"

"I promise you——"

"Words are easy. Work is different——"

Franc went on the run. Messer Gandolfi stamped the court-yard, watched by the helpless Council and the town guard in a body. He turned at sound of thudding feet, and stood square, fists on hip.

"Well?" he demanded. "What is toward?"

"One house in town is unopened because the owner threatened the searchers with loss of their work——"

"The name?"

"Corti——"

Messer Gandolfi pointed at Councilor Corti, standing in the front rank with Paolo behind, and looked at the Sergeant of the town guard.

"Into the dungeon, him and his son. Search his den brick by brick, and I will come with you!"

Councilor Corti made no argument, and when Paolo began to shout he knocked him silent, and father and son marched off with no word or any struggle.

"When the vicious bull is docile, then beware his horns," Messer Mayor whispered. "This Corti is too quiet. Go up on the walls and inspect all men-at-arms. See that nothing is wanting for the night watch."

Franc climbed the stair near the convent of the Little Brothers and walked toward the main gate, counting men and their arms and the stores of weapons, and saw that fire buckets were alight, and the lead was molten for throwing upon those venturing up a ladder, and arrowheads were white-hot to shoot at any coming in stretch of a bowstring.

Keeper Mozo and his goodwife sat beside the capstan house to enjoy the night air. The little white city of tents had all been packed, he said, after sunset. He had seen nobody near the tower and nothing of Toma after he had rung the alarm.

"Who gave him license to leave his post, and where is he?" Franc asked. "I have looked over all those who did the searching. But I saw no Toma——"

"I heard the alarm and drew up the bridge and fastened the postern, and Simone and his men raised a wall of stone behind," Keeper Mozo said. "From this place I saw nothing——"

"Tell me who stole the bells," the goodwife Clara said. "No sound heard and no move seen, and I was there on the wall. Who was this, except somebody thrown to magic?"

Franc made a tour of the walls and found all at post and ready. He went to Toma's house, but nobody answered his knocking, and a neighbor said the women were at the church. The house of Emantha's sisters was shut. Nobody among those he asked had seen Ubaldo. He went to report his tour to the Mayor and told of the absentees.

"Tell the Wand Bearer to go with a town guard and find Toma and Ubaldo," Mayor Gandolfi said. "This Ubaldo is little use outside his books——"

"If they were attacked when the bells were taken——"

"That was also my thought. Young Corti was taken from the courtyard to the dungeon. Ask his reason for absence from the tower. That lad must be taught a lesson, or he will grow worse than his papa——"

Franc went into the mayoral court and under the building to the dungeon. The turnkey took him through a long passage that stank of age and the sewers to a cell, lit by torches, covered with a carpet, and made comfortable by beds.

"These pieces were brought in during the past hour," the turnkey said. "He is a councilor and I had no order against——"

The elder Corti sat on a bed and said nothing.

Franc asked questions of Paolo Corti and asked again. But the younger Corti, also, had nothing to say. He sat on the bed and stared at the wall.

"This is the last time," Franc said patiently. "Why were you not in the tower——"

"Last or first, it was not his place!" his father shouted. "What, is my son born to stand up in the air watching others build a living and having none of his own——"

"This is not the question——"

"He answers no question of any starveling!"

"He shall answer to the Mayor Gandolfi!"

"Little time for Messer Mayor to pride himself. The Count d'Orosa will bring him to scream for mercy!"

Franc left him shouting. Memory of the visit to D'Orosa's lodging made him think back. The family of Corti were not noted for steady speech or any brave airs, but rather for speaking, mouth to ear, among their own kind.

"What makes him into such a ranter?" The Mayor frowned when Franc told him. "And why did you keep this matter of D'Orosa to yourself?"

"They have D'Orosa business in their keeping, and I thought it no great matter——"

"Search out Toma and that useless second man. I will speak with Messer Corti. He may busy himself with D'Orosa's affairs, but he treated in secret, and that is my affair!"

Word sped about the walls, in the streets, and in all the churches, but nowhere could Toma or Ubaldo be found, and neither had any seen them since the alarm.

Soffolo, of the Three Silver Men, came under the archway of the Mayor's court and pointed a finger.

"What of Leda?" he demanded. "This night I have searched through the hours. She is not in the churches or in any house!"

"When did you see her before this?"

"After the alarm, and I opened the inn yard to those coming in the walls. She went then with Messer Dante to the studio of Messer Giotto. The apprentice, Tivi, took Messer Dante to his master in the lower church, and Leda went away. But where?"

Soffolo looked at the walls, at the sky, at the houses, and uphill toward the Three Silver Men. No longer was he the rough smiler, strong in thought of many a pewter platter and service of silver, and ready for all with a pat on the back, but pale, soft of speech, and hands together ready to fall on his knees.

"Go back to the tavern," Franc said. "I will go to the studio and there start afresh——"

He waited for no thanks, though Soffolo's voice followed him across the courtyard. The studio building was shut, and no light came from the paint-room windows. He ran down to the churches and into the dip and along to the sacristy postern. The Brothers crowded, chanting at prayer, and he pushed his way around the walls and into the tower church by the side door. Women and children sat in every space among the goods of their households. Nuns stepped, giving food and drink, or taking children from tired mothers. Candles burned, though few, for most of the families slept. He saw his mother holding a child and went to her.

"I stayed with the Abbess," she whispered. "All in the house is out. The Cathayans sent soldiers to help us move stick, pot, and loom——"

"The Cathayans carried our goods?"

"And everybody's. In that way, we were all out and in the churches within the space of two chimes. And nothing left for thief or picker——"

"Did you see Leda?"

"Yesterday, in passing. What of Emantha?"

Franc smiled at her gray eyes.

"I shall go in the morning to plead with the Princess to release her from the bond——"

His mother looked at the sleeping child.

"Come and tell me what passed," she said softly. "Make sure to go to the house of Il Cardinale. Hortensia cooks for us all. She will find you a supper."

He kissed her and went through the length of the church, stepping over and around the huddles on the floor. The nuns guarding the outer postern had seen nothing of Leda, but they pointed out the heap of goods taken from the inn and the ring of wenches sleeping round about. Nobody in the upper church had seen Messer Giotto or any of his senior apprentices. He went across the space to Il Cardinale's house and found Hortensia and Maldina working at fires in the yard with a dozen other women, and more women slept under the walls.

He told them all they asked about Emantha and promised

to go with them and Rosina to the encampment on the following morning. They had seen nothing of Leda and had no interest.

"No finger has she lifted to help us," Maldina whispered. "Let the street open and swallow her. No tear comes from me!"

"We need tears for ourselves," Hortensia said with good humor. "Not a chime ago we thought we would go mad from the watchtower bells that some say are stolen——"

"You had a fly in the ears," Franc said, thinking of an empty belfry.

"They were the watchtower bells," Hortensia said, tapping ladle to pot. "Think you we have lived our lives in the town without knowing the toll of Great William?"

"All in here heard them together," Maldina said. "From far away, as though we slept. If they were stolen, how can we hear them?"

Franc ran out to the space of grass and wet a finger and held it up to tell the way of the wind. It blew across the town from the northeast, over the mountains and across the lights of the new Cathayan encampment. He listened, and heard only the sounds from the stables and the whine of breeze among the builders' ropes and poles.

It came clear, first, that there was purpose in the Cathayans' help for the townspeople, for the watchtower must have been entered and robbed at about the time they were carrying goods to the churches. It was plain, then, that Hortensia and the other women had heard the sound of bells wind-borne from the direction of the Cathayan camp.

He went uphill among the boulders, following a path fresh-cut by Cathayan engineers, and came upon their sentries perched up on the rocks. He opened his hands in sign of peace, and walked on to a cave where officers of the guard sat at a fire behind a screen of branches.

He said Messer Polo's name and mimed a long mustache and

236

a feathered hat, and the officers laughed, and one got up, taking a lanthorn. They went through a tunnel, also fresh-cut, and entered an open space ringed about by rock that went up on every side almost as high as the watchtower. Pavilions were lit down three lanes in the middle, with smaller tents at the ends, and the palanquins ranked in darkness further on.

The officer passed through the sentries at the third pavilion, and Messer Polo came out a moment later in Cathayan robes, with torchlight shining on the curved nail sheaths in covering his eyes.

"Well then, Franc!" he hailed. "What may I do?"

"Give back the bells you stole, with all that kept them in place," Franc said. "And with them, the curulis. The twigs you may keep since we can cut more——"

"Stay, remembering where you stand. Say nothing you are not sure of proving——"

The bells tolled soft across the words. They turned in the way the breeze blew, facing a pavilion set apart. The bells played unsure and not in proper order, as if the player had no wrist to use a hammer. But another hand rang correct order and a sharper tone and, after a period, as if the hammer had passed across, the unsure hand began again.

"Here is something I had not known," Messer Polo said. "Are these the bells you mean?"

"Stolen from the watchtower——"

"On what evidence?"

"That the watchtower is empty and my ears point to them here——"

"They shall be returned——"

"I should inspect them. A forging can crack with ill handling——"

"Proper sums shall be paid in penalty for any damage and for the trespass. Wait, and I will order their return."

The length of Messer Polo's robe made small dust in light of the torches. He went to the pavilion set apart and sent away the women running out of the darkness to crowd about him. Light shone when the hangings were raised, and Great William tolled in a long, humming sigh, muted when the hangings dropped in darkness, though the echo traveled about the quarry walls and at last was still.

First one shadow, and then two more ran from behind the pavilion set apart, and a fourth followed them, calling softly, and yet loud enough to tell the voice of Emantha. They ran among the lanes of small tents, appearing in the gaps and going on, though never in the light, but it was easy to see Hsi-Soong in the first shadow, and One-piece and Two-piece in the pair behind, and Emantha, a giantess catching them up two paces for one.

To follow them or to wait for Messer Polo argued in his mind, but the town's affairs came first and, in any event, it was not proper for him to take part in some girls' game within the Cathayan encampment. The first shadows passed through the tunnel, and Emantha almost caught them, though where laughter and shrieks might have been expected, there was silence.

Time passed, and a moon skimmed the top of the rocks and made silver light about the trees.

The hangings of the pavilion were parted, and a group of men struggled under a weight, with one calling orders in Cathayan. Messer Polo came and, with him, two others wearing Cathayan robes.

"Ah, Franc, what you must think!" Toma moaned, trying to find his hands among the folds of the gown. "Set upon and flung into women's garb——"

"You thought us idle ones?" Ubaldo laughed. "But they climbed the tower and jumped upon us——"

"Climbed?"

"Scores came up the walls like ants, without ladder or any

238

help," Toma said. "We sat watching the plain and the Cathayan women on the wall. The soldiers climbed up from the back of the temple and had us in a twist of ropes before a fly could raise buzz. Then they took the bells and we were brought here to teach the little dolly and her jugglers——"

"Emantha tried to let us get away," Ubaldo whispered. "The little dancer was angry with her. Then Messer Polo came in and she made a great outcry and ran off——"

"Franc!" Messer Polo called. "Send your townsmen to guide these teams with the bells. I shall have others sent to put them back in the tower by morning. The curulis is here, last of all——"

"Then I will go with that, and nothing more will be said——"

"I shall come with you and myself make apology——"

"This Hsi-Soong and her pipkins are a costly crew——"

"A caprice of her exalted highness, which she can well afford. Did you, perhaps, think to speak with Emantha?"

"The morning will be better. Or I could have spoken to her some minutes since——"

Messer Polo turned about and looked at him, and torchlight sparked pale crystal in his eyes.

"She attends her exalted highness," he said from distance. "How could you have spoken to her?"

"When she ran after Hsi-Soong and the other two just now. They went into the tunnel——"

Messer Polo's golden claw hooked before his face in anger and he shouted in Cathayan, and all the soldiers in the tunnel entrance turned and ran through. Toma went with the first team of men carrying the smallest bell, and Ubaldo followed with the others. Great William took thirty men to lift, but even so they could barely walk beneath the weight, and more men were called, and while they waited Messer Polo tapped a fan on the nail sheath and looked up at the moon.

"It seems that your plea for Emantha cannot be heard," he

said quietly. "Her exalted highness has decided that her services are required——"

"But I shall ask!"

"And know yourself put aside with refusal——"

Franc looked at the long mustachios, at the pale eyes, and the brown face stained by the sun and sea and almost black by moonlight.

"I shall ask Messer Gandolfi and the Abbess of the Poor Clares to plead for us," he said. "I will ride through to Perugia to make appeal to Il Cardinale——"

"But his excellency set the terms and accepted the gold for the family."

"I will pay it back double!"

Messer Polo shook his head.

"Save breath," he said irritably. "Emantha serves with the suite of the Princess. She will then return to Venice, and there she will marry me!"

Chapter 19

Franc awoke before dawn on the lower step of the stones beneath the curulis, and while he stretched to ease his bones of chill he thought of Emantha and Messer Polo's threat, and memory brought new cold that rested in his blood and made him wish never to move again.

Stiro came over with hot broth from the guardhouse.

"Messer Mayor cannot be found," he announced. "Ciro and the Wand Bearer and a dozen of the guard are gone with him. Where? None can tell!"

"Did they search the Corti house?"

"If they did, it is barred and nobody moves near. The little Cathayan dancer is also gone. Messer Polo has ordered search through all the town and the land about——"

Franc put down the crock and stood.

"But is Emantha also of the lost?"

"Not only Emantha. Poor Soffolo cries about the streets for his Leda. Every gate in the town is shut and built with stone. Yet these, a dozen and more, cannot be found——"

Franc looked up at the curulis. If Messer Gandolfi was not

to be found, then on his order the Esquire was first man in Assisi with a duty to safeguard the town and all its citizens. Many of those citizens, as well as the Mayor himself, were missing.

His rank required him to act without delay.

He went to the sergeant-at-arms of the town guard and told him to call his men together and prepare to make closer search. Messer Gandolfi must have made his orders clear, because the sergeant obeyed with a salute, and Franc led a troop of men toward the Corti house, tasting at last the wine of authority.

Dawn was alight in the east. The town was silent. Only the calls of sentries came on the breeze. Franc ordered half of the men to dig out a small air hole on the ground floor. With the others he searched the garden behind the house. Nothing was found, and the wall was too high to climb over and there was no ladder. The diggers pulled out the stone frame and Franc went in first to the kitchen, as Goodwife Corti had left it. He sent the sergeant up to the shop and storerooms and himself went below to the cellars. Bales and crates were stacked in neat piles. A passage went all the way under the house, and corridors led off, dug out of the subsoil and bricked, to small rooms full of merchandise.

The sergeant came from upstairs and said he had found only what might be expected of a wealthy trader. From his face, it could be told that he thought himself in the wrong for obeying an order that would cause trouble. A trader and a councilor had power of his own and a vote that could lose a man his living.

"Take hammers," Franc said. "Go down and tap the walls for a hollow place——"

"Why should this house be so treated above any other?" the sergeant-at-arms demanded.

"First, because this is the last place known to have had a visit from Messer Gandolfi," Franc said. "Second, on his order you will do as you are told!"

The sergeant looked at his men and paused and shook his head.

"This is no esquire's work," he said. "I will take order from one of substance. Here is offense against a man not here to defend his house or goods——"

"Take your men away," Franc said. "Make your peace with Messer Gandolfi when he returns."

All the men left with the sergeant-at-arms, seemingly glad to go.

Franc went down with a torch and an iron bar and started on the left hand, tapping the wall at every other step. At the angle of two passages he found a hollow space behind a crate. He slid away other crates and bales to make room, and the bar tapped hollow from floor to low roof, but there were no marks on the stones. It might, he thought, be a place dug too near the sewer that ran beneath all the houses along the street.

He ran back to the guardhouse. Instead of the smiles there had been before, he got flat faces, and when he asked for the jail keys to talk to the Cortis, the sergeant turned his back.

"Leave," he said. "Or you will go into the jail, though not to visit!"

"Where is this order given?"

"Of my will. I am sergeant under the Mayor——"

"Mayor Gandolfi gave me authority——"

"Where is he?"

"We should make search for him——"

"Go, before search is also made for you!"

Franc went out to the archway and up the steps and sat in the cold metal of the curulis.

He saw that the sergeant had right on his side. A house belonging to a councilor had been broken into for no good reason, with nothing found and trouble of many kinds to come. Esquires were very well, in their way, when a Mayor Gandolfi gave the orders. Esquires on their own were the same stuff as any townsman. A warden of the watchtower was that, and no more. Francesco, son of Caterina, whatever he might think of himself, had far less to say in public matters than Fat Gil, a father of nine and a cordwainer with his own shop. A thousand pieces of gold, certainly, would give him a place and new respect, and two thousand might bring twice as much. But the gold was not yet in his pouch, and its handling was as much a dream as the offer. Nobody, much less sergeants-at-arms, took notice of dreams or dreamers.

In the quiet gray street glistening with heavy dew, he seemed to hear Messer Gandolfi telling him that the young men were with him. He thought first of Simone, then of Tivi, and, one after the other, the young men stood before him, beckoning.

He leaped out of the curulis and ran up on the walls. Cathayan guards had been withdrawn and townsmen patrolled with yeomen and men-at-arms, and groups stood about the fires. He ran down to the gate above the churches and slid the ladder to Messer di Rovigo's shelter. An elderly mason, a youthful friend of his father, took him on one side and looked over his shoulder to see if any were listening and said that Simone had secret work below the level of the lower church.

He climbed down through the timbers of the new tower, walking through cuts in the rock to a cavern. Torches burned at some distance inside, and Brother Dario sat with a score of his Brothers, all white with rock dust, warming at a small fire.

"You may not enter," he said. "I will fetch Simone, if he will come."

"If?"

"He works for the church. Of this, speak to no other!"

Brother Dario went into the opening and flattened against the wall to let carriers come out under baskets of rock. Franc turned away, unwilling to see what might be denied him. But he wondered if the tomb of the saint was near, and in the thought, raised prayer for its safety.

Simone came out, whiter than the others, and his grin split a mask of dust.

"How, when all the work is done, do you appear?" he chided. "Come, let me find a well and cool my head——"

"I looked for Tivi and Mok——"

"They work with me——"

"And Messer Giotto——"

"Certainly, and all in the paint room. Where were you?"

"Returning from Perugia. And asleep!"

"With us you would have had reason. We made a crypt beneath the lower church to hide the altar furniture. They may have the town and all in it. But the glory of the church, no!"

"What of Mayor Gandolfi?"

"Not with us, nor any word."

Franc stared at Simone's head under the splashing water. He told of the search in the Corti house and the change in the sergeant-at-arms.

"The house is a full twenty paces from the sewer, and there should be no hollowing from solid stone," Simone said.

"In the weeks of work I watched from the tower, and for all the masons in his employ, little has been done below," Franc said. "Is he the man to pay for nothing?"

"The men he paid were none of ours," Simone puffed, drying his head. "I was never allowed to watch them at their work. Why was this?"

"Let us enter and see!"

Simone ran back for a few of his lads with picks and bars, and they followed by the back lanes to the Corti house. But at the corner, where the lane entered the street, Franc halted, seeing town guards outside the house, and signed to the others to keep still.

"Let us enter the sewer behind the forum's trough," Simone whispered. "We shall then see how near it passes to the house."

They ran uphill to the cistern and climbed down into the

runway, walking bent-back through the tunnel under the street leading to the Mayor's court. A little way along and Simone pointed to an opening, and at the end, rapped a pick on an iron bar and ran his fingers around the timbers it held in place.

"This branch is new dug, and we are under the Corti house!" he shouted over the noise of water. "It can be opened and closed only from this way. Therefore, those entering or leaving came and went by the sewer——"

"That also passes beside the prison!" Franc shouted. "I know why vicious bulls were docile. These who worked for Corti were sappers of D'Orosa's, as the corporal-at-arms as good as told me!"

The main tunnel was wider, with a narrow paving, and the torch burned clear enough to see a white rag caught in a crevice of the water channel. Franc squeezed it dry and flattened the fringe and held up Leda's tall lace cap, seeing that it was known to the others, and with no word put it in his tunic and ran on. Light shone into the water from further down. They halted, and Franc signed that he would go first. The trap was open, a square cut out of the wall, and the cover lay inside the tunnel, faced on one side with stone and backed with timber.

He edged with care to the opening and looked into a cell with beds and a carpet, but no Cortis. The door hung open. He went inside and out to the passage and down as far as the jailer's box. All the cells were empty, and the jailer was gone. He went back and into the tunnel. Simone listened and nodded and led toward the outlet beyond the churches that came out in a brook, which dropped down the mountainside and joined the river, and went up a wild way to its spring near the Rock Castle.

They saw the trampled ground before they were out in the light. Hoofmarks cut the soil, all leading up through the bracken to the olive groves. A glint of silver beside the path brought One-piece's pipe out of the reeds.

But one of Simone's lads whistled and pointed into the gorge. With a rear guard of pack ponies still crossing the plain among the wheat, and the main body almost hidden among the vineyards, the head of a column of Perugians made slow way in a climb up the rocks on both sides of the brook.

Franc went to an outcrop for better view and saw that the leaders would be at the mouth of the outlet within the hour.

"If the city is entered here, we are lost," he said. "How shall we deal with these?"

"We can destroy the tunnel mouth," Simone said. "But it will take little time for them to dig through. If Corti's masons also opened other outlets, we work for nothing!"

"Send two of your lads with me. There are fire sticks in the tower——"

Simone's face creased deep and double in disappointment.

"I had prayed to save them for bringing down the castle," he whispered. "What I would give to see the ruin!"

"This you shall see, but by another hand," Franc said. "Use the fire sticks on the mountain and send the rock down upon them in the gorge——"

"Go teach your mother the arts of pot and pan," Simone said. "Leave me to mine!"

Franc had made up his mind not to raise alarm inside the town, since it might lead to panic among the women. He resolved to pass word to the Brothers and to the yeomen. From the way the sergeant-at-arms had changed coat he thought that Councilor Corti might have bribed the town guard, so that any word to them would be a favor.

With three of Simone's men he took the short cut over the hillside to the rocks above the churches and went up the ladder to the top of the town wall near the house of Il Cardinale and down to the forum. The other three puffed a long way behind by the time he had reached the tower window platform, and he stopped to look at the plain.

Perugian troops were grouped in companies among the wheat beyond the walls, but well out of bowshot. The bombards were being pulled up the path by teams of horses, helped along by hundreds of men bearing on long ropes, all heaving on a horn blast. Knights stood outside small tents flying their banners, and the great flag of Perugia hung above the tent of the Count de Gubbio, which glittered in a press of armor opening here and there to let the heralds greet messengers, or send them galloping off.

He looked up toward the Cathayan encampment. There were no Cathayans in the streets or among all the townsmen on the walls, and nothing showed at the quarry, nor any flag. Behind, at the Rock Castle, men-at-arms' helmets flashed in the keep. A company of D'Orosa's men spread over the rough ground between the castle and the town wall, but they sat about on rocks, talking, and smoke showed where they cooked their soup.

He put his head through the trap, and the twigs heaped in the middle of the bell-tower platform were a friendly shock, and the bells hanging above his head all seemed to be opening their mouths in a silent shout of welcome. The packages were on top of the leathern blanket, as he had last seen them.

"This come-and-go in the wheat is byplay to hold us on the walls while their men-at-arms enter by the tunnel," he told the others, loading them with the packages. "Have you now flint and steel?"

"All of us," one grinned. "And in rare scratch to use them!"

"Then off, and din take their ears!"

He watched them, footing with care on the flights, and out to the forum and into the tunnel behind the cistern, nearest, because it went steep down to the outlet. He took off his tunic and flexed his arms. All the bell tunes his father had taught him, which he had practiced on dummy ropes for hours through the years, began ringing in his mind.

First, he decided on the warning chime to the Brothers of the Order that trespassers lurked at the chapel on the plain. Add to that the further warning that bandits were riding toward the churches, and finish with a general warning to guard themselves from harm.

The bells rang easily and sweet. The Cathayans had rehung them on scraped beams, and not a bat flew out or speck of dust drifted down. In a pause he saw that the townsmen were gathering near the gatehouse to watch him. Swinging up on Little Tom's bell rope, he saw a waving cloth at a window of the convent of the Little Brothers telling him that his warning was taken, and he rang thrice to show that he had seen.

He rested, thinking of the strange Cathayan whistle of many notes. All of them could not be rung on the bells, but some of them could, and the rhythm could be got in the pull. He sprang at Great William and tolled hard, using tricks of legs and arms to beat a tempo, and from that to the smaller bells, until he was ringing a fair copy, and the men on the walls whistled with him. He tolled again on Great William, straight strokes to clear the air, and, after a measure on Little Tom, he tried to pick out the tune One-piece had always played while Hsi-Soong danced.

A horn flourish in the street brought him to the parapet. A giant Cathayan officer he knew waved to him to come down. He took his tunic and wiped off sweat, jumping the flights and out, to a ready hand that swung him up behind. They went at a gallop toward the quarry at the back of the town, and bent low to go through the shaft, and pulled up in a cloud of blown grit.

The space inside the rocky ring was bare except for a string of horses and a pavilion without side walls. A group of officers stood about a table, and Messer Polo sat in the middle, wearing a golden corslet and a helmet with ear flaps. His eyes stared hard without a smile.

"These bell notes I thought a message for me," he began.

"If Emantha is not with you, she is at the Rock Castle," Franc said without a breath. "And if not there, then on the plain and prisoner with the others——"

Messer Polo stood, and the officers gathered close. Franc told what had passed, taking One-piece's pipe from his pouch.

A thunderclap shook the ground. Some of the officers began to speak, but Messer Polo silenced them and spoke himself, sending away all but four.

"We have searched house, hut, and byway since the early hours for the gracious Hsi-Soong and her two attendants, and for the Lady Nanou," he said. "They passed from the earth clean as if plucked by eagles. But now we know, and now you shall see an end of this Di Gubbio and all with him——"

"One favor——"

"Make it known——"

"They are held in the castle, because all the tracks went up to the peak. I am of small use in the town. Let me join you and claim first place at the wall!"

Messer Polo nodded at the horses held by an orderly.

"Ride the black beside me, and take your favor as you will!"

They mounted and rode up to the end of the quarries and on to the wild ground between the town wall and the castle. Franc almost pulled his horse to a standstill in astonishment.

The rocks were alive with Cathayans running up to the assault. The D'Orosa men-at-arms were gone. Helmets massed in the keep, and their arrows flew from the archers' slots. The Cathayans advanced, thirty men at a time, under thick shields of timber and hardened leather, to chosen places beneath the walls, and there sat under cover and let the arrows shaft down until the shields were stuck thick, though none pierced.

A shout from behind turned them about. Simone and his men were hurrying up the slope, laughing as if they were going to a feast, and waving their caps at friends watching from the town wall.

"We sent the mountain atop of those Perugian dogs!" Simone shouted. "Not one crawled out, and the shaft is blocked for a month or two of digging. We came up because we couldn't go down——"

Messer Polo touched his hat to Simone's bow and asked him questions about the gunpowder, displeased that any had been stolen.

"These are the Grand Khan's secret and not for other hands," he said.

"Other hands or not, it works the same, and I have four sticks left," Simone said, squinting an eye at the keep. "I know where they should go. That redoubt will fall at any touch. The keystone in the main arch wants no more than a whisper——"

"This has the tone of entering into a doll box," Messer Polo smiled, looking at the tall stone walls. "I think we shall not walk in there with the ease of pushing a satin curtain——"

"Give me a shield for roof," Simone said, straight-faced, and throwing down all he carried except a small package. "Cathayans may boast themselves great ones with a gold piece and a fur cap. But if there are matters of stone in question, then look to some of us in Assisi!"

"Success attend you!" Messer Polo called. "If you should fail, my engineers shall teach you more of your mystery!"

Franc dismounted and held out a hand.

"I shall go with him," he said. "If we should meet inside, it will be good fortune. If not, Messer Polo, let me thank you for kindly words and many gentle acts."

Messer Polo took off a glove, and the nail sheaths made a clumsy handshake.

"If we succeed and her exalted highness lives, you will have nothing to want for the future," he said. "If we fail, we shall die upon our sabers. Farewell!"

Simone had joined a small team of carriers under a shield. He made no comment when Franc went in, and the men started up the rocky ground to the place where Simone pointed. Arrows hit into the roofing with force enough to make the men lose step, but none came through more than a tip. They stopped short of the postern in the main redoubt and squatted. Simone got tinder in flame and lit a torch. He took two sticks from the package and gave them to Franc, and himself took a crowbar and hammer.

"I will run first," he said. "When I call, you run with the sticks and the torch. But keep them separate!"

"And do you stop short at the wall!" Franc shouted after him. "Or if your pate meets it, what need to waste good powder?"

Simone poked out his tongue and skipped aside to dodge a boulder flung from above. The postern door offered toe hold, and he climbed, with crowbar and hammer in his belt, over the arch and on to the stones around the main gate and up, hand over hand, to the carved design and a place over the keystone, forty or more feet from the ground.

Molten lead dripped from above and smoked into the grass and gravel, but Simone was covered by the jutting stone. He dug and levered for a short time, and then threw the tools down and signed to bring the sticks.

D'Orosa's men on the walls were waiting. Boulders rained as giant hail and pounded all about, but Franc kept eye on the falling shadows and side-stepped, hopped and skipped, and feinted a run forward and paused, and so missed a shower of white-hot metal that set fire where it splashed, and ran on to climb as Simone had done, torch between teeth, and the sticks with Leda's cap in his tunic.

He reached up the sticks and watched Simone push them into places he had dug.

"Go back," Simone warned, taking the torch. "Lead the men

fivescore paces out and on the other side of the wild-rose thicket. When you are there, I will light. This warren will fall down the mountain——"

"But those inside!" Franc shouted. "I had forgot!"

"They will be in the great hall, or playing guest in D'Orosa's parlor below," Simone grinned. "This haven of rats is known to me, inch by inch. Now hear them squeal!"

Franc climbed down part and jumped the rest and ran out too fast to be hit by thrown rocks, and the arrows loosed at him all struck the shield. He turned the carriers, and they jogged down the mountainside beyond the wild roses and stood clear of cover to watch. The torch flame was held up to light the strings in the sticks. Simone climbed down and waited in the wall's shadow, making sure the strings were sparking. He ran downhill, and the arrows followed, and one took him in the back and he fell. Franc ran and Cathayans moved the shield to guard him.

Simone opened his eyes and made sounds, trying to speak.

"Run!" he whispered. "It will reach——"

Franc picked him up while the arrows cracked into the cover and signed to the carriers to run. He saw the flash of the fire sticks from the corner of his eye, but the small, flat reports were almost lost in the shouts of the Cathayans massed for attack.

The great keep appeared to tremble as if in a haze. Stone fell out over the archway and more stone fell from above. Pebbles seemed to drop, and a piece of the arch design. A strange sound became louder than the shouts of the Cathayans. The men-at-arms on the top turret of the keep were running down the stairway. Some looked out of the archers' slots, and others ran along the main wall. The flagpole on top leaned over one way, and the turret leaned another. Halfway down, a crack burst black and opened wide as if it laughed. Lower, the trim split apart and pieces flew. In a moment the mass of stone was falling into the dale and the flagpole followed, into rolling red powder.

Franc waited for a Cathayan surgeon to attend Simone, and ran into the dust at the base of the keep and over the split rocks into the main courtyard.

Many of D'Orosa's troop were giving themselves up on the lower level, but others on the wall were listening to the screams of one telling them to stand fast until the Count de Gubbio sent help, and to rest easy in thought of victory and a fat reward.

Franc recognized the voice of D'Orosa.

The outer courtyard went up fifty feet to the first battlements, and another thirty feet or more to a second all around the four sides, each crowded with men-at-arms, some beginning to draw bowstrings, and others moving the metal pots from the outer wall.

The great hall could be reached only from the inner courtyard, barred by the iron door and grille, with hot metal already dribbling from vents overhead to cover the ground below and burn the feet off any attempting foray with scaling ladders or battering-rams.

Teams of Cathayan bowmen ran in under shields. Their bows were smaller, but they shot quicker and hit oftener. Under the flights of arrows D'Orosa's men stood away from the battlements and slots and shot into the air so that the shafts came down on Cathayan shields or bounced on the stones.

A company of Cathayans threw off their furs, and a rank stood at the foot of the inner wall, locking arms. Another rank leaped on their shoulders and stood, linking their hands, and as fast as one rank was in position another went up, and still another, and more, all climbing up the men in position and standing on their shoulders firm as the wall behind their backs. D'Orosa's marksmen picked off many in place and among those climbing up, but others filled their shoes, until the top men could almost grasp the battlements.

Franc had watched the climbers go up. He noticed they put a foot on the outside of a stander's knee, gripping the next man's shoulder, and keeping their heads lowered so that any weight was thrown toward the wall. The next step was on the hip, and the next to the shoulder, gripping the ankle of the man above to haul up.

He ran forward before the whistle called the next wave of Cathayans and went up, keeping his mind on what he had seen the others do, and finding himself climbing as if he had been part of a human tower lifelong. Hard muscle, trained to stepping cat-footed, and a head for heights took him up with no pause, and when an arrow hit a man he had just grasped, he let him slip between his legs, holding to the next, and waited until another climbed to fill the gap, and then went on.

A slicing blade might have taken off his head as he threw a leg over the top, but he fell on his hands and kicked out with both heels, and the swordsman grunted and reeled back into a flaming pot. More Cathayans had climbed over, reaching hands to those coming up. D'Orosa's men had all run to the top battlements, closing the grille at the head of the stairway. The iron door guarding the steps down to the inner courtyard was shut.

Franc looked at the stone arch. It crumbled at touch, and the pointing was loose around the frame. A shortsword and an ax made a good crowbar and hammer. The point drove in as to gravel, and he levered until he had room to push in a fire stick. A coal from under a fire pot set light to the string, and he shouted to the Cathayans to stand away, and made them an example by running the length of the battlements and crouching in a corner.

The thunderclap brought ringing ears because of the enclosed space. The stone about the doorway piled in dust, but the door stood twisted in its iron frame, and he climbed round it to clear the stairway of fallen rocks and covered his face from the dust to go down.

No door barred the way below, but the arch was under solid flight of arrows from three sides.

A thunderclap shook every stone in the building. A second, louder than the first, split the wall outside the arch. No more arrows cracked into the cobbles. Franc ran, followed by Cathayans, into the courtyard, and stopped short.

The outer wall and the roof of the great hall had fallen in. Over the rolling dust, sunlight glowed on Tivi's painting of St. Francis holding out his arms in appeal.

Franc ran into the ruin, over the great blocks, feeling his way toward the door beside the fireplace. It was barred. He battered it with the hilt of the sword.

"Send the man Polo to me!" a voice screamed from close behind the small grille. "I am the Count d'Orosa——"

"Open up!" Franc shouted, putting his mouth close. "I am Esquire of Assisi——"

There came the sound of a spit.

Franc took out the last fire stick. A couple of Cathayans dug a hole beside the lock, and another brought out flint and steel. They all ran behind the fireplace until the clap brought a red light in the dust. The door was bent outward, and much of the stone had fallen. Franc leaped down the narrow stairway and fell across a heap of rock. Even through the dust he saw the gleam of golden armor beneath the pile, and stood, wrenching the body clear and pulling it down to the floor level.

But the Cathayans behind set up a great shout and ran to fall on their knees and bow their heads to the ground before a veiled woman sitting in one of the chairs. Hsi-Soong sat, bound and gagged, in another. One-piece and Two-piece were tied to a ring in a wall. Mayor Gandolfi sagged in chains on the stretching frame, from the state of his back, weak from a flogging. Leda sat in a chair apart, roped at feet and arms.

Emantha stood, half fainting, on tiptoe, chained taut by the neck to a pulley overhead.

Franc found the control and gently eased until she could stand flat on her feet. She went to her knees and fell forward, but he caught her.

He looked at the lines of pain marked between her eyes and beside her mouth and at the scars about her throat and under the chin where the chain had cut. The Cathayans had begun a chant and many were dancing, with Hsi-Soong to give them the lead and One-piece and Two-piece not far behind. He barely noticed them. He put Emantha carefully on a Cathayan's fur robe and strode across to the figure in golden armor lying on the pile of stones near the stairway.

He heard a groan in turning the body over, but he made no pause. With a hand inside the collar of the corslet, he ripped off the white hood.

Amazement froze his hands. A cry went up behind him. The singing stopped and a silence came and none moved.

Golden curls poured out over the golden armor. The face was perfect, full in the lip and unlined, and if the eyes that began to open were a she-devil's, nothing could disguise a woman, or make her less than a mirror's image and fairest twin of Emantha.

Chapter 20

Franc went up on the wall above the towngate and looked over the plain, spotted black by a thousand dead campfires, and spread about with the litter of battle, mounded in many places to tell where the nameless were buried, and restless with many a grazing war horse enjoying freedom and ready to gallop off at any approach. Down in the wheat, townsmen and their women chopped the bombards' timbers for winter fuel. Smoke went up black from the furnace where Ob and his men had begun to smelt the heap of Perugian arms, from dagger to spear tip, down to the merest toe-piece and gauntlet of armor. Over at the river, the last company of Perugian men-at-arms crossed under the eyes of Assisi's yeomen mounted on horses taken from the Count de Gubbio's cavalcade of knights and esquires. A gray square of the Little Brothers stood about the chapel of St. Francis, and their litany of praise came on the sighing wheat as cooling salve to a wound. Below, some of Simone's men took away the last blocks to free the gateway. Far out on the plain, Cathayans guarded their caravan, in two long northbound lines, waiting for the palanquins ranked before the Mayor's court. The churches flew flags and streamers, and flower garlands linked every pole about them and hung from all the poles lining the path to the Mayor's garden. The cage of the White Bird shone a golden dome above the trees, and the great pennon of the Khan's daughter curled white and gold in the breeze, with a golden dragon floating beside it. Behind, at the camp in the quarries, Messer Polo's flag of a carp on a field of scarlet blew squarely in the hills' stronger drafts.

Assisi's banner stood brave in the ruin of the Rock Castle on the mountain. There was no keep or redoubt, and the only flash of steel came from the shovels of men clearing a space for the town's new watchtower.

Down in the streets, Messer Giotto's apprentices worked to light the way for the procession of the White Bird. Every house front was painted in a different color and, if three walls showed, each was another hue. The roadways were painted white, and the pavings, and every front and back door and chimney were daubed in the housewife's choice, so that from on high the town bloomed as a garden, and those in the streets danced instead of walking and sang instead of talking, perhaps because the color brought gaiety and a lifting of hearts.

Franc looked up at the old bell tower, at the faces of the elder and younger Corti standing watch, and raised his hand in answer to their salutes. At court that morning, when they had expected death for themselves and their family and loss of all their goods, he had sentenced them to stand in the tower for three months, with an hour's freedom once very day. His hand burned from the goodwife Corti's kiss of thanks that her men were spared, with a house still hers, and nothing taken of goods or money, except the fine which went to the school of the Poor Clares.

Keeper Mozo came, taking off his cap and making a knee.

"The last stones are gone, Messer Mayor," he grinned. "The

roadway is swept clear. Shall I lower the bridge and open the gates in a trial?"

"Leave open the bridge and the postern," Franc said. "Open the gates only to Il Cardinale. Send one to tell me when he passes the chapel."

He walked along the walls to the gate of the Little Brothers and down to the garden, answering all the workmen's salutes with a raised hand. His cap set with the Esquire's plume was sign of authority, but the Mayor's seal that hung about his neck by order of Messer Gandolfi was more and, if they were not enough, he carried over his arm Il Cardinale's threadbare red hat, sent to him that morning filled with the linden flowers of Perugia. All three together took doubt from any mind, and even the most crotchety graybeards made him a bow and went in haste to do as they were told.

Messer Gandolfi rested in his bed, with the goodwife at his side fanning flies away with a leaf. His face had fallen with pain and fever, and the red beard showed how pale he was, but light was in his eyes and growing stronger. The flogging with iron whips and the stretching on the rack had left him as a child, though without a child's strength. Will alone carried him, and he had willed, by whisper, that Franc was to be Mayor in his place. From that moment the goodwife allowed no other word or any question that wanted answer, and she made it plain that Franc might enter only to let her man know how went the town's affairs.

"Messer Gandolfi," Franc began, "all within the walls is now repaired and in order. Water flows in every duct, and all the outlets are built and free. The Count de Gubbio has left his banner and the town flag of Perugia in our keeping, until the Council votes the sum of their fines. After the noon chime, Il Cardinale will enter the town with the children, and we shall form a procession of the White Bird in honor of the departure

261

of the Khan's daughter. I am asked by Messer Polo to say that he wishes to say farewell——"

"Nobody!" the goodwife said, raising the leaf. "You, because you bring the news he wants to hear. Il Cardinale, when he returns. Others, no!"

Messer Gandolfi's smile showed his strength.

"Cathayans at Hsi-Soong's order helped to build the school of the Poor Clares," Franc went on. "The garden and cloister are repaired and planted. The capstan house and gatehouse on the walls are rebuilt. The old ones are stuck as full of shafts as any hen of feathers. Of the wounded, only Corporal Stiro of the town guard is still abed of cramps got from falling down the forum steps after a bout of free wine given by Soffolo, on the finding of his Leda. She is up and serving as ever and in good screech with the wenches. The Lady Nanou, who was our Emantha, is with the gracious Hsi-Soong, and is dearly nursed and ready to walk. The sister, nameless so far, but once called the Count Althasar d'Orosa, is held in the hospital of the Poor Clares. Her voice may be heard even over the sound of the work at the school. What else, then? Messer Dante has promised a canto in our honor. The crypt beneath the lower church is filled in, and nobody knows how to find the mouth except one of the Brothers, and his name is unknown to all except one of the Order. Simone is yet abed, but shouting to be up——"

"I share his plight!" Messer Gandolfi whispered.

"Sshh!" the goodwife scolded, and pointed the leaf at the door. "Enough! Outside until tomorrow!"

Franc grasped the hand on the quilt and bowed to her and left with no other word.

A score or more townsmen waited for judgment below the curulis, and the councilors in their robes, with the Purser and the Wand Bearer, stood about the steps.

Franc took off the Esquire's cap, wearing only the Mayor's

seal, and gave the Cardinal's hat to the Purser. He sat in the worn metal seat, feeling its rounded back hard against his spine, and holding the lions' heads on the ends of the arm rests.

"First!" he invited.

All, as always, began to shout at once. He pointed to a farmer and listened to a complaint about five pigs, lost during the alarm, and found hanging in joints on a stall in the market. The stall-holder stood forward to swear that they were his own, bred on his land. But the farmer said they carried his sign painted in Mok's red dye, which no boiling or scraping could hide. Franc gave him the pork, together with enough money to buy five live pigs, and sent the Wand Bearer to see that the order was obeyed. Most of the rest had claims against the D'Orosa estate, but he told them he could make no order until the Council held a meeting and decided on punishment.

"How, if this is a woman, shall she be punished?" Councilor Starace asked above the murmur. "A man might be flayed, or burned over green wood, or in other ways made to pay for his crime——"

"We shall listen to Il Cardinale in this," Franc said. "And are you free of crime? Did you plot with Corti that sappers of the Count de Gubbio's army might enter these walls as masons and bricklayers——"

"This was not my work!" Councilor Starace shouted. "Nothing was known to me——"

"Yet the work they did passed under your house," Franc smiled. "They cut a branch from the main channel beneath the bend of the street under your house to Corti's. Through that branch were taken the Khan's daughter, and the gracious Hsi-Soong, and our Emantha, with others captured off the street. Through that branch and others the Perugians might have taken us without a battle. You knew nothing? Heard nothing? Should we put you over burning charcoal to find out?"

263

Councilor Starace went to his knees and crawled forward, mouthing, in too great a fright to speak.

"Take him home," Franc told the sergeant-at-arms. "He is too old for punishment. Bring back his councilor's robe and all signs that he held honor among us."

"I serve only the elected Mayor," the sergeant-at-arms said, grinning at Councilor Starace. "I am an elected officer of the Council in session——"

"You are nobody, elected by none," Franc told him. "The Council we had was almost all a creature of the maid D'Orosa. You were a creature of the Council's, and I should have dealt with you before this, but we had need of a town guard——"

"You say so because I refused help in the search of the Corti house——"

"I now understand that you came meekly with me to see if there was sign that Mayor Gandolfi and all with him had been taken down to the tunnel by De Gubbio's men-at-arms. Do you deny me?"

Franc looked at the sergeant's sidelong stare and feet astride. At the earlier court that morning, all the townsmen had been in to listen to the trial of the Cortis and to hear the plan for working the D'Orosa lands. Now they were out, working beyond the walls, and the town guard was led by a man well able to see that with Mayor Gandolfi and a few more out of the way, the town could pass into his charge. Messer Polo and the Cathayans would have nothing to say. Il Cardinale might say much, but he could do little.

Franc watched the thumbs hooked in the sword belt and thought of his sword hanging in the Mayor's parlor. The townsmen crowding in the court were silent. From their faces he knew they had the same mind as himself, but feared to move lest they never move again.

The sergeant's cold eye roved along the rank of his men. He had more than enough help to do all he wanted. On the one

264

hand, he must lose his rank and leave the town, knowing that he would be lucky to find a lowly place in a troop of men-at-arms. On the other, he could exert himself to try his fortune by killing Mayor Gandolfi and the few loyal to him and giving the town back into the hands of the Cortis and Staraces, and relying upon their favor to keep his place, with rich gifts and higher pay for reward.

A stone jar flew between the open panes of the parlor window and struck the sergeant in the mouth. He fell against two of his men, and instantly Franc was on him, wresting the sword from its sheath, and standing, point ready for any attack.

"That, from me!" Goodwife Gandolfi whispered, staring out of the window. "And if he take less in punishment than my man from duty, you shall all hear more!"

She slammed the window shut, and everybody breathed deep. Franc whirled the sword, but none of the town guards made a move, and he walked back to the curulis.

"Those of you who worked with the Corti side, take your belongings and leave the walls," he said. "Or stay, and be questioned. Those found guilty will suffer. Go!"

The townsmen raised a cheer. Franc stopped some ready to wreak harm on the sergeant, and many of the guards held about him and went out as whipped dogs.

"Ciro, you will be sergeant-at-arms," Franc said. "Take this Starace home and see he stays there. For the rest, there will be no more judgment at the curulis until Il Cardinale gives word!"

He went into the parlor and buckled on his sword, swearing to himself never again to take it off until all was at peace. The street whispered with people listening to those coming away from the court. They cheered when he past, but if he smiled at them, he knew that they would also have cheered the sergeant-at-arms if he had won the day.

The cloister of the Poor Clares had been rebuilt, and new plants climbed sticks, and the archway to the school beyond the walls dried a coat of plaster. A nun went to find the Abbess, and while he stood in the silence, he heard the screams of the maid D'Orosa. But instead of the Abbess, his mother hurried across the garden to him.

"Find other lodging for this wretch!" she whispered. "She is used to having her will among men. Listen to her and learn the language of the stables!"

"No stableman would so misuse his horses," Franc said. "Let me see her!"

She led him along the cloister, to a stairway, and up to the top floor of the convent, which looked over the walls. All the cells along the corridor were empty.

"None would stay near," she told him. "She curses all and demands men's clothing. Beware as you go in!"

A nun got up from a chair outside the door and turned the key in the lock. He walked in, and the door slammed behind.

The maid D'Orosa stood in a long white shift, without belt or shape. She was unbathed and uncombed and her feet were bare. A bed pallet and covers had been torn to shreds over the floor, and the marks of her nails were on the walls.

She stared at him, wide and blue and stony fierce, but he saw Emantha, and laughed.

"You were right to cover your head with a hood," he said. "Men would find you ugly——"

She screamed curses and stamped, and he stood smiling at her.

"If you are ready to spend your life locked in a cell, dirty in body and mind and mouth, you shall be moved to the town dungeon," he went on. "There, only the jailer will see you, and only jailbirds will hear you——"

"Give me my own clothes!" she said, hoarse from shouting, but quieter. "Shall I dress as a serving wench?"

"Yes," Franc said. "As a serving wench you shall spend a

month or two at the Three Silver Men, where you plotted with Corti to overthrow us——"

She screamed and flew, claws out, and he felt himself in a grip well drilled by sword and longbow, and a body strong with carrying a weight of armor. He saw the scar on the right hand and took it in both fists and threw her over his hip. She fell on the rags of the pallet and sat, but force of the fall made her weak, and she covered her face and wept, and the curls tangled long about her hands.

"Il Cardinale will decide how the D'Orosa property is to be divided between your sister and yourself," he said. "You are not male and therefore you are female. If you are neither, you are nothing. While you are nothing you cannot own property. One other matter. For every word you say that should not be heard in these walls you shall lose one gold piece of your share. Each time you scream you will lose another gold piece. If you leave this convent nameless and of no substance, know that you swore yourself away!"

"Wait!" she called when he was at the door. "Where is the Count Schiavon?"

"In the hospital of the Little Brothers——"

"Does he suffer?"

"Enough. He was dragged off his horse by a rope——"

"I would see him!"

"In what name?"

She stood and held the wall and turned her back, looking out of the window.

"The Countess D'Orosa," she said in a small voice, and went to her knees, weeping.

"This means, then, that your sister is also a Countess?" he asked gently. "She is your twin——"

"I want no speech or any dealing with her!"

"This is well. But would you speak to her and in other ways

behave as a sister if I promised you speech with the Count Schiavon?"

"Is this in your power?"

"Prove me!"

She laid her head on her arms upon the window sill, and he saw the lines of her face lose anger.

"Bring the Count Schiavon to me," she began.

"No terms!" he said, sharp. "Bathe, and dress in the clothing brought to you. Be ready within the hour. Do you agree?"

She nodded once, and he went to the door and out to his mother's smile.

"Pity this one is not Emantha," she said, after he told her what had passed. "Her sisters cannot enter the camp to speak to her. She cannot leave. Will she go with the caravan, and no farewell?"

"I have a word to say," Franc smiled. "Now that the town's business goes apace, I may attend my own!"

He hurried along the wall to the convent of the Little Brothers and found Brother Egidio in the pharmacy.

"The Count is fit to move," Brother Egidio said, watching a mixture dripping in a bottle. "But he is a dangerous man, I must warn you. He threatens all who fought against the D'Orosa banner and prates day and night of his duty to protect his patron."

"Tell him that he shall speak to the Countess d'Orosa on condition he keeps the peace and abides by the law!"

Brother Egidio never moved his eyes from the bubbling in the red bottle.

"And if he refuses?" he asked. "Does he know his patron is a woman?"

"Yes!" Franc said with certainty. "For what other reason would he take her place in the jousts? Who met the Perugians? Yes, he knows!"

He ran through the gay streets to Messer Giotto's paint

room. Apprentices mixed washes and filled buckets, and lads ran in with empties and plodded out with the full. Tivi worked in the studio with Mok and Laz, preparing gold paint for the middle of the street where Il Cardinale would walk.

"A touch of the Mayor's seal for luck!" Laz shouted, setting aside a mortar. "See this primper in his fancies!"

"A small word of sense here," Franc said severely. "You three are now beyond apprenticeship. Before you become journeymen, you must have your parchments——"

"We dread this day," Mok said. "It will cost us three years of work in free wine alone!"

"But far more in Florence or Padua or Bologna, where a hundred and more thirsty journeymen's throats wait to drink you a welcome," Franc said. "What if your parchments came free? What would you do for Assisi?"

The three looked at each other and back at him.

"The seal of this town is as fair as any," Tivi said cautiously. "But what if the Master refuses his name?"

Franc touched the seal about his neck.

"This is no fancy," he said. "This is the seal, and I am Mayor. Would Messer Giotto refuse if I put the parchments before him, properly signed and sealed? This I promise you, free of all charge, for one small favor!"

"Name it!" Laz whispered.

"I need excuse to enter the Cathayan camp without being taken to Messer Polo," Franc said. "Their guards are strict, and I am known."

"Our parchments hang proud upon the wall!" Tivi laughed. "We will take in colors to paint the way for the White Bird. Come, pots of gold, black and scarlet for each of us, and a ladder for the Mayor!"

They took time only to give the juniors gold paint for the street, and Franc followed them out with a ladder and a length of plain cloth that flapped about his head and hid his face. The guards at the quarry chattered among themselves, but Tivi drew a white bird on the wall, and they laughed and gave way. The four went into the shaft alone and out to the open space. Most of the pavilions were being rolled and loaded into wains. Franc turned away from the flag of Messer Polo and went instead toward the long pavilion where many women hurried out with packs and baskets, placing them in lines for servitors to label.

Through the ladder's rungs, Franc saw two faces he knew among a crowd sorting the baggage, and hissed at Tivi.

"The two sniplocks!" he whispered. "Those two of Messer Polo's suite in your fable, remember, of a ladder and Emantha's blushes? Ask them to tell us where she is!"

Mok went across, hidden by all the boxes and bales, and came back with the older of the two.

"This is Jeroldo," he announced. "He knows where to find Emantha!"

"I shall also know where to find your heads!" Jeroldo warned. "They will grin from the tent poles——"

"Make us no jokes," Franc said. "Place this ladder against the wall of her pavilion and leave us. At a later time, come to me for reward!"

Jeroldo looked fearful, but he took the ladder and trotted behind the long pavilion to another further off, flanked by small tents. All the doorways were guarded by Cathayans, either resting on spears or standing with the long swords held in both hands.

They watched him stop at a tent on the right of the pavilion. The guards gave him no look, and he put the ladder against the rope at the back and ran.

"Tivi, bring a crowd around you with a drawing of birds on the nearest pavilion," Franc said. "You others, use your color. If I fall foul of any, say no word and make no move——"

"Fortune attend you!" Mok whispered. "What if you bring her out?"

"She runs as one of us and climbs as a goat. Attend your paint till we are gone!"

He went behind all the boxes and bales as Jeroldo had done, but instead of walking across the space, he held the paint cloth over his head and went the long way around, behind the far pavilion. The ladder was steady, and he mounted a rung, pretending to hang the cloth from the tent's circular rim. A couple of guards came to see what he was doing, but his earnestness in work satisfied them and they went back to their places.

Under the cloth he drew his knife and sliced into the tent wall, draping a loop over his head to see in. The tent was dark, with a small wick burning from a pot hanging in the center pole. He saw movement from a pallet and heard a little shriek of surprise.

"No noise!" he whispered. "When I cut the canvas, step through and run behind the pavilion to the sheep track by the churches. See nobody, say nothing. If any prevent you, scream!"

"I have no clothes!" Emantha moaned. "Furs and blankets——"

"Wrap this about you!" He pretended to sing, pushing the paint cloth through the hole. "Make a pack of the furs and carry it, hiding your face. Go to my mother at the Poor Clares."

He sliced the canvas down to the ground, but close to the pole where it showed least. She came through, with the cloth in folds of gray and colors about her, and an end hiding her face with a bundle of blankets on her head, barelegged and barefoot, waiting only to kiss him warm and soft on the cheek, and running full tilt for the pavilion and on behind the tents. He gave her time, sick in thought of any outcry. But the crowd still held about the painters, and more ran to join them and clap their hands.

Quiet piping and drumming started at his elbow. He dare not turn about. He looked at the slit canvas, at the ladder, at the sky. Still there came no warning shout and by that time,

271

he knew Emantha must be climbing the track and out of sight.

He swung about, and Hsi-Soong smiled with her hands in her sleeves, and One-piece and Two-piece bowed low with her.

"I came for the White Bird," he said.

"You speak, Hon'ble Flamp," Hsi-Soong smiled, turning toward Messer Polo's pavilion. "We make talk-talk, one piece, chu, say plenty words!"

He followed her, marveling that she had not called the guards. She walked into the pavilion flying the silver carp, and Messer Polo stood up among his officers and came around the table, clasping his jeweled claws to bow, looking his surprise.

Hsi-Soong spoke in Cathayan and he replied, and she spoke again.

"The gracious Hsi-Soong instructs me to tell you that she speaks for her exalted highness," Messer Polo said in hard tone. "They wish you to know, first, their admiration that above all the Khan's soldiers you were first to pierce the defense, first to scale the wall, and first to reach the prison. But you were wanting in courtesy by releasing the Lady Nanou before the ladies of the Court, and afterward helping one we learn is her sister——"

"I loosened the chain about Emantha's neck. I went to put it about the neck of that other!"

"It was never your desire to affront the ladies of the Court?"

"If the other had been a man, she would have swung from the tower!"

Messer Polo spoke to Hsi-Soong, and she laughed and chattered.

"I am required to say that you once more enjoy the favor of her exalted highness," Messer Polo began. "The gracious Hsi-Soong wishes to perform an immediate ceremony of forgiveness——"

"I came to invite the Khan's daughter to meet his excellency at the gates and to join our carnival in her honor. His noble years, perhaps, forbid any thought that he should be kept waiting?"

Messer Polo spoke to Hsi-Soong, and she spoke to One-piece and Two-piece and after they had piped and drummed, she spoke again.

"The gracious Hsi-Soong considers respect for age most proper," Messer Polo said. "Her suite shall be called together and I shall lead the procession to the gateway——"

"And the White Bird?" Franc asked, finely careless. "We have flowers and a speech prepared——"

"The Lady Nanou is now tirewoman to her exalted highness," Messer Polo said without speaking to Hsi-Soong. "She will not appear in public."

"Then we may borrow the robe of white feathers that another shall wear it?"

Messer Polo spoke again, and Hsi-Soong laughed and clapped her hands.

"Hon'ble Flamp, I go, take one-piece dress," she said in the baby voice. "You go, we meet one-piece house, six-piece bell, smoke-smoke? So-so!"

She danced out, and all bowed until her shadow was off the canvas wall. Messer Polo gave an order, and an officer hurried away.

"One of my suite will meet you with the robe," Messer Polo said, pleasant again, and smiling at the mayoral seal. "I am happy at your promotion, but sad that you shall not be with us. Have no fear of the one you call Emantha. She is cared for and happy in her new life——"

"This was my only doubt, and now I am at peace," Franc said with great seriousness. "Let me wish you well, Messer Polo, and go to my duty!"

They bowed, and Franc left the pavilion in a show of energy, seeing that a crowd was yet about the painters, and half the pavilion wall in a pattern of scarlet branches, black leaves, and golden birds.

On the other side of the tunnel through the quarry, an officer came behind and thrust a cloth bundle into his hands and turned away. The sentries gave him cheerful smiles and spoke in Cathayan, and he wished them long and happy lives and short of sprinting, put as much distance as he could between himself and them and stood, winded, behind Il Cardinale's house, listening to cheers and singing from beyond the walls, and thankful for silence along the way to the quarry.

He went through back lanes to the forum and down to the Poor Clares. His mother waited under the cloister and came laughing, holding out her arms to greet him.

"Emantha is here and singing to be with us!" she called. "What if the Khan's men search for her?"

"I have yet an answer for them. Bring out her sister and say nothing. Have they met?"

"Should I put a spark to tinder?"

"Go with Emantha to the Mayor's garden and wait in hiding until I call!"

She went away and he listened to the cheers outside the walls, seeing in his mind's eye the procession of Il Cardinale almost at the rise before the gate.

Footsteps echoed behind, and he turned. But he was far from ready to believe that the beauty in a dress of gray wool was not Emantha, of the wheat-tip hair and springtime-blue eyes, except that her smile was uncertain, and she walked as if she feared her skirts might blow away.

"These are not a comfort," she said, direct as a man. "Let us find a hidden way to be out of the stares of those in the street!"

"They shall look their fill," he told her, short. "You had no mercy on them when they were helpless. Be thankful the stares are not hot irons!"

"Where is the Count Schiavon?" she stamped.

"Safe, until you have done your part. Put this about your shoulders and follow me!"

He took the feathered robe from the cloth cover and held it out.

"The cap will hide your face from any stare," he said. "Wear it, say what you are bid, and do all you are told!"

She looked at the robe and might have thrown it down. But she thought better and with no look for him, put it on and pulled the golden beak of the cap over her eyes. He gave her no time to think, but hurried her along the back lanes to the stable of Scabbard and Spada.

"Make no noise until you are sent for," he told her. "Remember that if these mothers came to know who you were, nothing could help you!"

He saw fear in the blue eyes under the great gold beak and watched her crouch back against the manger.

"Leave me!" she whispered. "I wait for the Count Schiavon!"

He locked the door against idlers and went into the forum and down the steps.

"Ee-hai, Messer Mayor!" Keeper Mozo shouted from the wall. "I sent Ubaldo to give you warning a chime ago. His excellency is almost at the bridge!"

Franc held up the mayoral seal, and Keeper Mozo leaped to put his weight in the turn. The gates opened in oiled ease, and through the arch came a din of shouting and singing from parents greeting their children in the long line of flower-hung farm carts.

Il Cardinale rode a gray mule at the head. He wore the gray habit of the Order and if his arms were busy with blessings on every side, his face smiled, at rest.

Franc called over the purser-sergeant-at-arms and took the threadbare red hat. He went out into the sun, holding it up, and Il Cardinale laughed aloud.

"Well met, Messer Franc, goodly Mayor of our beloved Assisi!" he greeted. "Here's a prophecy come true, then? I sent the hat to you filled with the linden flowers of Perugia as sign of our peace. Why this somber face on so happy a day?"

"Your excellency," Franc began. "Two questions require quick thought. One is Emantha and the other is her sister. The Cathayans leave us within the hour!"

Il Cardinale pulled the gray mule to the side of the path and slid off, stretching arms and legs.

"Too old for long journeys," he murmured. "Let us walk then. I was a little overhasty. I thought Emantha in great danger from the moment her sister saw her twin when they both sat at my table. It seemed to me the better of two evils to let Emantha go with the Princess and have chance of life and happier living. Let us find a quill and an inkhorn and a sheet of that miracle paper!"

They went through the cheering crowds to the Mayor's parlor. All the older girls and boys were crowding in toward the cage of the White Bird, and mothers were thick in every path, giving their children a combing before sending them to the nuns to be put in place for the procession.

Cathayan horns blared and drums beat, and squadrons of cavalry galloped toward the forum and turned down the steps. Other squadrons rode from the quarry at slower pace and under the flags and pennons and floating emblems, the feathers in Messer Polo's hat bobbed before a troop of giants with the long swords.

"Here is trouble, Excellency!" Franc whispered. "The White Bird is flown and I believe they seek her!"

Il Cardinale shook thin shoulders in thinner laughter.

"Let them find her in her cage," he said. "I told the reverend Abbess what should be done!"

He passed into the parlor, and Franc went out to the roadway before the mayoral court, calling to the Wand Bearer to bring his robe of office.

Messer Polo saw him and trotted out of line, pulling up at his side.

"The Lady Nanou is missed from the encampment," he said quietly. "It were better she returned——"

"If you speak of Emantha, she knows the country as well as any bird, white or not!" Franc said loudly, knowing that Il Cardinale could hear through the parlor window. "How should we of Assisi help you?"

Messer Polo's jeweled claws crept along the length of the scarlet reins.

"A contract was drawn, and signed by Il Cardinale and the Mayor, on which certain sums were paid," he said. "We require that your part should be fulfilled——"

Franc pointed to the waiting palanquins.

"Are we to put off our homage to her exalted highness to look for a discontented girl?" he demanded. "Let us first have our ceremony——"

Drumming and piping got loud enough to make him shout. Around the curve of the road a troop of horse carried banners and the gold dragon of the Khan's daughter. A dozen Cathayans carried a curtained chair on their shoulders, and Hsi-Soong on a white pony and One-piece and Two-piece on blacks came behind, and after, a long line of men held up the tent wall painted with golden buds on scarlet branches of black leaves, and Tivi, Mok, and Laz marching before, all dressed in rich Cathayan robes.

The crowds in the garden streamed out to cheer and throw flowers, and in moments the press was so great that nobody could move. But the sound of the Mayor's mallet on the block cut through the noise, and all turned toward the parlor window.

"A word before we gladly show our guests the warmest side of our hearts!" Il Cardinale called, standing on a stool inside the parlor. "Most of us welcome our peace. But some of us are troubled. Let us remember our own Emantha!"

The crowd set up a great shout, but Il Cardinale calmed them and started to speak another language, from the faces of the Cathayans, their own. Hsi-Soong clapped her hands and got off the pony without help and made way through the willing crowd with One-piece and Two-piece close behind.

"As a young man I passed many years as a novice in the Khan's dominions," Il Cardinale told the crowd. "We were called Nestorians, as Messer Polo may remember?"

"I knew many," Messer Polo whispered in sharp surprise.

"Then let me speak in two languages," Il Cardinale smiled. "Know, then, that we in Assisi were afflicted by a monster called the Count Althasar d'Orosa——"

In the crowd's sullen murmur, he spoke in Cathayan.

"He wished for sons to carry his name, but his Countess died with the birth of twin daughters. He chose one child to be brought up as a boy and ordered his steward to destroy the other."

He spoke to Hsi-Soong in Cathayan, each small sound clear in the silence.

"The steward's heart misgave him. He stole the unwanted child out of the castle and brought her into his own family, here in the town. But his neighbors prattled, and word got to the Count. The poor steward came to me with the child, and I brought her in to the church. As most of us know, he was taken back to the castle and there perished. That brave man was known to us as Emantha's father. It was I who gave the baby into keeping of Hortensia's mother. She grew up among us, called Emantha!"

He raised his arms to quell the shouting, and spoke again to Hsi-Soong. Messer Polo got off his horse and pushed closer to hear.

"The other poor girl was put into armor as soon as she began to show herself a maid," Il Cardinale told the crowd. "When her beauty bloomed, her monster father put her into a hood and told a tale that horrid scars made her an eyesore. She spent her days hooded and in armor, knowing nothing of women or womanliness. She went to the Crusade wars, but suffered a wound when her father was killed. After small travel she came back to the Rock Castle. Consider, then, that cruelty has been her share all her life. What is to be done with her?"

"Death!" a voice screamed, and the crowd went forward.

Il Cardinale shook his head.

"Death pays no debts," he called. "Shall we kill this girl and so prove ourselves as cruel as her father?"

The crowd moved, and the shouts of denial got louder, and Il Cardinale raised his hands.

"Very well," he said gently. "Let her be put in keeping of her sister Emantha——"

"A moment!" Messer Polo said, sharp. "Remember, Excellency, this one, Emantha, is bought in service of her exalted highness——"

Il Cardinale reached into a pocket and took out two scrolls, giving one to Hsi-Soong and the other to Messer Polo.

"Here are the terms of her contract in our language and in Cathayan," he said. "Let the gracious Hsi-Soong read the Cathayan, and do you, Messer Polo, read aloud to us under what terms Emantha was to serve the Khan's daughter!"

Messer Polo opened the scroll, but instead of reading it aloud, he let it slip back into its roll and tucked it under the gold chains between the buttons of his tunic.

"The terms are clear," he said scarcely above a whisper, and turned away to mount his horse. Hsi-Soong chattered to One-piece and Two-piece, and the crowd began to move into the garden, hearing the Abbess calling the children. Il Cardinale came out of the parlor and beckoned.

"Get both sisters and let them enter the cage together," he whispered. "Tell Emantha to keep silent, and let her sister read the speech to the Princess. She is the better scholar——"

"Why did Messer Polo turn from reading to us?"

"He does well enough with the Cathayan language in speech and with the brush," Il Cardinale smiled. "But he neither reads nor writes in his own. Why did he offer you a place in the caravan, except that you have letters? Go, get the sisters!"

The procession started with long lines of children winding about the paths toward the cage of the White Bird. Girls in their bird costumes sat on all the perches except one, and that was in the middle, entwined with flowers. Franc hurried past, seeing Leda, in kingfisher feathers, swinging on her perch, and waved to her blown kiss. Many of the children were coated with pink or white sugar stuck with sugared petals, and they picked pieces off each other as they walked. Some wore silvered sugar, and others were gilded, and some were spread in many colors by Messer Giotto's paint boys, with a few in rich design by Tivi, Mok, and Laz. Mothers all wore the dress of their villages, with towers of lace on their heads, and stomachers of many-colored velvet, and so many lace skirts that they took the room of three. Franc ran among them, calling to this one and that, and on down to the tower.

But the door was splintered, and the mules pulled at hay, and the feathered robe lay on the cobbles. He ran inside the tower, shouting up.

Paolo Corti looked through the trap.

"We saw only a man and a woman making way together through the postern," he called down. "We can still see them going toward the river!"

Franc picked up the robe of feathers and ran over to the convent of the Little Brothers, but the look on Brother Dario's face was enough.

"We brought the Count Schiavon from the hospital and gave him fresh clothing," he said. "Then he was gone——"

"How could he know about the stable?"

"Is the door smashed from the inside? She knew where he was. Why would he escape us, except that she called him?"

Franc went through the garden to the space where the Princess Na-Nou had lived in her palanquin. The shape of the golden boat was in the grass, but the curtained chair stood in its place and, before it, the woman with the tired, withered face talked to his mother and Emantha.

He stood, staring, for only a little time at the Court of the Khan's daughter had brought a wondrous change, and he no longer saw a play-sister or the barefoot serving wench, but a grown beauty, paler through being out of the sun, and softer, and her eyes seemed larger and bluer, and her hair shone a brighter wheat tip, and she looked even slimmer in linen that he knew his mother had spun, and a white cap almost as tall as any Leda had ever worn. They all looked up, listening to a long-drawn blast of Cathayan horns. Carriers ran in to lift the chair, and he held out the feathered robe.

"If the Princess will spare the White Bird, she is wanted in the cage," he told them. "The Cathayans are impatient to go!"

Emantha and his mother ran with the robe, but he stayed beside the curtained chair and guided the carriers toward the cage.

Hsi-Soong met Emantha on the silver stairway and kissed her on both cheeks, and One-piece and Two-piece followed them into the cage and held the perch while the White Bird sat.

Franc opened the curtains of the chair and invited the Khan's daughter to step down. She crouched back in a corner, and he thought her shy and took her hand, pulling her gently out, and walked, while she hobbled, up the steps and stood before the cage door.

The Wand Bearer gave the town's scroll to Emantha and she started to read, but not a word could be heard for the cheering, and the children began throwing flowers, running up the stairway and getting in everybody's way.

In all the confusion of noise and the storm of flowers, Messer Polo forced a way into the cage.

"Let me lead the gracious Hsi-Soong away," he said urgently. "We are half a day late as it is——"

"But the Princess Na-Nou," Franc began, looking at the frightened, withered face at his side. "Should she not be thanked——"

"That is her tirewoman!" Messer Polo smiled. "She embodies the Princess, in solitude and regal distance. If you please, she is the Princess Na-Nou's conscience, partaking of no disorder or worldly commotion, but living alone, thinking only the highest thoughts, and arriving at the most delicate truths. The gracious Hsi-Soong is the poetess and dancer, and her province is the world. She may go where she will and do as she desires at all times and in all places, and why not? Her exalted highness gives permission. And who is her exalted highness? The gracious Hsi-Soong herself!"

He bowed before her, and she danced out, with One-piece and Two-piece behind.

Franc looked at Emantha and caught her hand when she would follow.

"Say one word," he whispered, close to the wheat-tip hair. "There are many more questions later and in proper time. Are you ready to plight troth with me?"

His voice was loud in a great silence. The smile in Emantha's eyes grew bluer. He turned to the quiet crowd and saw the reason. Il Cardinale stood behind with raised arms, smiling.

"Answer, Emantha!" he called. "Let us hear you!"

Emantha took her hand away and stepped back, slipping out of the feathered robe and throwing it over the perch.

"No!" she said, straight-faced. "The time for plighting troth is gone. I am not the one you used to know——"

.

A scream brought all turning toward a robe of kingfisher feathers and Leda hanging on to her perch and crowing with delight.

"My wager is won as I told you, Franc!" she shrieked. "You see these airs of hers and how she answered you? I claim my kiss, arms about the waist, in a place of my choosing, and the place is here!"

"But the kiss is mine!" Emantha laughed. "We'll plight no troth, or swear to share our worldly goods. I will marry or nothing!"

"And my mother wins a kerchief!" Franc bellowed.

Even the Cathayan horns and drums made no sound in the shouting. Franc and Emantha were picked up by the paint boys, led by Tivi, Mok, and Laz, and carried out to the front of the procession going down to the forum.

The palanquins were filled and carried off. Hsi-Soong and One-piece and Two-piece mounted their ponies and rode in front of Messer Polo. Cavalry and foot went by, all mixed with running children in a pelt of flowers.

Keeper Mozo opened the gate, and the town crowded out and stood at the wheat's edge, cheering and waving. Franc leaped down and ran to Messer Polo's side, reaching up a hand.

"Farewell, Franc!" Messer Polo coughed, covering his mouth from dust. "I sent a coffer to your house with the gold you won and other prizes from her exalted highness. Be happy with Emantha. If you should come to Venice, ask for me in the Square of St. Mark at the Bank of Cathay!"

The dust rolled pale gold, hiding the marchers and filling the rise with clouds that blew high over the wheat. Keeper Mozo closed the gates, and all outside waited turn to pass in through the narrow postern. Franc and Emantha hurried hand in hand up the forum steps and almost without thinking, ran for the tower.

The Cortis wanted no second telling to take an extra hour

off. Franc helped Emantha up the wooden stair to the bell platform, and they walked to the parapet, saying nothing, content to link arms and lean, watching the Cathayan caravan start toward the river.

Emantha pointed below, among the homing people, to Leda walking beside Tivi with their arms about each other, and in following them he saw his mother enter the tower doorway.

He went to the trap and looked down.

"I knew where to find you!" she laughed from the lower stair. "Come home and eat a dish of Cathayan spaghetti——"

"Good wardens eat in the tower," he called. "You said so!"

"No more waste in this land of birds and bells," Emantha said, going past him into the trap. "The work is all below. Come, Messer Mayor!"

Franc looked across the wheat to the chapel of St. Francis, and at the line of pilgrims walking out of the dust rolling away from the caravan. He reached up to touch the ropes, and in the echo of each bell heard good-by to the highest man in Assisi.

"Pax!" he whispered. "Adio!"